No Fortunes

Also by Peter Anastas

Glooskap's Children: Encounters with the Penobscot Indians of Maine

When Gloucester was Gloucester: Toward an Oral History of the City (with Peter Parsons)

Landscape with Boy (novella)

Siva Dancing (memoir)

Maximus to Gloucester: The Letters and Poems of Charles Olson to the Editor of the Gloucester Daily Times, 1962–1969

At the Cut: Growing Up in Gloucester, Massachusetts in the 1940s (memoir)

Broken Trip (novel)

No Fortunes

A NOVEL BY

PETER ANASTAS

First Edition

ISBN 0-9762638-0-7

Book design by Ruth Maassen
Rockport, Massachusetts

Printed in the USA.

Cover photo courtesy of George J. Mitchell, Department of Special Collections, Bowdoin College Library.

Quotation on pp. 121–122 from *The Long Goodbye*, by Raymond Chandler, copyrighted in 1953 and 1981, and published in 1988 by Random House/Vintage Books.

Back Shore Books are published by Back Shore Writers' Collaborative.

Back Shore Press
P.O. Box 211
Gloucester, MA 01931-0211
Tel. 978-283-4582

To Peter W. Denzer
vecchio amico ritrovato

There are no fortunes to be told;
there is no advice to be given.

—HENRY JAMES

I believe that most of an entire generation
will go to ruin...voluntarily, even enthusi-
astically. What will happen afterwards I don't
know, but for the next ten years or so we are
going to have to cope with the youth we, my
generation, put through the atom smasher.

—KENNETH REXROTH, 1959

1

$\mathcal{F}$rank Crow was an enigmatic guy. He spent most of his time hunched over the bridge table in a corner of the TD house living room. That is, when he wasn't trying to drag anyone who'd listen into a discussion of existential theology. Frank had an uneven crew cut that made the back of his head look like a coxcomb. His plastic-rimmed glasses were too small for his narrow face, while the thickness of their circular lenses seemed to force his pale blue eyes closer together, giving him an invariable expression of quizzical concentration.

Frank chain smoked Camels. Sometimes he'd have two or three lighted simultaneously around the lip of an overflowing ashtray. When he was involved in heavy bidding, ashes dropped at random or flew about him. As a consequence, his rumpled blue Oxford cloth shirts were peppered with cigarette burns, the holes multiplying over time. Like the rest of us, Frank wore sloppy chinos. But instead of the usual dirty white tennis shoes or spit-shined loafers, which were *de rigueur* among the brothers, he favored a pair of battered black Navy dress shoes he'd swiped from the PX at the Brunswick Naval Air Station. At one point the soles were so worn the brothers took to calling him "Adlai."

Nevertheless, everyone seemed to tolerate Frank. Maybe they only feigned interest when he went on about Berdyaev and Christian mysticism. In a house full of men who scarcely cracked a textbook, let alone read a newspaper or even *Time* magazine, I'm sure many found it odd to see Frank with the latest paper-back translations of Sartre or Camus. He had a habit of locking himself in the bathroom to read. Just as often, he'd leave one of his books behind on the floor, where the dampness of countless showers soon reduced it to a limp bundle of mildewed pages.

I suspect that Frank's pre-theological status granted him a certain immunity from the insults the rest of us got for being discovered with books at all, never mind daring to engage in talk beyond the obligatory subjects of exams and "nookie." Whatever the reason, I always found Frank at the bridge table just before lunch, smoking and laying out his cards; and after dinner, when he was the first to return to that round oak refuge, he never lacked for partners. Aside from cigarettes and his apparent addiction to bridge, Frank always seemed to lead an ascetic life.

He was a year ahead of me in college. We weren't close at first, although any discussion with Frank was revealing. He knew what he was talking about—and that went beyond existentialism, which I'd been attracted to since my freshman year. He was born in a Chicago suburb, into a family of Unitarian ministers; and he grew up in South Portland, where his father led a congregation for many years. With Frank's interest in religion and his major in philosophy, we expected that he would go into the ministry himself. When he disappeared with the rest of the senior class the year before, I assumed he'd be attending Harvard Divinity School. But I was wrong.

Frank turned up again at the beginning of first semester of my senior year. He hadn't graduated after all. In fact, what kept him from receiving his degree was a lack of credits in physical education. Although the Dean had warned him about the deficit, Frank still hadn't shown his face at the gym. Now he was back to get his degree, he announced; he'd returned to Brunswick to make up two idiotic hours of "cal" a week. Naturally, we figured he'd spend the rest of his time at the bridge table, regaling a captive audience with one of his marathon accounts of Marcel's "creative fidelity."

But the Frank who appeared after that summer was a transformed person. Outwardly, he had the same pointed nose that stuck out below those fingerprinted lenses like the proboscis of some house pest. And his voice was just as squeaky, an odd cross between a Maine coast nasal twang and a Henry Aldrich crack, as he reached for the upper registers in his habitual enthusiasm. In fact, it was precisely that excitement in which he seemed different. He still played bridge at the house, though he now lived off campus in a little room over Lucy's Cash Market on Page Street, where we bought our beer after the other stores had closed. Instead of Kierkegaard, Frank was now talking about revolution. His new hero was Fidel Castro. Before Frank's return Castro had only been a name to us, with a face of course—the unkempt beard and the jungle fatigues—but still not an authentic presence.

Frank changed all that. I remember the first time I laid eyes on him after his return. I was drinking coffee in the big front window of Clayton's Food Shop, diagonally across Maine Street from the campus. St. Pierre, my former roommate, was at the table, along with Bob Mendel, who lived with him in the Zeta house. Bill Mueller was with us, too. Except for Bill, who was a junior, the rest of us would be graduating the following June. I'm not sure if it was the unstated fact of that event, or merely our resistance to returning to the classroom after summer vacation. But everyone seemed withdrawn.

Suddenly I saw a short, skinny guy bundled up in a red and black lumber jacket, even though it was a warm afternoon in mid-September. He was heading toward the coffee shop, a cigarette stuck in the corner of his mouth. It was Frank. One minute he was squinting through the steamy window at us, and the next he was at the table talking a blue streak about Castro and the techniques of insurgency.

I never did discover what sparked Frank's interest in the Cuban Revolution, but during those few weeks he remained on campus I learned a lot about what preoccupied him. He took to visiting me on Federal Street. Frank knew I liked to read late at night after returning from my job at the library. He would come up to the second floor room, in a wing of the large, white nine-

4

teenth century faculty house where I lived, and tap softly on the door. I always knew it was Frank from the shuffle of his footsteps and the acrid smell of his cigarette smoke.

We talked a lot there, especially since I'd left the TD house at the end of my junior year to become an Independent. Night after night Frank outlined his theories of political action. He gave me Arturo Barea's memoir of the Spanish Civil War. And with great cogency he explained Camus' vision of *l'homme revolté*, based in part upon the French writer's involvement in partisan activities and his editorship of the underground paper *Combat*. Frank spoke with passion and authority about translating existential theory into direct action.

"It's time to put away the books," he would often declare. "We've got to change the world and sweep away oppression. It's imperative that we open up the space for people to remake themselves."

My only experience of politics had been as a member of Students for Stevenson during the 1956 presidential campaign. I was drawn to Stevenson because I couldn't abide the spectacle of Eisenhower and Nixon. I adored Stevenson's speeches, especially since I'd learned that he wrote most of them himself. But after I had a few doors slammed in my face while canvassing for Stevenson in Brunswick and Topsham ("Don't expect me to vote for that bald-headed pinko!" one otherwise gentle looking old lady screamed at me); and after only sixteen of us had voted for the Democratic ticket in a student mock election, I was so discouraged at the thought of another four years of soporific Ikeism that I returned to my books and my daydreaming.

Frank never tried to convert us to his way of thinking, though. He'd merely share what was on his mind if he happened to meet us between classes at the coffee shop or over at the student union late at night. Yet it was clear to me that Frank meant business when he talked about trying to sneak into Cuba. None of us considered that fighting with Castro might entail killing people. Naively, perhaps, we thought about it as an opportunity to change Cuba from a dictatorship of thugs and grafters into a democratic society. But Frank wasn't sanguine about that possibility. He'd read his Malraux and he knew that political change often had to come from the barrel of a gun.

All during the rest of September and into October Frank seemed obsessed with escaping to Cuba. He planned to travel to Mexico, hoping to find a way to sneak onto the island from there. He'd been to Mexico before and he spoke some Spanish, which he learned at St. Paul's. Mostly he'd show me revolutionary literature that got into the country through France. He seemed aware of everything that was going on in Cuba, especially where the significant action was taking place. Then he left. He didn't complete his credits in "cal." He didn't wait to graduate. One day in mid-October Frank simply disappeared.

✣ There was a big picture of Fidel Castro entering Havana on the front page of that morning's *Boston Globe*.

"Do you think that bastard really made it?" St. Pierre was lighting up another Lucky from the butt he held in his small dark fingers.

"If he did, you can bet your ass we'll hear about it," I said.

"Imagine watching the news," he said. "Suddenly you catch a glimpse of Frank sitting on the tailgate of some truck with a bunch of guerrillas—or driving a Jeep!"

"With that crazy crewcut," Mueller interjected, "and a shit-eating grin on his face."

Mendel was quiet as usual. A black curl bisected his forehead. His sharp blue eyes followed our conversation, darting from one speaker to another.

"Hold on," he broke in. "You guys think it's some kind of movie. If he made it down there, if he *actually* got through to Castro in the Sierra Maestra, do you think for one minute they'd be silly enough to give him a gun?"

"Frank's a good shot," I said.

"Hunting's not warfare," Mendel replied dismissively. "Besides, with his eyesight he couldn't even pass a draft board physical."

"Fuck the American army!" Mueller shouted. "Pretty soon they'll be going in against Castro."

"I can see it now," St. Pierre said. "The president comes on national TV with a stern look on that baby face of his: 'We have to intervene because the Cuban Revolution is threatening our national security—'"

"Security, my ass," said Mueller, doing a bongo roll on the edge of the Formica table top. "It's cutting off the gambling take. Next thing you know they'll be nationalizing the sugar industry."

It was the first day of the new semester. We were sitting in the window of Clayton's Food Shop. Ten o'clock classes had let out and you could see everyone's breath on the cold air. Calls and shouts came to us through the plate glass, partially fogged with moisture. They seemed to echo off the old stone buildings in the gray light. It had snowed again the night before, and now it was hard packed on Maine Street, with drifts still white along the sidewalks.

Only four of us remained from a group of six friends. Frank was gone. And just before Christmas Roonie Reardon, a Korean War vet on the GI bill, had blown a hole the size of a melon in the living room wall of the TD house with his .357 Magnum pistol. For that indulgence, he'd been expelled, leaving St. Pierre, myself, Mendel and Mueller.

We sat around three sides of the table, elbows jammed in among saucers and textbooks. The big bay window in front of the luncheonette jutted out over the sidewalk. From our vantage point you could see the entrance to Fairfield's Book Shop next door to the right of us, and King's Barber Shop and the Parkview Cleaners and Laundromat down the street on the left. Directly across the street was the white facade of the First Parish Church. On the other side of the Bath Road, which was perpendicular to Maine Street, was the entrance to the campus, where the Franklin Robinson Memorial gate hung perpetually open on two granite pillars. A brick walk began there and led to Massachusetts Hall, which housed the administrative offices. Spread out beyond that around the "quad" were the classroom buildings, the chapel, the library, the art museum and the dorms.

"I told my parents I wasn't going to medical school."

St. Pierre lit up another Lucky, jabbing the previous butt out in his cup. The cup and saucer rattled against the table top. His hand shook against the cup as he tried to fit it back into the saucer. That set the cup to rattling again and some more of the gray-colored coffee spilled into the well of the saucer.

"Fuck it," he said, pushing both cup and saucer away. With a crumpled paper napkin he dabbed at the circle of moisture in front of him.

"It was pandemonium. My father cracked the kitchen table with his fist and my little sister went screaming into her room. The message was clear—I'd disappointed them again."

"We had the same argument all over," he continued, leaning his chair back against the window frame. "I told them that I wasn't cut out to be a doctor, that I wanted to go to New York to study acting."

"'But you've just completed three and half years of pre-med,' my father bellowed. 'What do you mean you're not cut out?'"

"'I'm passing by the skin of my teeth,' I said. And when I tried to explain the whole thing had been a lie, that I never really wanted to go to medical school, and that I'd only started applying to please *them*—to go along with my uncle who was the family success story—it was like adding insult to injury."

"But the worst part of it," he said, and his coal black eyes sought mine—"the worst was my father looking at me with unbelievable contempt. 'Go to New York,' he said, 'you'll end up nothing but a queer.'"

St. Pierre dropped his cigarette into the last of the cold coffee. He pushed the cup and saucer even farther away from him.

"That's what happens," Mueller said, smoothing his goatee down under his chin. "You try to come clean with them and it blows up in your face. Just don't tell your family anything. Do what Frank did."

St. Pierre shook his head.

"It doesn't work. They start reminding you who's paying the bills."

"So what?" Mueller said. "Don't you remember the letter I got from my father when he tried to convince me to shave? He threatened to stop my allowance if I didn't get rid of the beard. I said, 'Great, I'll drop out and hitchhike to San Francisco. See what the neighbors think of that.' The next thing you know my mother's on the phone begging me to stay in school."

"I hate that kind of blackmail," I said.

"Yeah, but whose parents live without duplicity?" Mendel said.

"I can't take it anymore," St. Pierre yelled. "I can't *be* the way they want me to be!"

"You were gung-ho about applying to med school," Mendel insisted. "Don't deny it."

"It's meaningless to me now. All I want to do is act. I think I've discovered my true vocation."

While they talked, I drifted away. Frank was on my mind. The photograph in the *Globe* had brought back the poignancy of our midnight talks that past fall, Frank's nonstop theorizing about existential action. I wondered if he'd actually made it into Cuba. He hadn't said anything about writing to us. I didn't expect he'd be able to get a letter out of a country engaged in civil war, even if he wanted to communicate. But the fall seemed years behind me. With the snow on the ground and my last semester ahead of me, it felt like another time.

Now I was haunted by endings. Returning to Brunswick the previous night on the train out of Boston, I experienced a new pressure. As I sat over a beer in the stifling clubcar, platforms of deserted railroad stations stacked with wet newspapers flying past me in the newly fallen snow, I imagined myself away from it all and wanting it back before I'd even lost it. I felt the loss even more acutely as I trudged through the snow from the station up to my cold room.

"Where will I go?" I asked myself in the purple dark of the mercury vapor lamps. "Who will I be?"

I knew the answer to the first question; I suspected that the answer to the second depended upon what happened to me at my next destination.

"Come by tonight and listen to some Bartok." Mendel leaned over the table as he pulled his sweater back on. "I've found the most extraordinary recordings of the first four quartets!"

Mueller bummed a Lucky off St. Pierre and slipped out. I lingered, sensing that Henri wanted to talk some more.

"Your folks will get over it," I said.

"Jason, it was hell. Only you could know that. My father will probably never speak to me again. All he's talked about for four years at the fire station is me going to medical school like my uncle did, a poor French Canadian boy making good. Now I've dashed his dreams. How can he tell those guys his son wants to be an actor in New York City?"

"Listen, if we've learned anything at all from Frank it's that we're free to choose, condemned to, even."

St. Pierre only shook his head.

"They probably won't come to see me graduate."

"They'll be here," I said. "Wait and see."

St. Pierre grabbed my sleeve as I got up to leave.

"Tell me the truth, Jason. Do you think I'm effeminate?"

"Don't be silly!"

"No, really, tell me because something happened to me just before we left for Christmas break. It was right after we did *Streetcar* and I was walking back to the house one Sunday morning with the *Times* under my arm. As I passed Winthrop Hall someone yelled, 'Faggot!' out the window. I knew it was intended for me because the campus was deserted. I stood there and I shouted back, 'Show your face, you fucking asshole!' But no one did, and I felt like an idiot standing there all by myself."

"Henri, forget about it. You and I are misfits."

"But I played football! What more do they want?"

"Abject conformity," I said.

"It's driving me crazy, Jason. I don't know if I can hang on until June."

"Listen, six months, a year from now, this will all seem like a bad dream. You'll be in New York, I'll be in Europe."

I wanted to put my arm around St. Pierre as we both gathered up our books. I felt an enormous kinship with him, a closeness born of nearly four years of friendship. Instead, we walked back to the campus in uneasy silence, the snow lying all around us in frozen drifts.

2

*R*eturning to my room after class, I put Fats Navarro's "Lady-bird" on the turntable and kicked off my soggy engineer's boots. There were only two of us in the Dante seminar, Kruchel, a junior majoring in French, and myself. During the first semester we had concentrated on early Italian poetry, the Sicilian School and the *Stil Novisti*, before proceeding to *La Vita Nuova*. This semester our teacher, Jeff Cotton, would have us reading the entire *Inferno* and most of the major cantos in the *Purgatorio* and *Paradiso*. I laid my copy of Grandgent's edition of the *Commedia* on the desk and pulled the typewriter table over so I could begin writing to my girlfriend Leslie.

Even though I didn't get much heat from the single register in the floor until evening, the room felt comfortable. I hadn't made the bed yet, and my suitcase was still packed. The closet, which faced the foot of my bed, was open with some dirty laundry I'd forgotten to bring home strewn on the floor. I could smell the sourness of the rag socks from my desk, so I lit up a Pall Mall.

I hadn't seen Leslie since the last day of Christmas break when we'd driven to Front Beach in Rockport. As we sat in the front seat of my parents' '57 Chevy with the windows steaming up around us, I read to her from my new play. It was called *Summer's End* and I'd written it for submission in the annual student one-act play contest.

The play focused on an aspiring writer in his mid-twenties, also named Jason, who's given up a career in advertising to return to his home town to work as a ship's carpenter. Jason's conflict arises when he begins to date a student named Pat, employed for the summer as a waitress at the Rockaway Hotel, a seaside inn, just up the street from where my family and I lived on Rocky Neck in East Gloucester, behind my father's S. S. Pierce grocery store and luncheonette. Though Pat is majoring in English and they have much in common, Jason is reluctant to reveal his feelings.

The action of the play unfolds near the end of summer, just before Labor Day, when the hotel closes and Pat is about to return to college for her final year. Jason will have to declare his love or risk losing Pat, who is also being pursued by a slick undergraduate named Rick. But Jason's unwillingness to take a

stand, as I tried to show, is less a result of shyness than of his am
bivalence about commitment. In the end, he's torn between
wanting to live alone and write or open himself to a relationship
with its own emotional risks.

Leslie liked the play. After I'd finished reading from the manuscript, she bent over and kissed me softly, locks of fine blond
hair tumbling over the collars of her English woolen cape.

"It sounds familiar," she said.

"I tried to imagine what it might be like if I came back home
to work after college."

"You've had this fascination with physical labor ever since
I've known you," she said.

"I'm getting sick of just using my mind."

Leslie had been a secretary for two years before starting college.

"There's nothing magical about working with your hands,"
she said. "Our fathers have done it all their lives."

"I've got to find some way to make a living while I write."

"I happen to think you'd make a great teacher."

"I'd be chasing degrees and tenure. When would I have time
to write?"

"You'd be so tired after a day on the waterfront you wouldn't
be *able* to write."

"But my head wouldn't be full of Keats and Shelley."

"You don't have to teach literature. You could teach Italian."

"I've considered that... Listen." I hesitated. "I have some
news to tell you. A letter came from Florence yesterday. I've been
accepted at the university."

Leslie was suddenly quiet. She pulled the black cape tightly
around her as if it had gotten colder in the car.

"That means I won't see you for a year." She was biting her lower lip.

"The time will go by quickly," I said. "We'll both be in school."

"We're just a train ride apart now. It won't be that easy when you're in Europe."

"I want to go very badly," I said. "You've already been."

"You could study Italian at Harvard. We have a great department."

"But I have this *need* to go to Italy. Ever since I started reading Lawrence—"

"Lawrence will be the death of our relationship," Leslie said bitterly.

"You like him! You've said so!"

"In the abstract," she answered. "But here he is taking you away from me just as we've begun to get close."

"We can still be close."

"A lot can happen in a year. You could meet someone in Europe. Don't tell me you haven't entertained fantasies of some ravishing Italian beauty."

"Oh, Les," I said, "I love you more than anyone in the world."

"Now, maybe. But what about in the heat of a passionate moment, in a romantic place?"

"I'm only going to Florence to be a student, to get a better feeling for the language."

"That's what you say now," she said.

✢ I had wanted to tell Leslie that I did love her and that I fully expected we'd marry when I returned. She would have finished

Radcliffe by then, and maybe we could both get fellowships and go to graduate school together on the West Coast. Perhaps I could write while she taught. We had spoken about that possibility many times before.

I slid a sheet of Manila paper under the roller and I lit up another Pall Mall. Then I put on Dinah Washington singing "A Foggy Day," with Clark Terry in the background with a wah-wah mute. Instead of beginning the letter, I started imagining what London might look like in the haze of an October morning. Of course, I had to see England. Maybe I could travel north during the Christmas holidays. I expected I'd be able to earn enough money for visiting England or France if I worked on the waterfront again that summer. But then another fantasy obtruded, one that I dared not share with Leslie. It embarrassed me even to think about it.

I imagined the room I would rent in Florence, somewhere near the university, in a narrow street or alleyway shadowed by the twelfth century towers of the medieval quarter. Maybe it would be a small room looking out on a busy piazza. There would be a bed, and near the single window with its view of red-tiled roofs and church cupolas I would have a desk. My books would be lined up on the desk, Dante and some Italian concordances, along with Old French and Latin texts. Perhaps the room would have a ceramic stove for cool Florentine nights, and I would sit at my desk and write or read close by it in an old leather chair. When I pictured the room, there was a yellow glow about it. It resembled a nineteenth century German student's garret I'd once seen depicted on an old bookplate: Gothic buildings viewed through the window, leather-bound folios stacked on the desk, an oil lamp to study or read by.

There was something else in my fantasy, or rather, someone else. I would meet an Italian girl at the university. She would have long black hair and flashing dark eyes. We would walk along the Arno after class, stopping at a café in late afternoon for *espresso* or a glass of Punt'e Mes. We'd discuss the lecture we had just heard on Renaissance humanism; or maybe our philology professor would have carefully conducted us through an arcane passage in *The Romance of the Rose*. We'd sit talking in Italian and our conversation would take us into the dinner hour, which we'd share. Then I would accompany Francesca or Rosalba, for I had even given my fantasy friend a name, back to her room. Or maybe—this was always the difficult part, the one I shied away from when it came into my mind—maybe she would come back to my room with me and we would make a fire and mull some wine and I would undress her in the firelight and she would kiss me and we would fall into my bed together and make love with great abandon. And afterwards, I would hear her husky voice in my ear: *"Jason, ti amo tanto..."*

It was difficult. The fantasy got in the way of the letter and I stood up and flipped the Dinah Washington record over and sat on my bed.

"If you could see me now, you'd know how blue I am," Dinah sang.

It was dark already and the street lamps along Federal Street and the Bath Road highlighted the drifts of snow in front of the big white houses with their dark green shutters. I would have to hurry if I wanted some dinner.

I sat down once more and I wrote:

"Believe me, Les. I'm not running away from you. I need to put some distance between this place and myself, not between the two of us. You could come with me if you wanted. I just feel a terrible need to see Europe, to be in a foreign environment, to hear another language. I won't be happy until I do it; and I won't be good for you or for myself until I have that adventure. You know I have to pass it off as graduate study or the draft board won't let me go."

I wasn't pleased with what I'd written. The point was I did love Leslie. I couldn't conceive of our not getting married and settling down to a life together. Nevertheless, there was something that called me to Europe—not to abandon Leslie but to obey a voice I seemed to be hearing deep within me, a voice beckoning me to another continent, to a place of ancient palaces and narrow streets, to a city of rivers and quays with dimly lighted cafés. Leslie and I could travel there, we might even live there together. But I had to go first. I had to go alone. I didn't quite know why, but I felt that if I didn't go alone I'd never go anyplace in my life. I wanted desperately to leave America behind, the way Frank had gone to Cuba, only I didn't want to fight in a revolution. I wanted to lose myself so that I could find myself, even though I couldn't fully explain what that meant. Somehow it had to do with Francesca or Rosalba. Although she was only a figment of my imagination, I had become obsessed with her dark flesh and soft breath, her sharp heels on the cobblestones of a Florentine street at night, her knowing laughter in my ear as we ascended the stairway to my room in Piazza San Marco, where we would make love until morning and I would be freed of whatever it was that held me in chains.

✢ Bartok's "First Quartet" was already playing when I got to Mendel's room on the second floor of the Zeta house. An architect's lamp, its shade reflecting a circle of white light onto the adjacent wall, barely illuminated the large single room. In the quiet dark I could see Mueller leaning forward in Mendel's reading chair, his head bent nearly between his legs. St. Pierre occupied his usual place on the floor, a pillow under his head. Mendel sat by the cabinet, which contained the hi-fi turntable and receiver. Four speakers were set up, one in each corner of the room.

The room itself was different from the other rooms in the fraternity house. In place of polar bear banners and Playboy center-folds, Mendel had hung finely mounted and framed reproductions of two Cezanne landscapes and Picasso's *Demoiselles d'Auvignon* on his carefully painted white walls. None of his books were visible and the bed looked like a perfectly made military cot.

When you listened to music with Mendel you had to obey his rules. There was no drinking or smoking allowed and there could be no talk that didn't have to do with the music itself. Usually Mendel, who had an encyclopedic knowledge of modern music, would introduce the piece. After it concluded he might comment, briefly but always trenchantly. At that point a conversation could begin. But if Mendel was anxious to share a related work, there was no further dialogue. He would simply put the new record on. Requests were entertained if Mendel felt they didn't break the mood established by the evening's main event, a collection of works by an individual composer or one long performance of a single opus. Otherwise, we stayed until Mendel felt the evening was over, not usually too late, for he liked to get up early to walk by himself, no matter what the weather.

No one ever dared to question Mendel's rules. He was small and well-built, the dark haired only child of older parents from Brooklyn. His father was an insurance adjuster; his mother taught high school math. Easily the most accomplished student in the college, he had long exhausted the offerings of both the math and physics departments. He'd also completed the equivalent of a major in philosophy. This final semester, during which he had no classes, he was being allowed time to "think" for a senior thesis on unified field theory. He described it derisively as "a couple of pages of equations." Mendel had already been accepted for doctoral study in theoretical physics at Stanford. But just before Christmas he'd attended a campus interview with a representative from the Defense Department and had been offered a job doing weapons research for the Pentagon, which would begin immediately upon graduation in June. To the dismay of all his professors he took the job.

It was hard getting to know Mendel. During our first two years I'd been afraid to speak with him because of the impatient way he responded to whatever anyone said. He didn't actually criticize you. The quality and depth of his comments merely made you feel stupid. But he and St Pierre had roomed together in Appleton Hall during our freshman year and Mendel seemed to accept me, although whenever we had spoken I felt utterly inadequate. It was music, especially jazz, that sealed our friendship. Mendel first invited me to his room to listen to his extensive be-bop collection. When he learned that I also enjoyed the music of the Vienna School and Stravinsky's *Histoire du Soldat*, he began to treat me with as much warmth as he treated anyone, which was little enough.

The program for the evening consisted of the first two quartets of Bartok, recently recorded for Angel Records by the Vegh String Quartet. We had heard other recordings, one in particular by the Fine Arts Quartet. But Mendel said the Vegh Quartet's reading of Bartok was more incisive. As I relaxed into the one remaining chair and let the music take me in, I realized that he was right.

Many of Mendel's fraternity brothers who heard this music through the walls of the Zeta house thought we were all crazy. They referred to what we were listening to as "noise." But Bartok's music always seemed lucid to me and deeply moving. As I let the strains of the quartet lead me down into my mind, the precise dissonances, the spare phrases never too endlessly repeated, the melodies and echoes of melodies of Hungarian folk songs helped to sharpen my thinking rather than to diffuse it. Each tone was like an image projected onto the screen of my consciousness, and I seemed both to hear and to see the music as it played.

Mendel said nothing before turning the record over for the second quartet. I kept my eyes closed and found myself struggling with the letter to Leslie, only this time the words came easily, the thoughts were not impeded, for there were no words to try me, only images to lead me on as I freely associated.

I began by thinking it was odd that Leslie and I came from the same town. Most of my college classmates were meeting girls from places as disparate as Washington, D.C. or St. Louis during their undergraduate years. Although I had dated occasionally, I hadn't met anyone who combined the qualities of mind and physical beauty I found in Leslie. I loved her worldliness, her sophistication, born of a summer in Europe on an American Field Service scholarship and two years in a State Street investment bank. Leslie and I had shared only one formal date in high school. I'd asked her to our senior prom, where, instead of dancing or drinking, we spent the whole time discussing the novels of Aldous Huxley. After that we'd double-dated a bit. One of those summer nights we ended up necking in the back seat of our classmate Dave's '49 Ford. Then, at the insistence of parents, who thought college was a waste of money on a daughter they believed would soon marry, Leslie started secretarial school in Boston and we lost touch.

Toward the end of the summer before my junior year, we ran into each other one afternoon on Good Harbor Beach. Leslie was wearing a black one piece bathing suit, which made her ivory skin and long blond hair look all the more striking. She gave me a big hug, something no girl had ever done to me in public. When we sat down on her blanket, I saw that she was reading *Death in Venice* in the original. Then she told me what she'd been up to. Over her parents' objections, Leslie had applied to Harvard. Radcliffe had offered her a full scholarship, so she'd enrolled for September, quitting her job in the city. She planned to major in comparative literature.

We discovered that we shared so many interests we couldn't stop talking. That night we went to see *La Strada* at the Little Art Cinema; the following evening I took her to a Count Basie concert at Castle Hill. She was waiting on tables at the Peg Leg restaurant in Rockport and I started picking her up after work each night. Pretty soon we were talking about seeing each other during the winter. By Homecoming we were going steady; during Winter Houseparty she accepted my fraternity pin.

As the music of Bartok filled the space of Mendel's room and my own mind as well, I felt the deepest pangs of love for Leslie. A far quicker student than I, she had amazed my professors when I brought her to Saturday morning classes during party weekends. Right away her hand would be up as she responded to tough questions about Conrad's narrative baffles or symbols of the Eucharist in the *Four Quartets*. It made me feel proud to know her.

But that wasn't what I wanted to write Leslie about. What I wanted to say had equally to do with us and Bartok, for it was this music, always, that transported me to a world where anything seemed possible. It was like when you're drunk and you come reeling back to your room and fall heavily down on the bed, your head spinning, the bed whirling around you. Even during that alcoholic dizziness you begin to see yourself and your dreams in a more ample dimension. You feel that you could actually accomplish what you only barely think you're capable of when you're sober. The music made me feel as though I could become the writer I wanted to be, that I could write something large and important.

Bartok's music, or Schoenberg's, when I was caught up in it, seemed an example of the highest form of human creativity. It was what I imagined Michelangelo's sculpture to be; and being immersed, totally lost in it, I seemed to find the best in myself, even if it was only a fantasy. The music let me dream, it allowed me to leave my mind and body and observe them both from an external and seemingly more objective distance. It made me understand that it, too, had come from the same stuff of dreams and desires.

That's what I wanted to share with Leslie. I wanted to write it to her or whisper it in answer to our troubled conversation in the cold car at Front Beach. I wanted to tell her that suddenly I understood it was all right, it was going to be fine between us if she only trusted me to come back to her, if she only understood that I had to go away from her first.

✜ The music was over. Mendel was in a trance. St. Pierre still had his eyes closed. Mueller was shaking his head as if in disbelief. Silently we left Mendel to himself and I made my way across the campus. I had no desire to stop in the Union for coffee, no need to see anyone or to speak to anyone. My breath expanded in the gelid air like steam. My lungs ached when I inhaled. The snow was an iridescent blue under the moonlight as I approached Adams Hall, stopping for a moment to contemplate the familiar illuminated windows of Anton Schrebner's office on the second floor.

Schrebner, who had been a former teaching assistant of Ernst Cassirer's in Hamburg before the Nazis forced them both to leave Germany, taught philosophy by making us philosophize. "Meester Makrides, to *feel* is not to theenk!" he once exhorted me in his thick Germanic English. We laughed when he pronounced Kant "cunt" and took weeks to get our papers back. But when they were finally returned, covered with comments in a spidery Gothic calligraphy, we found that he had entered into profound dialogue with us rather than simply having graded our efforts. In class he walked up and down, bags under his deep-set brown eyes, chain-smoking as he conducted us through the pre-Socratics, chalking up relevant terms in Greek on the blackboard, then transliterating them into English. He never lectured, choosing instead to question gently and to probe; and we responded by engaging each other and our teacher. Even in winter Schrebner rode to class on an old English bicycle, staying up half the night in his office, pacing the floor. You could see him framed by that office window night after night, pacing, thinking, pausing to jot down notes, which would form the basis of the next day's discussion.

Passing Adams, I walked through the Presidents' Gate out to the Bath Road, devoid of traffic. Soon I was looking up at the dark window of my room on Federal Street. My mind was amazingly clear. Yet I felt mesmerized by the music, which continued to sound in my ears, in my head, carrying me to worlds I could not even imagine. I paused on the steps to scrape my boots, listening to the gritty sound they made on the frozen wood. Here I was back in school. Leslie was in Cambridge, probably already asleep in her dorm. A highway connected us, or a single ribbon of railroad tracks between Brunswick, Maine and Boston; and yet the distance seemed so far, or I envisioned it suddenly so enormous, that I felt like a speck of dust in the wheeling cosmos over my head. I wanted to tell Leslie that, or write it to her. But I knew that once I was in my room I would only climb into a cold bed and fall into a sleep of eons.

3

*A*dvanced Writing met on Wednesday afternoons in the Chase Barn, across Maine Street from the campus. Fitted out like a miniature Elizabethan theater, the chamber had been part of a Shakespearean scholar's home, left to the college after his death. Opposite the stage was a large, stone fireplace with a couch and some easy chairs arranged around it. Lou Diehl, the Longfellow Professor of Poetry, sat warming his hands in front of the fire.

Most of us had studied with Lou before. His own verse was traditional—he was rumored to be working on an epic poem about the war in the Pacific, cast in heroic couplets. But we considered him a hot ticket personally. He came from an old New England family and had graduated from Princeton. At Harvard, where he co-authored a stage version of *Bartleby, The Scrivener*, he'd been a Junior Fellow. After teaching at the University of Michigan, Lou had assumed the Longfellow chair, beginning our freshman year, upon the death of its incumbent, Sherwood Harlan Crocker Thompson. Thompson, one of whose many affectations was rolling his own cigarettes, was reputed to have lectured in blank verse while often drunk. Hence the nickname "Crock," given him by students. It may also have referred to the content of those lectures.

Lou wore horn-rimmed glasses. His habitual costume consisted of baggy flannels and a gray, moth-eaten Shetland sweater. He referred to Kimon Friar and John Malcolm Brinnin, the editors of the text we had used in his modern poetry course, as "the Greek fairy and the American fairy," and he was always ready with some slander about the poets we were studying. How much money they earned, whom they slept with, and what they said behind each other's backs.

This irreverence endeared him to most of the English majors. We especially enjoyed his cutting remarks about the other members of the English Department, and the fact that he didn't seem to mind what he said. All of it delivered with a patrician offhandedness and a dirty mouth.

The class was small, three juniors and three seniors. Mueller sat slumped across from me in tight blue jeans and a red and black stripped silk shirt. He was already on his second Camel. With his wispy goatee and curly, close-cropped hair, he looked like a Zen monk in the fading light. Next to him was Dell Beverly, the only Negro on campus and easily the best writer among us. Sitting cross-legged in the corner of the couch, his hair slicked back across a slender mahogany head, Dell eyed the rest of us as if he were minding a bunch of children about to shit their pants. The third junior was Tim Lindner, a poet, who had arrived on campus from Florida already writing like Wallace Stevens. Under Lou's tutelage he now sounded like William Meredith.

Of the seniors, beside myself there was Fred Foster, who was tall and skinny and idolized James Gould Cozzens. After reading *The Just and the Unjust,* he had decided to forego literature for law school. The other senior was Hal Quoins, who wore black turtle neck sweaters and had a Pulcinella profile. Quoins wrote verse plays mostly under the influence of Archibald MacLeish, with whom he corresponded. He had just succeeded me as editor-in-chief of *The Quill,* the campus literary magazine.

Lou seemed pleased there were a couple of poets in the class, so he began by asking Mueller and Tim if they felt like reading. Tim poked his black-rimmed glasses back up on his nose and started reading from a long poem he'd been working on all fall. I could still hear some Stevens in it, especially cadences from "The Idea of Order at Key West." But Tim had also found another voice since I'd last heard him read in his room before Christmas. The poem, called simply "Mendacities," was an examination of an affair from the point of view of a jilted woman and it was powerful.

As he read, the fire crackled in the fireplace. Through the mullioned windows of the chamber I could see a winter sky the color of pewter. I lit a cigarette and closed my eyes. The poem made me think of Leslie and I pictured her alone in Cambridge after I had left for Europe. I saw her walking in Harvard Yard in a full tweed skirt and black leotards, her golden hair trailing behind her in the autumn wind. There was someone coming to meet her. He was tall and fair. She smiled and let him kiss her in front of Widener. Taking his arm, she joined him in walking...

Once Tim had finished Lou was saying that he ought to let the poem go wherever it wanted. He felt it was a big break-through for Tim and he shouldn't inhibit himself. Tim, whose face was mottled by acne scars, just nodded and smiled in embarrassment. When Lou asked if we had anything to say, I felt like telling Tim that the poem had really touched something in me, but I decided against it.

Mueller's poem was more political and was meant to be recited to the rhythm of bongo drums. It had a nice beat to it, but you could tell Lou wasn't impressed.

"Don't be so preachy," he said to Mueller after he had finished reading. "Try to evoke or elicit feelings instead of describing them."

"Sometimes you just need to say things right out," Mueller responded diffidently.

"Not in poetry," Lou snapped back. "What makes verse different is its suggestivity. Tim is writing about an affair gone awry, but he's not telling us that. We discover it by indirection. It's like it's happening to us. We relate to the speaker rather than simply receiving an idea or an opinion."

Dell raised his hand to speak.

"There is a poetry emerging." He pronounced it "poi-tree," the way a Southerner would. "It's direct, if not conversational, in its expression of anger, dismay and disapprobation of society."

"Auden and Spender were writing that way in the Thirties," Lou broke in, "and Auden used slang quite effectively."

"I think Bill's trying to deal with a more *pressing* reality," Dell replied, catching my eye, "the way Ginsberg and Corso are."

"You know what I think of those jokers," Lou said, terminating the discussion.

Dell was from Washington, D.C. where his father practiced law. He dressed more formally than the rest of us, often in a rep tie, a white Oxford cloth shirt and a smartly tailored brown tweed jacket, in contrast to our rumpled blue button-downs. Faculty members seemed to show him greater respect, not entirely because he was a Negro, I suspected, but because he seemed to possess a maturity, or at least the semblance of one, that made them hold back in the often arch demeanor they habitually adopted with the rest of us.

During his freshman year Dell had belonged to the now defunct Manuscript Club, an informal group of writers who met once a month with Sean Minturn, a former English instructor, who was also working on a novel. Dell's first story was about a young academic on his way to meet an agent in New York City with the manuscript of his first novel. Reviewing his work in the train, along with his marriage, the writer realizes that he hasn't confronted his own life, therefore, the novel is a sham. He gets off the train, leaving the manuscript behind him. When the conductor reminds him that he's forgotten his package, he replies, "Not mine." The story had affected all of us. It had particularly moved Sean, who wrote a note on it afterward telling Dell the question was not whether he was a good writer, but what he was going to do with his talent.

Quoins had his hand up to read the first scene of a play that sounded a lot like MacLeish's *This Music Crept by Me upon the Waters*. He read lugubriously, his face buried in the manuscript, sandy hair falling over his eyes. Quoins had gone to Milton, expecting an automatic acceptance from Harvard. Compared to that failed hope, Bowdoin always seemed to him like rustication. By senior year, when his parents bought him a car, he was spending most of his weekends in Cambridge, working backstage at the Poets' Theatre and staying at Eliot House with his friends from boarding school.

When it came my turn, I read from the first section of a long story I'd begun the semester before, based on the marriage of an Italian girl I'd known in high school. My classmate Rosalie was bright, but her parents, much like Leslie's, wouldn't let her go to a liberal arts college. Instead, they forced her to attend the same secretarial school in Boston that Leslie's parents had sent her to. After graduating, she came home to Gloucester to work in the office of the Empire Fish Company. But she continued to date a classmate of ours who had gone to Amherst. Vinnie was also Italian, and he was wild about opera. Rosalie was hoping that she and Vinnie would eventually marry; she seemed content to wait until he finished graduate school as well. But her family put a lot of pressure on her to break up with Vinnie, implying that because he loved music and studied literature he wouldn't be a good provider. They even impugned his masculinity. Rosalie finally gave up and agreed to marry a Sicilian-born fisherman she'd met at a Christmas party. Vinnie had been so hurt by her rejection that he stopped coming home. When Leslie and I heard the news, we couldn't conceive of Rosalie married to someone who was barely literate.

Their marriage is what I tried to imagine in the story, which I hoped might be part of a sequence of stories about Gloucester, stretching back to my childhood. I called the young woman Grace, which was actually Rosalie's cousin's name, and I began the story with a scene from her marriage night. From there I would flash back to her high school days, describing her relationship first with Vinnie and then with Sal, the man she married. Just as she has waited for Vinnie to finish school, Grace discovers that, as the wife of a fisherman, often at sea for weeks, she will join her mother and her sisters in a continual waiting game. In her husband's absence, she will be the one to raise the children and manage the household. I particularly wanted to depict her inner life as the consequences of her choice became apparent to her—a life spent largely alone or talking with other women about children, furniture and the redecoration of houses. I had discussed my story a lot with Leslie, the two of us writing back and forth excitedly as I began to draft it.

When I got through reading, Dell said, "This is the first time I've heard you write about everyday life in Gloucester. I like it. I hear Lawrence in the prose, but that's better than Farrell."

"Better than Kerouac, too," Quoins muttered.

"It's no secret that I've been reading Lawrence," I replied. My senior thesis was going to be on *The Plumed Serpent*.

"D. H. Lawrence in Gloucester, Massachusetts!" Quoins added sarcastically.

I shot back:

33

"He came from a mining family and my hometown is a working class city."

"Proletarian literature is *passé*," Quoins said, "like existentialism."

"Lawrence is not a proletarian writer!"

Lou intervened:

"If a model helps you, by all means use it. I'm not partial to Lawrence, he's too mystical for my taste. But I can understand the attraction he holds for some of you—Kerouac too, considering the strong dose of Henry James you've been given by this department."

✝ After class I walked Mueller back to his fraternity house on my way to the book store.

"Son of a bitch stuck it to both of us," he said angrily. "I'm dropping the fucking course."

"And leave me in there alone?"

"How can you stand Quoins and those other effete bastards?" Mueller shouted as we stopped in front of the ARU porch.

"It's an easy three credits," I said. "Besides, I like Lou's sense of humor."

"He's the worst offender of all! He has no toleration for anything that isn't like what he writes."

"I don't go to Lou for advice," I said. "I can get that from Murray."

Mueller took me by the arm.

"You can't have it both ways," he said. "You're either in the academic world or out of it. If you accept it, you'll only end up writing like Lou, a pale imitation of E. A. Robinson. I can't believe anyone is still rhyming in this day and age!"

"Look," I said, "we'll print your stuff in *The Quill*, no cutting."

"Alongside of Lindner's, right?"

"Tim's good," I reminded him.

"He was better freshman year."

"And he'll be even better after he graduates," I said.

"If he survives."

✝ Fairfield's Book Shop was owned by the former town manager of Brunswick, who also operated a Laundromat and sold real estate on the side. Lou liked to quip that Lloyd McLeod had read a book once and didn't like it. Still, he'd had enough sense to save the best bookstore for miles around, when Ken Andreotti, who first opened it, put the business hastily on the market the year before as part of a divorce settlement. Ken had majored in history after returning from Korea. His book store was a Mecca for the small group of writers and artists who lived in the surrounding communities. Once Lloyd had acquired it, he was wise enough to hire a manager, who continued Ken's practice of carrying a wide variety of good books. Ken had kept the fireplace glowing on winter afternoons and you could count on finding the latest Sartre and Simone de Beauvoir on the shelves. When Murray Aarons took over as manager, the atmosphere and inventory remained the same.

From the start Murray and I hit it off. He was a burly, Hemingway-bearded man, who had already published three novels. I liked him because he didn't try to play the part of the established writer. His wife Aune was a painter, who wrote and illustrated children's books, one of which had won the Caldecott Medal. Besides managing the bookstore, where he spent each afternoon behind the counter, Murray free-lanced for magazines and wrote an occasional "masturbator" for Gold Medal or Monarch books to help make ends meet. This earned him the disdain of purists among the faculty like Lou. But Mueller and I never lost the opportunity to point out that Murray had been consistently well reviewed in the *Times,* as Lou had not. In fact, Murray's latest book, *Of Heroes Gone*, had been hailed by Alfred Kazin as one of a small group of recent novels that dealt powerfully with contemporary Jewish-American life.

Murray let me take whatever I wanted from the book racks, keeping my own account and paying at the end of the semester, or even during the summer when I had more cash. Beyond that, our talks nearly every afternoon, brightened by dinners in the apartment he and Aune rented with their two children at the Mill End of town, made me feel there was something in life besides term papers and exams.

Murray had dropped out of Oberlin in 1939 to wander the country working on farms and in factories. Once the war broke out, he served with the army in the European Theater. Afterwards, he returned to Germany, first as a press officer for SHAEF and then to edit and publish the first English-language newspaper in Berlin. Later he became a broadcast journalist in Chicago, relocating to New York to work in the early days of television. When he was thirty, he published his first novel, about a young Jewish-American GI who has a psychotic breakdown during basic training, quickly following that book up with two more.

He and Aune, who was his second wife (his first had been German), had abandoned their Bleecker Street apartment for Maine, where they felt it was healthier to bring up their two sons.

"Your Spengler's in." Murray looked up smiling from his desk near the fireplace at the rear of the bookstore. In one large hand he held up both volumes of the tan and light blue Knopf edition of *The Decline of the West*.

"Pay me when you can," he added in anticipation of my protest that I couldn't come up with $16.50 for the set all at once.

We shook hands.

"Aune asked when you'd be back. She wants to put the sauce on for another big spaghetti dinner."

"You name it," I said, sitting down in the old easy chair that had been Roonie's for the entire year he was with us after transferring to Bowdoin from NYU. I could smell the hardwood smoke from the burning logs. It made me feel at home again with Murray, who sat behind his desk in a dark red Pendleton shirt and faded jeans.

"Come down Saturday night. We'll have the kids in bed early and the wine on the table. Bring the gang... What's up? You look glum."

"I just came from Lou's class," I answered. "He's already started in again on the Beats. Mueller's talking about dropping the course. It's too bad we couldn't draft you to teach it."

Murray shook his head.

"Writing can't be taught. You can only sit down and work at it the way Jack London did...after living a bit. That's what guys like Lou don't seem to understand, even though they may be up on their scansion."

"Try to convince *them*," I said, kicking my boot toe against the fire screen.

Murray pushed his chair back against the wall.

"Don't waste your time in a futile exercise. Here, read this." He tossed me an envelope with a couple of hastily typed pages in it.

It was a letter from Roonie. He'd left his parents' house in Garden City to move into a cold water walk-up on East 10th Street with an old Navy buddy. They were both taking courses at the New School.

"Tell Jason it's his cup of tea," Roonie wrote. "The teacher knows everybody—Kerouac, Gaddis…"

Roonie described a poetry reading he'd attended at the Gaslight Cafe:

"Diane di Prima's sitting on the top of an upright piano in a pair of tight white toreador pants. Jet black hair. An Italian madonna with a mouth like a longshoreman, and can she write. Like she has this jazzy, hesitating voice and she's reading this poem about going to the post office in Provincetown to pick up a package with salami in it her mother sent her from New York because she's starving. But they won't let her have it unless she presents the right ID, which she hasn't got or can't find, and it's paranoia city all the way. Suddenly the mangy small-town post office is the State and you ain't getting nothin' without them knowing who you are and why you want what came to you legally in the first place."

Roonie went on:

"I'm staying in the Apple till the course is over. Then I'm heading for the Coast, San Fran I think, depending on where I can apply my GI bill. But Berkeley seems a likely destination. A lot of the vets I know are heading out there. I've had it with the East. When I first saw California in the service I knew I'd be living there someday. Screw this cold in New York. I left the Caddie in Garden City, all clean and ready for the road. I may fall by for one last drink before I leave."

"I envy him," I said, handing the letter back to Murray.

"You'd soon tire of Village life," he said, stroking his graying beard. "It's fine when you're trying to get your bearings and it was great after the war, I mean frantic. But if you want to get any serious work done you can't beat the boondocks."

Murray looked at his watch.

"Time to close." He smiled. "Let's continue this on Saturday."

⊹ Independents ate cafeteria style in the Moulton Union. We weren't required to wear jackets and ties and we could spread out in the dining room to our heart's content. John, who served our food from behind the shiny steam table, didn't complain if you were late and he was generous with seconds. White-haired, with a pink face and rimless bifocals, he always had a good word for you, unlike Walt, the cook at the TD house, who was constantly dropping cigarette ashes into the mashed potatoes.

What I appreciated most was the peace and quiet. There were no more than thirty Independents, referred to as "turkeys" by the fraternity brothers, and we were a reserved group. Unable to face the ostracism of not pledging, I had scorned the idea of becoming Independent during my freshman year. But after three years of listening to the brothers belch and fart at the dinner table, and refer to those of us who objected to their vulgarity as "fags," I had decided to go inactive. It was like living alone. At first I couldn't imagine it, but when St. Pierre's father insisted he move into the Zeta house for his senior year, I reluctantly gave up our attic loft at 83 Federal Street and took a single room downstairs, only to discover that I relished the solitude. I read more, I wrote more, and I thought more…and it was the freedom to think that I discovered I liked so much.

At six-fifty-five I carried my chicken bones and coffee cup back to the kitchen and set off for the library where I had the shift until midnight. I saw my breath on the sharp air as I left the Union and cut between Appleton and Hyde halls on the short walk to Hubbard Hall. Behind the circulation desk I leaned back in my chair to wait for the evening's rush of students, once dinner and cards were over at the fraternity houses. The cavernous entrance hall of the library was flanked on either side by larger than life portraits of Hawthorne and Longfellow. It looked and felt like a cathedral, the lights dim, the sounds of footsteps and voices echoing off nineteenth century stone walls. I liked being surrounded by the books on reserve in back of me and the immense card catalogue on the left side of the hall. There was a "new books" section to my right teeming with the latest English novels by Kingsley Amis and John Wain. The younger faculty wives usually gathered in front of that bookcase, whispering breathlessly about the erotic passages they'd discovered the night before in *The Alexandria Quartet*. I liked to watch them in their plaid wool skirts and knee socks, wondering what it was like being a Smith or Radcliffe graduate and sitting home all day while their husbands taught.

I had done my job for a couple of years now and it was simple. I charged out books and kept track of the reserves. I could study or read as I worked. I also got to look over all the recent acquisitions that would be shelved in a nearby alcove where the librarian who prepared them for circulation worked. As usual, the night passed quickly and uneventfully. At eleven-thirty I'd ring the first buzzer. By eleven-forty-five everyone had to be out. One of the other student assistants would make the rounds to see if all the upstairs rooms were empty and the carrels had been abandoned. On weekends there might be the odd couple making out on one of the leather couches in the second floor lounge. Occasionally you'd find a used rubber on the floor. Otherwise, we began putting the lights out. By midnight I was the last to leave, locking the double front doors from within and the side door from without as I headed home, usually with a new book or two to sample under my arm.

My room was in a separate wing of the three-floor Victorian faculty house. Luckily, I couldn't hear the radios or record players of the few students who lived in the main section along with the chairman of the biology department and his family. Once I'd lighted the floor lamp behind the easy chair at the foot of my bed, the room was suffused by a comforting yellow glow. Then I'd put my flannel bathrobe on and wrap a blanket around me. Warmed that way, I could study or read for as long as I wanted, which was often until the first light. Usually I slept until noon because I no longer had morning classes. In any event, I took breakfast and lunch together.

To the right of my old upholstered chair was a big bookcase with glass doors. It was there I kept the books I owned, the poetry of Pound, Eliot and Williams and some of the novels I was currently reading, including Lawrence's and the Modern

Library edition of Proust. The floor against the adjacent wall was lined with books I borrowed from the library. To the left of the single unlocked door to my room was my desk. Over it I'd tacked a large street map of Florence cut out of a Baedeker guide. Between my desk and single bed there was a window, and another at the foot of the bed and to the right of the closet. Over my bed I had a Vlaminck print of fishing boats tied to a wharf in Normandy because its dark browns and cerulean blues reminded me of the waterfront in Gloucester. On the opposite wall was a *gouache* done by a Greek artist friend of mine from Cambridge, who summered on Rocky Neck. It was of an ancient flute player with Byzantine beard and hair locks. A rug covered most of the floor. A hi-fi console sat between an old dresser and the bookcase on a table with cast iron legs. My collection of ten and twelve-inch long-playing jazz and classical albums was lined up under it. Attached to the dresser was a mirror that reflected my desk and the map of Florence. In the glow of my reading lamp the map appeared to be made of old parchment.

This was the room I had lived in since September. A single duct heated it irregularly. Sometimes through the register I could hear Professor Waddell and his wife, who taught high school English in Bath, talking quietly over dinner. My typewriter and typewriter table were nestled to the left of my desk under the big window. The sound of trailer trucks late at night on the Bath Road told me I wasn't isolated from the commerce of highways; and the roar of jet planes taking off or landing at the Brunswick Naval Air Station, a mile from the campus, reminded me that I was never very far from the instruments of war and those who operated them.

There had been no letter from Leslie on the mail table in the downstairs hallway, so I sat with Spengler in my lap and began to read: "The decline of the West, which at first sight may appear...a phenomenon limited in time and space, we now perceive to be a philosophical problem that, when comprehended in all its gravity, includes within itself every great question of Being."

4

It had snowed again on Saturday, but the roads were clear now and the drifts sparkled under the street lights. St. Pierre and Mueller led the way down Maine Street. Dell and I followed close behind, kicking up icy crystals underfoot. Shouting back and forth at each other, we passed Mike's sub shop, the First National, and the darkened windows of Benoit's and the Army and Navy store, just a block down and across the street from Murray's. Our voices echoed and reverberated off the darkened store fronts. It was seven o'clock and the town was already deserted.

Murray and Aune lived at the opposite end of Maine Street from the campus. The front windows of their apartment looked across the Androscoggin River to the ancient redbrick Cabot Mill, now silent. The Verney Corporation had departed Brunswick four years earlier, leaving most of the town's French-Canadian textile workers unemployed.

We found Murray beaming at the door. The smell of Aune's tomato sauce and freshly baked bread filled the hallway. Climbing the stairs to the warm second floor, we could hear the strains of Vivaldi from the record player.

"Benvenuti!"

Aune emerged from the kitchen in a black peasant skirt. Her hair was piled on top of her head. As she hugged me I could smell singed garlic in her gray-blond curls. Murray took our parkas.

"Oh, lovely," exclaimed Dell, catching sight of a big new painting in the living room. It was of Chris, who was a year old, taking his bath in a galvanized tub. Aune had allowed patches of white canvas to show through the yellows and oranges that predominated, giving the painting an equal sense of airiness and warmth.

Murray appeared with a pitcher of red wine. A platter of cheese and thick slices of French bread was already laid out on a sheet of glass covering the lobster trap that served as a coffee table in the long, narrow room.

"Dig in," he said, returning with wine glasses.

St. Pierre and Mueller had been to dinner here before, but this was Dell's first visit. Aune took him on a tour of her studio while the rest of us settled into our habitual seats. St. Pierre favored a couch made of an upholstered mattress set on a laminated door with black cast-iron legs. I lowered myself into a red canvas butterfly chair, and Mueller sat on the floor, his back against the flat white wall. Murray got up to stir the *sugo*. I could hear Dell exclaiming over the work in Aune's studio in the rear of the apartment. A life-sized painting of Murray, sitting up in bed naked to read, dominated one of the walls. Aune had painted it during their first summer in Maine, when they'd taken a cottage at Robinhood before moving into Brunswick.

I always felt at ease in this apartment. Occasionally I'd babysit for the boys while Murray and Aune had a rare evening out. I knew by heart the titles of the books in the unfinished pine floor-to-ceiling bookcase that stood at right angles with Aune's new painting. Murray's spare workroom was directly off the living room. He wrote at an old desk, his Hermes manual typewriter propped on a nearby crate.

Aune called us to dinner in the kitchen. The big, round table was set with steaming plates of *pasta*. The table cloth was Aune's own design, white with blue potato prints. A blue tureen of sauce occupied the center. Murray tossed the salad, placing a wedge of parmesan cheese and a hand grater in a bowl on the table. I poured some wine for Aune.

"This beats dinner at the Zeta house," St. Pierre said, taking his first forkful of *vermicelli*.

"It may not be kosher, but it sure tastes good." Mueller grinned at Murray.

"*Buon appetito,*" said Aune, deftly curling her *pasta* on a soup spoon.

"I wish I could learn to do that," Dell said.

"Aune picked it up in Rome, among other affectations."
Murray winked at his wife.

"Is that where you met?" Dell asked.

"We met in New York," Murray answered.

"In the Village, actually," Aune said, grating some cheese over her *pasta*. She gestured to the rest of us to join in.

"Those were the days," Murray said. "After the war everything was wide open."

"I traveled to Italy while I was in art school," Aune said. "Then I came back to New York. We met at a party."

"Where else?" said St. Pierre.

"I heard *you've* made up your mind," Aune said, turning to him.

St. Pierre nodded, chewing on a slice of bread.

"My family doesn't agree, but I'm going anyway."

"Mine didn't even want me going to art school. They thought it would be the end of me."

"Instead, it was the beginning," Murray said.

"It certainly coaxed me out of my cocoon."

"You were destined for finer things than cotillions."

"How would you know? You couldn't wait to get me into the kitchen!"

"Via the bedroom, or have you forgotten?"

"How could I have forgotten?" Aune reached over to tug Murray's beard. "Let's not bore these gentlemen or they may never come back."

"And forego the best *pasta* in town?" Murray passed the salad bowl.

"Is it true you knew Kerouac?" Mueller asked.

"Murray knew everybody," Aune said.

"The Village was a smaller place ten years ago," Murray explained. "It was easier to meet people. Everyone stayed up half the night drifting from party to party. But let me tell you, Kerouac was a very different guy from the one you've seen on the Steve Allen show reading poetry to that phony jazz."

"Actually he was quite shy," said Aune, "and oh so handsome with a lock of black hair over his forehead and those dark flashing eyes."

"Don't forget, his first novel was fairly conventional," Murray recalled. "It was a family saga quite a bit like *Look Homeward, Angel.*"

"Why is it that parents are so dead set against the arts?" Mueller asked.

"My father was a doctor," Murray said, "and he sent me to college to become a doctor. When I left to bum around the country we didn't speak for years. Even after I dedicated my first novel to him, he wouldn't acknowledge my decision to write."

"Mine drove a taxi in Mattapan," Mueller said. "He and a friend got this idea to start a business making silk-screened shower curtains. The next thing I knew we were living in a big house in Newton and my father was driving a white Cadillac. Now he wants me to take over the business."

"That's not unlike my father's dream for me," Murray said. "It's very much an immigrant's way. You keep what you've achieved in the family."

"But the arts subvert all that," Aune said. "If you have a child who wants to dance or paint, that doesn't fit the pattern."

"Because the arts are frivolous," I said, "at least to people whose lives they don't touch. When I told my father I wanted to be a writer, he said, 'Get your degree and a good teaching job. Then you can do what you want in your spare time.' As if novels could be written on weekends!"

St. Pierre leaned forward to speak:

"Art is not central to life in this society. If you tell anyone you want to be a writer or an actor, they think you're crazy. It's got nothing to do with making money."

"The arts are associated with deviance," Dell said, helping himself to more salad. "I think this society fears difference more than anything. To what else would you attribute McCarthyism?"

"Exactly," Murray said. "Underneath it all there's an absolute terror of otherness, if you want to couch it in existential terms. How else can you account for anti-Semitism or anti-communism, for that matter?"

"Castro isn't in power for one week and they're already calling him a commie dupe," Mueller said. "What the hell's wrong with us? He's overthrown a vicious dictator and we won't acknowledge his right to govern?"

"That's because we really don't want him in control," Murray responded. "We're much more comfortable with the Batistas of this world. They speak the same pro-business language we do. Why do you think Hitler went on for so long without opposition from Britain and the U.S? We prefer fascism to any form of collectivism. Didn't Eliot himself say that if he had to choose between the two systems he'd take fascism—and that was in the 1930s."

"Look," Murray continued, warming to the subject. "When I was a teenager all I wanted to do was join the International Brigades that were helping to fight Franco's insurrection in Spain. It was the great cause. Hemingway wrote the script for a film about it called *The Spanish Earth*. No one could understand why the United States wasn't supporting the Republicans. But it slowly emerged that we didn't want to be allied with the Soviets in Spain, that we preferred a fascist regime because we were afraid of provoking conflict with Hitler and Mussolini."

"I've always wondered why communism is so disturbing to Americans," I said.

"True socialism, which the Soviet system isn't, is deeply threatening to our myth of self-reliance," Murray answered. "Yet few people remember that Eugene Debs received a million votes when he ran for president on the socialist ticket in 1920. And he was in a federal prison at the time! We have a native socialist tradition in this country going all the way back to the early 19th century."

"Wasn't Brook Farm a socialist experiment?" I asked.

"You bet," Murray answered, "and don't forget the little communistic societies in upstate New York and Ohio. People came together to pool their resources and live a more meaningful life, away from the ravages of the Industrial Revolution."

"It's such a paradox," I said. "The House Un-American Activities Committee lists Abstract Expressionism as communist-inspired art, while Kruschev denounces it as bourgeois decadence!"

"Nobody points out the contradictions," Mueller said. "For example, I took economics hoping to learn something about how money works. All we got was an apology for capitalism. Not one word about other systems involving the exchange of goods. It was understood that what was meant by economics was free enterprise."

St. Pierre jumped in:

"The same thing happens when you study poli sci. The professor makes a few wisecracks about the Soviet Union. End of discussion. And the course focuses on what we do and how we think in the West."

As the others talked Dell and I gave Aune a hand clearing the table.

"It's nice to get off the campus," I said, stacking the plates by the sink. "The Deltas and the TD brothers had already started drinking this afternoon. Tonight they'll be barfing in the bushes."

Aune sighed:

"I don't know how you men do it. I'm lucky if I can finish a glass of wine."

"When we were children," I said, "we started taking wine with a little water at dinner. It seemed natural for us to drink."

"You see, your parents taught you *something*." Aune smiled.

Back in the living room we settled into our chairs. St. Pierre and Mueller lit up and Aune accepted one of my Pall Malls.

The dessert was lemon sponge cake with a cream sauce. I could smell the *espresso* beginning to steam on the stove. Murray brought out the demitasse cups and a bowl of sugar.

It was suddenly quiet. The music had stopped. The boys slept peacefully in their back room, alongside of Aune's studio. The rich smell of the sauce still filled the house, giving way now to the more pungent smell of our tobacco and the smokiness of the *espresso*.

Aune sat in the corner softly strumming her guitar.

"Please play," Dell said, his dessert in his lap, the silver fork in his long black fingers.

First Aune hummed "Greensleeves," then she sang the ancient words I'd first discovered in my English Lit textbook. Everyone sat silently. I closed my eyes and thought of Leslie. It was scarcely a week since we'd last been together, but it seemed like months. I hadn't gotten a letter from her that afternoon and I was beginning to worry. She might have been waiting for mine, which I'd mailed on Wednesday, but it wasn't like Leslie to let so much time go by without writing.

Aune was singing:

"I'm gonna moo-oo-oove, way on the outskirts of town..."
She had learned some blues in the Village, listening to Josh White, and she sang them with a wonderful lilting quality. *"Don't want that ice man hangin' around..."*

This was the kind of life I had once imagined for Leslie and me. But at Homecoming Weekend, during the past fall, I had taken Leslie to meet Murray and Aune, expecting that she'd like them immediately. Instead, she was quiet all through dinner. On the way back to her room on McKeen Street, I pressed her for a response.

"I don't see us living in squalor," Leslie said.

"They've chosen simplicity not destitution."

Leslie answered that she could see little difference between the two, and that what she pictured for us was much more like the house my Greek professor Barry and his wife had—a beautiful old Cape Cod cottage with a stone fireplace on the Mere Point Road.

"But Aune comes from a prominent New York family," I rejoined. "She gave all that up to paint."

53

"You can paint in better places than a shabby apartment in downtown Brunswick," she said.

"They're saving up for a farm. Murray wants to grow their own food. Aune's going to start weaving again."

Leslie said nothing.

"I know you don't care for them," I said. "I hoped that you would. You didn't approve of Roonie. Now you don't like Murray and Aune."

"It's the pretension I mind."

"But why?" I asked. "Why can't you accept someone who's part of my life, who means a lot to me? I try to like your friends."

"That's where we differ," Leslie said.

"Besides," I shouted in the dark, "I don't think Aune and Murray are pretentious. They live like artists. My friends back home on Rocky Neck live that way. You don't find fault with them!"

There was no point in pursuing the argument. We'd reached the front door of Mrs. Hill's house. She had left the outside light on and I started to go up the steps with Leslie, hoping that we could at least kiss and make up in the hallway. Leslie turned to me at the door.

"I'll see you tomorrow. I'm getting up early so I can study at the library before I catch my train."

Leslie closed the door after letting me brush the side of her face with my lips. Slowly I made my way back to Federal Street feeling like I'd spoiled something between us.

✢ It was after midnight when we left the Aarons. Aune had gone in to check the sleeping boys. Murray saw us down to the front door, stepping briefly outside with us to get a breath of fresh air. We all shook hands. The night was clear, the stars shone brightly above the mill chimneys out toward Topsham.

"Perfect, just perfect," Dell said, as we made our way down the center of Maine Street.

Mueller lit another cigarette. St. Pierre was singing "Greensleeves." At the cross lights on Maine and Middle streets we got up on the sidewalk again, Dell and I in the lead. A block ahead and just under the street light in front of Mike's there were four townies, who appeared to be our own age. One sat astride a motorcycle, the others were leaning against a car whose rear end was higher than its front. When I caught sight of them, I felt short of breath and I started talking compulsively.

"Oh, shit," St. Pierre said, picking up on my anxiety.

Usually there was little trouble with local kids during the day, but at night some became aggressive, especially if they'd been drinking. After four years' experience I had learned not to look at them in any kind of challenging or provocative way.

"Let's just walk by as though nothing was happening," Mueller said between his teeth. Dell kept quiet, but he didn't change his pace.

The townies, who had been talking and smoking amongst themselves, turned as we approached them. Two were wearing leather motorcycle jackets, their hair slicked back into DAs. They all had blue jeans on and heavy black boots. I recognized the short, bow-legged one as being a leader in various exchanges of taunts I'd been a party to, especially from the bar at Bill's on Mason Street where everyone went for pizza with their dates.

Mike's was closed and no one else was nearby. It was two blocks to the campus. I took a deep breath and pressed ahead. I wanted to say something to Dell but nothing came to mind. All I could think of was, *"There are four of them and four of us."*

We had almost passed them on our left when I heard the first remark:

"Too cold up here for niggers."

"Niggers and college *girls*," another voice said, slurring the word girls so that it sounded effeminate.

St. Pierre saw me starting to turn my head.

"Don't," he whispered.

I was seething with anger. I could feel my body shaking.

"Fucking bastards," Mueller said, as we reached the railroad tracks a block from the campus. The townies hadn't stirred to follow us.

"I'm sorry," I said to Dell.

"Forget it, Jason. I'm used to it."

"But they don't even know who we are."

"That's the sadness of it," Dell answered. "And we'll never know them."

"Why didn't we just stand up to them?"

"It wouldn't prove a thing," Mueller said. "If I fought with every jerk who called me a kike I'd be dead by now."

St. Pierre stopped to stamp his feet in the snow.

"Just once, wouldn't it be nice to beat the shit out of punks like that?"

"I can't wait to get out of this town," I said.

We separated in front of the First Parish Church. I took the Bath Road home alone, listening to my boot heels strike the frozen ground. There wasn't a car in sight. The campus was silent. As I turned onto Federal Street I noticed that the president's mansion was dark. The only light burning on the street was the one over my porch entrance.

5

*T*he word got out on Sunday. There'd been a gangbang the night before. By Monday everybody on campus knew about it. At first it was rumored that twenty students were involved. The victim was only fifteen, they said. A bunch of Deltas had gotten her drunk and taken her to the Sleepy Time Motel, across the highway from the Naval Air Station. At the motel they'd fed her more alcohol and each had taken a turn with her. Someone had driven her back toward town and let her out near the railroad station. The police found the girl wandering half naked in the cold, her underpants stuffed with dollar bills.

Then they said there were only eleven participants. A couple of them were well known jocks. The girl was seventeen or eighteen. She worked at Ernie's drive-in on the Bath Road. They said she was partially retarded. The guys had promised her money and beer. They claimed she went along with it at first, but that she'd started screaming when they got her into the motel room and began tearing her clothes off. Someone turned on a portable radio to drown out her cries. The management at the Sleepy Time didn't pay any attention to the commotion because they were used to renting rooms to men from the base, who took their dates there on weekends.

The Brunswick police had gotten the Dean out of bed at three in the morning. He'd gone with them to the Delta house after the girl had identified some of the brothers. On Sunday the president intervened. The ringleaders were isolated and immediately expelled. Everyone else had been suspended, awaiting the outcome of a joint investigation between college authorities and the police. By Sunday night all those who had taken part in the rape had left the campus.

When I got to Clayton's around eleven on Monday morning, St. Pierre was already there. He glanced up warily from Urmson's *Philosophical Analysis* as I approached with my coffee.

"What's the story," I asked. "Is it true they were all kicked out?"

"Every fucking one of them," he muttered, his pencil at work on the text.

"I can't imagine how you could even get it up under those circumstances."

"Not those animals," he said, shaking his head. "If it was my sister I'd have killed them with my bare hands. She was half-witted, too. Did you hear that?"

"What could they possibly feel with the girl lying there drunk and disheveled?"

"Beats the shit out of me." St. Pierre closed his book and placed the pencil stub behind his right ear.

"Was she a virgin?"

"Who knows?" he said. "She worked at Ernie's. I don't remember anyone retarded working there."

"She could just be a little slow."

"They left her naked on the Bath Road," St. Pierre said.

"I heard it was near the railroad tracks and they put money in her underwear."

"Pigs."

"I bet they'll have something to say about it this week in chapel."

"Don't count on it," St. Pierre said. "One of the guys' fathers is a big shot in the state legislature."

"It figures."

"The girl was under age. They said she was in such a state of shock that she couldn't even talk afterwards. They had her sedated at the Parkview Hospital."

✝ All through Lit Crit class that afternoon I couldn't keep the rape out of my mind. Even our professor, who was usually animated, seemed subdued. Loren Halley had long white hair. He combed it back on both sides of his head, keeping it in place with the bows of his steel-rimmed glasses. His green workpants often had the stains of anti-fouling compound on them from the boat yard he ran in his spare time on Orr's Island. Loren had graduated from Bowdoin, going directly to Yale to get his doctorate with a dissertation on Hawthorne's social criticism. Yale University Press had published it while Loren was stationed in the Pacific as a Lt. Commander in the Navy. After the war he taught for a while at Annapolis before coming back to Brunswick.

Even though I'd studied with Loren for three years, we'd hardly had a conversation that you could call intimate. In class he was witty, tough and informal. But when you had a conference with him, or during the rare occasions you ran into him on campus, it was always "Mr. Makrides," and spoken through strong white teeth in a tightly clenched jaw. If there was any one of my English instructors I'd wanted to get to know better it was Loren; but he kept his distance with everyone. What you found out about him was likely to be gossip, like the story that he and his next door neighbor had swapped wives, divorcing their own and marrying each other's. They were still said to be friends.

Loren announced that we'd be doing actual criticism in the course. He wanted to give us practice in various contemporary approaches, starting with I. A. Richards and the New Critics and progressing to the study of archetypes advanced by Northrop Frye. Frye's *Anatomy of Criticism* was one of our texts. It promised to be an exciting semester. Yet while Loren went over the syllabus, I kept returning obsessively to the girl who had been raped.

I wondered what she looked like. I pictured her, maybe dirty blond and pudgy like so many of the girls who worked at the drive-ins of Brunswick and Lewiston, lying naked on a motel bed.

This made me think of the first time I'd seen Leslie without clothes. It happened toward the end of the previous summer. As usual, I had picked her up from work and we'd grabbed a bite at the drive-in on Thacher Road. Instead of parking in the public lot across the street at Good Harbor Beach, I'd driven to a smaller and more hidden one at Brace Cove on Eastern Point. Symphony Sid was on radio—night time Sarah Vaughn singing "Moonlight in Vermont" in her throaty voice—-as we lay close together on the front seat of my parents' '57 Chevy, kissing and fondling each other.

Leslie often let me put my hands up under her waitress uniform to feel the smooth flesh of her thighs. Once or twice she even put her hand on my penis. We'd never gone beyond that, unless she let me caress her covered breasts. But that night we both seemed under the spell of a late August wind that swept across the water, blowing the tall beach grass back and forth with a nearly human moan. The moon was enormous, its light on the water splintered by the wind-riven sea. We could smell kelp in the high wind.

With our lips and tongues we kissed, Leslie sighing as we spoke of having to abandon each other to return to school. We were lying side by side. Then Leslie got up on her knees and began to unbutton her white blouse.

"Take your shirt off, Jason," she said breathlessly. "I want to feel you under me."

In the near darkness I watched her blouse fall back while she unfastened her bra. Then she lowered herself until her bare breasts were on my chest.

We lay like that until it was time for me to take her home. The next night she let me unbutton her Bermudas, and with trembling hands I pulled her white panties down. Then I kissed her naked stomach and her silky pubic hair. The smell of Leslie's body was intoxicating. As I leaned over her, she unbuttoned my shorts. Then she did what I had been dying for her to do all summer. She put one hand under my testicles and with the other she held me warmly. I had all I could do to keep from coming.

In the midst of this reverie, with Loren comparing the tragic and the comic modes, I started thinking again of the gangbang, which led to a feeling of discomfort about what Leslie and I had done. Our intimacies seemed somehow improper, although there had been nothing of rape or resistance about our behavior. We had done no more than undress, exploring each other's bodies with a keen sense of discovery.

Even though my probing had told me that Leslie was wet inside and I'd nearly ejaculated as she let her fingers trail across my erect penis, we had gone no farther, stopping ourselves or each other in subsequent moments, falling back, pulling away, the car window steamy with our breaths and the heat of our bodies.

"We have to wait," I'd say.

"Yes, it's too soon," Leslie would echo as she pulled her bra back on or buttoned a blouse.

"Let's not rush it," I'd say. "We'll have the rest of our lives to make beautiful love."

"I know," she'd answer. "Besides we have to be careful."

And even though we talked of buying Trojans, especially after the one time Leslie let me gently penetrate her as she straddled me, slowly, exquisitely moving up and down on me, we both agreed that once we did that we'd have entered the realm of intercourse and that was proscribed.

As Loren spoke of the practice of criticism, Mueller and St. Pierre jumped in to carry on a lively discussion with him, contrasting Edmund Wilson's belletristic approach with the more tough-minded one of John Aldridge. Quoins, who at first had seemed to be mumbling to himself in the corner of our Chase Barn classroom, joined them, and then Foster. But I kept drifting back to the raped girl and then to Leslie and me. The last thing in the universe I had intended was to violate Leslie. But I was suddenly afraid that I might have hurt her and she had not said so, or that I might in some manner of speaking have been raping her. Beneath those thoughts there lurked an anxiety mixed with not a little excitement that I could barely let myself bring to consciousness.

✢ I rushed back to my room after class and started writing a story about the rape. I decided to tell it from the point of view of a freshman named Ethan, who agrees to accompany some of the upperclassmen to the motel because he doesn't want them to think he's chicken. I began the narrative with a group of brothers arriving in one car outside the motel. Ethan sees the lights on and he hears loud music; there's a sense of excitement in the air, yet he's frightened. He doesn't know what to expect. He's a virgin and he's afraid of being forced to perform sexually in front of the other brothers.

I wrote furiously until dinner, my room filled with cigarette smoke. After my shift at the library, I resumed work at the typewriter, writing until my eyes watered and the chair under me felt so hard I couldn't sit on it any longer. I reached the point in the narrative where Ethan has to enter the bedroom alone. The other brothers are drinking and talking in a larger adjoining room. He finds the girl naked on a double bed, her arms tied to the posts with strips of cloth torn from the bed sheets. She seems in a trance, yet when he approaches the bed she looks at him with terror in her eyes. From the next room comes the loud music of a radio and the voices of the brothers drinking and boasting about what they'd done to the girl or made her do to them.

"Man, did you watch her taking that cock in her mouth!"

Ethan has never seen a naked girl before. Earlier that fall, at the Topsham Fair, he'd watched an older woman doing a strip-tease in front of a bunch of leering farmers and some fraternity brothers who were shitfaced. As she danced she rubbed her crotch up and down against one of the tent poles. After the show he and another Delta pledge had been sent backstage to get three cunt hairs as part of their initiation. Wrapped in a red kimono, the woman hardly appeared to notice them. Nonchalantly she'd plucked out the requested pubic hairs and handed them to Ethan with a wink, a cigarette dangling from the corner of her heavily painted mouth.

The girl who remains unnamed jerks her legs up so Ethan won't be able to see her genitals. He sits on the bed, fully dressed, his hands shaking. Nothing excites him about the naked girl. She is overweight and there is perspiration between her small breasts; she seems to be sobbing almost silently. He wonders how the other brothers can take their clothes off in front of her, how they can have any desire for this girl they've reduced to hysteria.

As Ethan sits on the bed beside the frightened girl, he hears the brothers outside singing, *"Roll me over, in the clover. Roll me over, lay me down, and do it again!"* He remembers a story that Ruth, the girl he's in love with, told him at Christmas. Ruth is a nursing student and she finds herself so ill one morning that she collapses in the ward with a high fever. This had actually happened to Leslie when she was in secretarial school, so I incorporated her experience into Ruth's story. Having fainted in class, Leslie had been rushed to New England Baptist Hospital. After moving her from the stretcher to a gurney, an intern had undressed her, presumably so that she could be examined. Another intern came by to watch as she lay shivering. She had felt utterly helpless, so sick that she was barely conscious, as the two men continued to stare at her white nakedness. Then one of the older nurses came into the room and covered Leslie with a sheet, admonishing the interns as she took over the case. Leslie was subsequently diagnosed with mononucleosis and sent home to recuperate. But for remainder of her brief hospital stay she never felt comfortable around the interns. I transferred Leslie's sense of having been violated to my character Ruth.

✝ The next day I left my room only to eat and to attend Dante class. I was back at work on my story in the afternoon, the rhythms of the first cantos of the *Inferno* throbbing in my head. I felt as though I were Ethan and, indeed, I became him as I wove Leslie's story and my outrage into the narrative. But there was another dimension, both to the story and to my own involvement in it. I had never seen Leslie naked when she told me how the resident had stripped her and left her lying on the gurney, and I had been excited by what she recounted.

Ethan recalls his own sense of impotence when Ruth tells him how she lay there helplessly, while the two interns cracked jokes about her figure. Fleetingly he remembers his arousal at the

67

thought of Ruth's nakedness. As he sits with the frightened girl in the motel, the brothers shouting that unless they hear some "action" on the bed they'll come in and "take over," he feels a sudden anger about what has been done to her. At the same time, he feels caught in a situation he abhors.

Realizing his hesitation, the girl looks at him imploringly. Softly she says, "Help me," and Ethan realizes that he must act...

Back from the library that night, I finished the story and began recopying its twenty pages. I typed until dawn, stopping to revise as I worked. Then I slept until noon on Wednesday, getting up in time to grab some lunch and head over to Lou's writing class.

I was the last to read. As tired as I was, I read my own words clearly and carefully. I began with the description of Ethan's arrival at the motel and the noise in the next room as he imagines one of the brothers "banging" the captive girl. Then I read the long central section, which describes Ethan alone in the room with the girl and his memory of Ruth's treatment by the interns. When the girl asks Ethan to help her, he realizes that he must, although he also knows that his aid to her will be viewed as an act of betrayal by his brothers. He realizes that he'll never be able to face them again; indeed, that no matter what happens he'll still be considered guilty of the rape because he willingly went along with the brothers in agreeing to accompany them to the motel.

Leaning forward in my arm chair, the fire going and the others in the class intent on my reading, I came to the end of the story:

"Ethan said nothing to the naked, frightened girl, who had now pulled herself up against the headboard as if to move as far away from him as her bonds allowed. He could have untied her. He could even have helped her get into what was left of her clothing on the floor. But he knew that both he and the girl would be the target of the brothers' retaliation if he attempted to get her out. Clearly they would prevent such an act on his part, knowing full well that they were already liable for what they had done to the girl. Instead, Ethan pulled the sheet up over the trembling red-haired teenager, gently covering her legs and her torso. He said nothing. He would go out into the next room among the drinking brothers. Perhaps he would even accept a beer and make some remark about what they had presumed he'd just accomplished. As soon as he could, he would slip out and call the police from the motel payphone. He supposed he could run then, back to the campus; but he knew that there would be no escaping for him. Best to meet the police car, best to face them, knowing that he would also have to confront the other brothers and eventually his classmates.

"Anxiously, he had a glimpse of his college career ending because of this act. Yet what did the brothers think would happen to theirs, especially those seniors who expected to graduate that spring? He had a sudden image of himself on the train back home. He would be telling Ruth what he'd done, how he'd covered the shaking girl and gone out to face the brothers.

"'Oh, she was a dog,' he'd have to say, 'but I dicked her just the same. I fucked her till she was blue in the face.'"

No one said anything after I finished reading, which had gone beyond the hour for the ending of the class. Lou just sat there gesturing with open palms. As I got up to leave, Mueller began softly snapping his fingers. Lou and the others joined in. It was a college tradition for quietly acknowledging that something had moved you.

I walked across campus alone, exhausted and drained of emotion. My initial elation at having completed and shared the story had given way to an obsession with details I could have added to make it better or more authentic. I thought maybe I should go take a look at the interior of a motel room to get the decor right. Then I blanked those thoughts out of my mind, as the last sunlight slanted across the snow that was crosshatched by the blue shadows of the trees. Behind me was the Walker Art Museum and ahead lay the chapel, its spire reflecting the dying light. All around me was stillness, the sky turning slowly to lead. I heard my footsteps on the frozen path, saw my breath in front of me. I felt the cold air on my gloveless hands as I clutched the notebook I had stuck the story into to protect it on the way to class.

✛ Waiting for me at my room there was a long letter from Leslie. I read it anxiously before rushing out to dinner and the library. She reported that classes had begun and that she was pleased to have gotten into Douglas Bush's seminar on the Metaphysical Poets. She was also taking Contemporary Philosophical Debate with Ralph Harper, whose book on existentialism we had read together.

"It's going to be tough," she wrote. "Lots of analytical philosophy, not much Kierkegaard or Sartre." She'd finally begun *The Mandarins* on her own and was loving it. "The central couple reminds me of us," she wrote. "But the French with all their *affaires de coeur* just frighten me. I don't want to live that way. I can't imagine our being unfaithful to each other..."

I read further in the dark room, pausing only to switch the desk lamp on. My desk was littered with Manila scrap paper.

Grandgent lay on the bed. Already I was falling behind in my assignments for Dante. Coming up, too, was a conference with Hubie Braun, my thesis advisor and the department chair. I knew he despised Lawrence, so I expected trouble as I worked with him on my paper.

Then an alarming sentence of Leslie's caught my eye.

"We need to talk," she said. "I have to tell you that your news about going to Italy alone next September, although not unexpected, disturbs me deeply. I didn't think it would hurt me so much, but once I got back to school I couldn't get it out of my mind. I don't want to say anything more about it now. When I come up for Winter Houseparty—assuming, of course, that I'm still invited—I hope we can talk about this big adjustment in our relationship..."

I wanted desperately to address Leslie's concerns. In fact, I made a move to pull my typewriter table over. But I knew that dinner was being served now in the Union and that if I didn't eat on time I'd be late for the library. I felt torn between rushing off to eat and writing Leslie, then I thought about calling her. Long ago we'd made an agreement to communicate only by letter, reserving the more costly telephone calls for absolute emergencies. Was this such an emergency? I didn't know. All I knew was that I was exhausted and that I hoped I wouldn't fall asleep at the circulation desk. As I made my way over to the Union, Leslie's words echoed in my head. What did she mean by "this big adjustment in our relationship?" I felt gripped by the same impotence and terror I'd experienced when she told me how she lay feverishly on the hospital gurney, miles from me or any power I might have had to shield her from the ravishing eyes of the interns, who stood menacingly over her exposed and defenseless body.

6

*O*n the last day of January I received word that my play had been one of three selected for performance in the Student One Act Play Contest. Quoins and Dell were the other two finalists. St. Pierre agreed immediately to direct *Summer's End*. Mueller would design the set; and Mendel offered to handle the technical details, including the music. We spent the first week in February mapping out the work ahead, while St. Pierre and I rounded up the cast.

Ruth Barry, a widow who owned a chicken farm in Bowdoinham, would play Martha, Pat's boss at the Rockaway Hotel, who tries to coax Jason out of his shell. That fall Ruth had been a brilliant Blanche Dubois in *A Streetcar Named Desire*, playing opposite St. Pierre as Stanley Kowalski. We thought that she would be perfect in the role of a middle-aged hotel hostess and go-between. To create even greater dramatic tension, St. Pierre suggested that Martha have a crush on Jason herself. Jessie Cranach, a married student, agreed to play the part of Jason, suggesting Amanda Swan, the wife of his Congregational minister in Yarmouth, for the role of Pat. As soon as we saw Mandy's round face framed by dark hair cut in bangs, we knew she was going to be perfect. In my search for someone to play Rick, the snotty undergraduate, I managed to prevail upon Dave Muncie, a former TD brother of mine whom I'd originally used as a model for the character. Finally, the walk-on roles—two waitresses at the Rockaway Hotel—would be played by the president's daughter Claire and her high school classmate, Jahna, the daughter of the head of the chemistry department.

Once the cast was settled, St. Pierre and I sat down to block out the action. We worked in his room at the Zeta house, dropping in on Mendel from time to time as he played for us some of the background music he was considering. It would all be jazz—Errol Garner's piano and the airy, summertime music of Stan Getz, but with a profounder, maybe even darker shading, a ground theme of impending fall. I suggested Stan Kenton's "Cuban Fire." With its throbbing Afro-Cuban rhythms and deep brass scoring for French horns, trombones and tuba, over which Lucky Thompson's tenor saxophone mournfully wailed, it seemed like the perfect theme music for the autumnal atmosphere of loss and change I'd hoped to achieve in *Summer's End*. The others agreed.

Then, suddenly, it was Winter Houseparty weekend and I was meeting Leslie at the Brunswick railroad station on Friday afternoon. Since morning I'd felt an electricity in the icy air, a hushed sense of anticipation as students rushed between classes. Here and there you caught a glimpse of the bright faces of dates, who had arrived early, making me all the more anxious to see Leslie.

She swung off the four o'clock train wearing the raccoon coat she'd bought the previous year at Morgan Memorial, her shapely legs in gray woolen knee socks. I conducted her immediately to Clayton's, feeling proud that we were on display in the big front window as the other students passed by with their dates.

We sat drinking coffee, Leslie's compact black suitcase next to the table. I offered her a Pall Mall, but she took out a box of Marlboros.

"You're not smoking our brand anymore?"

"They burn my tongue," she replied, moving her head away from me to let a plume of smoke out of her mouth.

I covered her still cold hand with mine.

"Not here," she whispered.

I cleared my throat.

"Do you want to talk now or should we wait until later?"

She shrugged her shoulders, letting the open raccoon coat fall back against the chair. Then she looked me in the face, her hazel-colored eyes catching me by surprise.

"First, tell me about the play, Jason." She tilted her head, a wistful smile on her bright lips. "I'm so happy for you."

As Leslie spoke I felt an overwhelming love for her surge up in me. I started to speak, but my voice choked up and my eyes filled with tears. Softly she placed her hand on mine.

"I don't love you any less because you're going away," she said gently. As she shook her coat further off, I saw that she was still wearing my fraternity pin over her heart on the gray cashmere sweater that matched her knee socks.

Just the same, I felt a tension between us. Over dinner at the Union we stuck to the safer topics of courses and instructors. When we made the preliminary round of houses, stopping first at ARU to have a drink with Mueller and his date Miriam, and then at the Zeta house to rendezvous with St. Pierre, Leslie seemed her old confident self, talking a blue streak about her new professors. But on the way back to her room at Mrs. Hill's she was quiet again. The air was freezing as we held hands through our gloves. I wanted to kiss her, to touch her all over, to tell her I adored her. But at the door we kissed only once, our cheeks glancing off each other like sheets of cold metal as we said good night. And I returned home to masturbate in the chilly confinement of my bed, only to feel afterward that I'd betrayed Leslie with yet another willful act.

✝ On Saturday afternoon the editorial board of *The Quill* met at Quoins' room on School Street, just around the corner from mine. There was liquor in abundance, even tequila, and we all brought our dates. Leslie and I sat on a big couch. St. Pierre and his blind date Nancy occupied a loveseat across from us. Quoins and Hillary Wainwright, his date from Bennington, sat on the floor, Quoins, as usual, in a black turtleneck and baggy flannels. The manuscripts of the poems and stories that had been submitted for the spring issue of the magazine were spread out on the cottee table in front of us. We'd all given them a preliminary reading. Now it was time for a joint selection.

"What dogshit!" Hillary drawled, as she tossed a poem back on the pile. She had long black hair that fell halfway down her back. From time to time she would toss her head to get it out of her eyes. Her lips were painted a red that seemed almost black, and she wore a long black woolen skirt over black dancer's tights. St. Pierre hadn't been able to take his eyes off her since he'd arrived.

"Well, don't expect this to be Bennington," Quoins said in his sleepiest voice.

"I'll never forget a date I had there once," St. Pierre began giddily. "I was visiting my friend Anthony at Williams. He'd fixed me up with his girlfriend's roommate. When I went to their cottage to pick her up on Saturday morning, she stood in the window waving her bra at me."

Hillary gave St. Pierre a bored look.

"Most of the girls I know don't even *wear* them," she said dryly.

Quoins poured himself another screwdriver. I helped myself to the tequila. Leslie sat back surveying the room. I was sure she'd hated Hillary on sight. Nancy, who was from Westbrook Junior College, remained silent. She was wearing a pink woolen sweater, her hands clasped together in the lap of her red plaid kilt.

I wanted to push for the inclusion of Mueller's poem, but I didn't want it to seem obvious.

"Try this," I said, handing it to Hillary.

She squinted over its three pages, finally smiling.

"The Village comes to Brunswick, Maine!" she intoned, but not without a hint of appreciation in her theatrically deep voice.

"Mueller's trying for a sound of his own," St. Pierre said.

"Ah, you guys are always pushing your beloved Beats!" Quoins sighed.

"But what *are* the other models?" Hillary gestured to the room at large. "Surely the days of the Fugitives are over. If I have to read another poem by Ransom about some *dead* student I'll barf... And don't even mention MacLeish." She peered down her beautiful long nose in Quoins' direction.

"I don't think it's an either/or," Leslie said calmly. She took one of my Pall Malls, snapped open her lighter, and drew deeply on the cigarette.

"I happen to be reading Denise Levertov just now," she continued, exhaling the smoke through her nostrils. "There's some wonderful poetry being written outside of the academic world and it doesn't have to be Beat, although I must say I adore the Beats." Leslie looked in Hillary's direction. "Do you know Diane di Prima? She's only a few years older than we are. I suppose you could call her Beat by association, but mostly she's herself."

As Quoins called us back to order, I gave Leslie what I hoped she would accept as an admiring look. How I loved her in those moments when her intelligence shone forth!

We chose a number of poems, trying to achieve a balance between the traditional and the experimental. Everyone agreed that the excerpts from Lindner's long poem were incredible. We decided to publish those along with Mueller's poem and some diamond-like translations from the Chinese, which I'd persuaded

Bobby Wong Yee, a physics major, to submit. Since Quoins was editor, we had to vote to include the verse play he'd read in Lou's class, even though I hated it. I was relieved when nobody asked about my story. Although I desperately wanted to see it in print, I wasn't ready yet to share it with Leslie. Instead, we opted for a translation I'd made from a tale in Italian by Grazia Deledda about a summer encounter on a Riviera resort beach. We took a few more poems by underclassmen and a brilliant vignette by a junior from Bath named Skraeling, who was said to leave his room in Moore Hall only to buy booze. Everyone voted to publish a story that St. Pierre had written about the summer after our freshman year, when he'd traveled to the Pacific Northwest to pick peas for the Green Giant company.

I poured some more tequila into Leslie's small glass, after rubbing a bit of lime around the rim and dipping it into a plate of salt. I was thirsty from the salt in my own drink so I made myself a screwdriver. St. Pierre and Nancy stuck to tequila. As yet Nancy had said nothing, and no one had made any effort to draw her out.

"If you like the Beats, have you read this?" St. Pierre handed Hillary Quoins' copy of *The Outsider*, by Colin Wilson.

"Oh, spare me!" she shouted. "It was required reading in practically every course at Bennington last year. What a fraud!"

St. Pierre's eyes blazed.

"How can you say that?"

"Well, I mean the whole mystique about how he lived in a *sleeping* bag on Hampstead Heath while writing the book in the *British* Museum. And he's barely educated!"

"That's the point of the book's attraction," St. Pierre rejoined. "It's an incredible study of alienation, but it's not academic. In fact, you could say that it's by a truly alienated person."

"I'd call him an English equivalent of the Beats," I chimed in.

"I believe they're dubbed 'The Angry Young Men'," Hillary said condescendingly.

"Whatever you want to call him," St. Pierre persisted, "I've never read a clearer analysis of what it means to be on the outside socially and intellectually."

"But alienation is so *fashionable* now. Once it's in the classroom it's no longer a lived feeling, it's only a pose."

Leslie intervened:

"They said the same thing about existentialism. When I was in Europe all you saw in Berlin or Paris were boys in little black berets—and woman wearing their hair in bangs like Juliette Greco. But that didn't take away from the power of what Sartre and de Beauvoir were writing or how they were *living* anymore than it does from the Beats' message."

"Which is?" Hillary asked in a voice both bored and aggressive.

"Which *is*," Leslie responded with sarcasm, "that crass materialism kills what's human in each one of us, and that in a fatuous society like ours the place of honor is on the outside."

"Brava!" St. Pierre shouted, raising his drink.

"I don't disagree," Hillary said, smiling faintly. "Where did you say you were in school?"

"I didn't," Leslie replied, getting up to find her raccoon coat.

Once we all hit the air, we could feel the effects of our drinks. I grabbed the porch railing to steady myself.

"Jason, I think I'm drunk." Leslie began sliding toward me on the icy sidewalk. I let her collapse into my arms.

"Let's stop for a minute at my room," I said, as the others piled into St. Pierre's car heading for the Zeta house cocktail party.

"But I can't come up with you." Leslie seemed alarmed.

"It's getting dark," I said. "No one will notice. We'll only stay for a minute. I've got to piss and I can't do it on the street."

The house was empty as I led Leslie up to my room, which she'd seen only briefly during last fall's Homecoming, when parents and dates were allowed a perfunctory inspection of off campus housing. I'd fantasized our being together in this cozy setting, although I knew it would be too small for a couple to share. But just the thought of Leslie here with me had been enough to help me imagine it on a cold February afternoon like this one.

"I love it, Jason," she said, as I closed the door quietly behind us and snapped on the desk lamp sending a soft glow over the room.

"This is the scene of all my letters to you."

"It doesn't seem as cold as you've described it to me—right out of *Crime and Punishment*.

"Today they put the heat on," I said. "You can sneak across the hall if you want."

I pulled the shades down while Leslie used the bathroom. Then she came back to sit on my bed.

"I can tell you live here," she said in a hushed voice when I returned from peeing. "I know your books and paintings by heart. The room even smells of you!"

"Not too badly I hope." I still felt dizzy even though I'd splashed cold water on my face and brushed my teeth to get rid of the salty taste from the tequila.

"Come hold me," Leslie said, "just for a second."

I dropped my army surplus parka on the floor and went to join her on the bed.

"I was wondering if I'd ever kiss you again," I said, as we lay back on my cold pillow. Leslie let me slip her coat off, but our boots were cumbersome on the bed and I was afraid that my landlord would return and find us together. So we lay still in the semi-dark, our bodies gradually warming from our embrace.

"You were wonderful at Quoins'," I whispered in Leslie's ear.

"I sort of like Hillary," she said. "She reminds me of some of the boarding school kids I met that summer in Paris. She's better, though, because she's got real opinions."

"I think St. Pierre's smitten."

"He deserves an interesting woman," Leslie said.

"I've already got one, and I'm so happy to have you."

"Then why are you running away from me?"

I couldn't tell if the tone in her voice was humorous or angry.

"Oh God I'm not, Les. I'm right here this minute holding you."

"Forgive me." Leslie started rubbing my back. "I've had too much to drink and I'm feeling sad about myself."

"Don't be sad," I said. "I meant what I wrote you. I'll come back to you. You must know that."

"I do and I don't," she said with an almost wary sound to her voice. "Part of me knows you have to go to Europe just like

I did. The other part is jealous of you because you'll be gone longer and you'll be alone."

"And what does that mean?" Suddenly I wished we were naked and under the sheets.

"It means that you'll be free to do whatever you want and see whomever you choose."

"So will you," I said, with the sudden fear that we were actually talking about breaking up.

"I don't want to. I'm perfectly content loving you."

"Maybe I won't go after all," I said, knowing full well that I could think of little else, that is, when I wasn't thinking about Leslie.

"No, you have to go," she said, "and that's the sadness of it. Because if you don't you'll always wish you had and you'll blame me. You'll take your anger out on us and our life together will be a disaster."

I could smell our warm bodies and the fumes of the tequila in our breaths.

"Let's just stay here," I said, holding her close. "Let's not go anywhere tonight...or if you want we can go to a motel. St. Pierre will lend me his car."

"I don't want to consummate our love in some dump, Jason. But I do love you, no matter what."

Leslie squeezed my hand as I cupped her face and we kissed tenderly.

✝ When we got to the Zeta house, the party was in full swing. Ross Kimball and his quartet were playing a raunchy "Black and

Blue," Ross's trumpet smearing the blue notes in a fine imitation of Satchmo.

"Hey!" St. Pierre motioned us over. "Where in hell have you guys been?"

"In the sack where they belong." Hillary grinned, as she grabbed St. Pierre away from Nancy and danced him out into the middle of the room in front of the band. Quoins sat off to the side in a leather chair, hunched over his drink.

Without even taking off her coat Leslie maneuvered me onto the dance floor in a slow jitterbug. As we danced we accepted beers from Mueller, who was being handed them by Miriam at the bar behind him.

"Oh shit, this is all I need." Leslie and I wiggled out of our coats.

"Thank God we stopped for a bite," she said, hugging me into a fox-trot as the band took the tempo down another peg.

There was a fire roaring in the corner of the room, the bar was lined with beers. Slowly we worked our way back to where our friends were sitting.

"You smell so good," I said to Leslie as we left off dancing with another hug.

A sudden hush came over the room as the band took a break. Leslie retrieved our coats from where we'd dropped them on the dance floor and we both collapsed in a couple of armchairs that had been vacated when everyone rushed to the bar.

Mueller came over to shake my hand, his bright black eyes fixing mine.

"Thanks," he said.

"For the poem? It's first rate. Everyone thought so."

"I loved it." Leslie nodded enthusiastically. Miriam joined us. She had short curly black hair and a piercing voice.

"Where's this Mendel I've been hearing about?"

"Bob never socializes," I answered.

"Let's go drag him down then."

Mueller sat on the arm of Miriam's chair.

"He wouldn't appreciate it," he said.

"What is he, some kind of recluse?"

"He's who he is." St. Pierre pulled his chair over so that we were all knee to knee.

"I've met him and I love him," Hillary said. "He's the most authentic person on this campus. He doesn't abide by any of the bullshit norms around here."

Quoins materialized, looking dolefully at Hillary.

"What do you say we disappear?"

"Don't be ridiculous!" she shrieked.

The music started again with an uptempo "Undecided." The women wanted to dance so we all got into a circle. It enabled us to move and talk as a group, breaking off into couples when Ron pointed the bell of his trumpet at us and swung into a furious "How High the Moon."

St. Pierre and Hillary did a strut right through all the dancers. Hillary was hanging onto his neck, her dark hair flying behind her.

"I might have predicted this," Leslie whispered in my ear.

"I just feel badly for Hal."

"He encouraged it. He may even be enjoying it."

Mueller and Miriam had disappeared into the darkened Zeta library. As Leslie and I made our way across the floor, I caught sight of my Greek teacher Barry and his wife Jan.

"No making out!" he said, barring our way to the Zeta library, his face red with excitement.

"Don't pay any attention to him," said Jan. She was dressed in a flower print Villager dress and flats, her round horn-rimmed glasses giving her the look of an owl. "Two beers and he's worse than an undergraduate."

"I *am* an undergraduate," Barry protested.

"You're a baby is what you are," she said.

Barry stepped back and bowed to Jan, his blond curls wet with perspiration.

"This, my loves, is marriage, if you are tempted to try it."

"Home we go," Jan said. "I don't want to spend all day Sunday listening to your recriminations."

We groped around for an armchair in the Zeta library, bumping against knees, tripping over bodies supine on the thickly carpeted floor. But there wasn't an empty one. Holding Leslie's hand I led her back out into the party. The upstairs rooms were off limits and the kitchen was closed, so we headed out again into the cold on our way to Moulton Union.

The dining room was packed with couples. Girls tried to sober up their comatose dates with black coffee. Guys sipped whiskey out of hip flasks, pouring liquor into their dates' coffee cups. People shouted back and forth from table to table, their faces heated and their voices rising or falling, depending upon the state of their inebriation. We took our coffee into the lounge where someone's date was playing Cole Porter tunes on the grand piano, while others were kissing in the leather arm chairs that ringed the enormous room. Two couples occupied the big sofa in front of the fireplace, one buried under a mound of coats, another drunk or asleep, their arms and legs intertwined.

In the darkened corner near the piano we finally located a chair. Leslie collapsed into it immediately. I sat on the arm rest. The pianist was singing "You Are my Everything." Her voice had a wonderful, hoarse, Mabel Mercer quality to it. I couldn't take my eyes off her as she played and sang in the semi-dark, no male companion in sight, a mink coat falling around the leather-upholstered piano stool she sat on. Then someone blinked the lights to signal that the Union was closing for the night and we were all ejected into the cold.

When Leslie and I got back to Mrs. Hill's, there was a light on upstairs in the old lady's bedroom. Sneaking up to the room Leslie occupied next to it was out of the question. Hesitantly we kissed good night in the freezing, echoey hallway. Alone I crossed the campus. The drunken shouts of students and their dates leaving house parties around the quad mingled with the din of dateless revelers in the dorms. Lights flashed on and off, while every variety of music emanated from radios and hi fi systems in a pandemonium of noise. Yet through it all the lamp still burned in Schrebner's office. I paused beneath it as if to salute his solitary vigil.

Once I was back in my inhospitable room, I seemed to hear again the breathy voice of the girl, who sat alone at the grand piano in the Union, her lipsticked mouth the only prominent feature of her face in the half-light, the mink coat encircling her. Who was she, I wondered, and what was she doing all by herself singing "You Are my Everything?"

✝ It was Sunday afternoon and snowing again. Reluctantly I'd put Leslie on the two o'clock train to Boston. I was sitting in my room gloomily making notes on *The Plumed Serpent* when St. Pierre burst in, his hair and black duffel coat wet with snowflakes.

"Jason, you're not going to believe this. I had to come and tell you." He was unshaven and I could smell beer on his breath. He grabbed a cigarette from my desk and sat on my bed, his back against the wall.

"I did it," he said. "I spent the night with Hillary!"

"Where was Hal?"

"He dropped her off at the motel. We arranged to meet there as soon as Hal left and I'd dumped Nancy. I was gone by the time he came to pick Hillary up in the morning. She's fantastic! We made passionate love all night long."

I shook my head.

"I know what you're thinking," St. Pierre said. "But they hardly know each other. They met through friends in Cambridge. She only came up here out of boredom."

I continued to stare at him.

"Jason, it was wonderful. When I knocked on the door she was waiting for me naked. We didn't say a thing. She just undressed me and we got into bed. She wrapped her legs around me. My God, she put them up around my neck. I thought I was going to die!"

Suddenly I pictured Quoins, back in his room sound asleep while Hillary had her legs wrapped around St. Pierre. I started to laugh.

"Are you going to tell him anything? I mean, what's going to happen if she shows up here with you?"

"We'll meet for a while in Cambridge," St. Pierre said. "We've already made plans for next weekend."

"What if you run into Hal?"

"Shit, Jason, I don't know." He got up to stamp out his cigarette in my ashtray.

I laughed again. I knew it wasn't funny. St. Pierre had bird-dogged a mutual friend and here I was making light of it. But it probably served Quoins right for being so blasé about everything.

"She's certainly a character," I said. "Leslie likes her, too. At first I thought she was a phony, but then I started to warm up to her."

"Hillary enjoyed you both. She wants us all to get together." St. Pierre got up to leave. He hugged me. "Jason, I needed this. I need someone to like me. I didn't do it to hurt Hal. I wasn't even thinking about him."

Long after he'd left, clomping down the stairs in his joy, I sat at my desk thinking about the weekend, a cigarette gone cold between my fingers. I wondered what Leslie would say about St. Pierre and Hillary. By now her train would be arriving at North Station in the dark, the snow on Beacon Hill and Boston Common already in drifts that reflected the lights of the city in winter. I wondered if she would wrap her legs around my neck. Would we ever get to make love?

7

St. Pierre had tiny hands for a man over six feet tall. He directed *Summer's End* as though he were conducting a chamber work. Those small hands, fine and dark, marked time while sculpting the space around each character as they entered and spoke, until the play burst off the page into sound the way music does once it's performed. We worked together to rewrite the first scene, adding more animation to the swift exchange of its opening lines between the two waitresses. Then we shortened the speeches between Pat and Jason, which had seemed too literary when I first heard them. Suddenly they came to life, along with the characters themselves.

It was a new experience for me, watching my words take form on a stage, spoken by actors, who were playing characters I myself had actually conceived. I'd read my own plays aloud before, in English 47, the playwriting course I took the previous year. But sitting in on rehearsals for the One Act Play Contest was a revelation. It was especially exciting to observe St. Pierre, who had three summers' training in The Method at Ogunquit, as he helped the actors prepare for their roles through an elaborate series of exercises dedicated to increasing their concentration. Already I was planning my next play, a full length drama about a jazz trumpeter, who returns to his mother's house on Portagee Hill in Gloucester to drink and remonstrate about his failed career. I would call the play *Sonny's Blues*. I could imagine St. Pierre in the lead, much in the manner of Jimmy Porter in John Osborne's *Look Back in Anger*. When I told Henri about my idea during a break, he cut me off impatiently.

"For Christ's sake, Jason, let's do this play before we get lost in another one!"

So I held myself back in the near delirium I felt each night as we rehearsed. It was a heady experience watching Jessie and Mandy as they mastered the dialogue, adding a line here, dropping another, changing a word whose tone St. Pierre didn't like. Suddenly I saw the play as a fluid thing, quite unlike a story or a novel. I understood the role of the director, indeed of the actors, as they brought something of their own immediate emotions to the characters they were creating. I realized that once the script had left the writer's hands it entered a separate community, a place of collaboration, not only between actors and directors but among set designers and technicians.

We weren't allowed to attend rehearsals for the other two plays. Each was allotted its own time and place in Pickard Theater, so that the writers and the participants could proceed without interference. Still, we knew that Quoins and Dell were just as deeply engaged in rehearsal as we were. It created an atmosphere of tension emanating both from a sense of competition and from our own excitement at the growing reality of *Summer's End*.

Then, in the middle of rehearsals, I had to see Hubie Braun to discuss the progress of my senior thesis. I'd been putting this conference off for weeks, not only because I hadn't done much work on the paper, but because I hated Hubie and I knew he had no great love for me. Those mutual feelings had their origin, I suspected, in the Shakespeare course Roonie and I had taken with Hubie the year before. It was required for the English major and he was the only person in the department who taught it. Hubie would arrive each morning at nine with a stack of ancient faded blue books out of which he'd read his interminable lectures on the plays. Often we would appear late to find Hubie already sitting at his raised desk in front of a class made up mostly of jocks and Ec majors, who considered the course a gut.

Hubie was short. To compensate for his lack of height he wore elevator shoes. Their built up heels made a thwacking noise on the polished wooden floors each morning when he entered the classroom. Habitually he dressed in a herring bone sport jacket and gray flannels, which his wife Rachel—a "classic yenta," according to Mueller—kept pressed to a knife-edge. On his balding head was an old brown felt hat. In winter Hubie exchanged that outfit for a beige woolen car coat and galoshes. The boot clasps jangled while he lectured. He would generally be accompanied to class by his dog Pepper, a small black and white mongrel, who wandered up and down the aisles sniffing and scratching himself while Hubie droned on about Shakespeare's use of character foils.

One day I reached over to pet Pepper while Hubie was deep in an exposition of Harbage's view of tragedy (Lou always referred to him as "Garbage.") Then I slipped the eraser end of my pencil up the dog's rectum. The pencil was long and Pepper didn't seem to notice it. He kept on walking around the room with the sharpened pencil point dragging on the wooden floor. When the other students heard the sound of the bouncing pencil and caught sight of its yellow shaft sticking out of Pepper's ass, they started laughing. St. Pierre had to jam his hand over his mouth to keep from exploding. Roonie's face got redder and redder. Finally Hubie noticed the disturbance. Then he caught sight of Pepper hauling the pencil around. By that time the class was in hysterics. Before Hubie could say anything the chapel bells rang to signal the end of class and we all bolted.

About a week later, Roonie talked two friends of his into dressing in Elizabethan costumes, including plumed hats and long capes, which were kept in the Pickard Theater building where our Shakespeare class met. At a certain point in the class—we were reading the fencing scene in the last act of *Hamlet*—they were to enter masked on one side of the room, begin their sword play, and leave by the other side still flashing their rapiers. They remained just long enough to disrupt Hubie's lecture. Again, the class went wild, and the prank was timed so that the bell would ring to save us from Hubie's wrath.

I always felt that Hubie suspected me of being implicated in those gambits, even though he never let on. Each of our subsequent encounters had been stiff. When I learned that he would be my thesis advisor, instead of Loren or Lou, I knew I was in for a hard time of it. I also knew he didn't like Lawrence, or much modern literature for that matter. At our initial meeting to discuss my thesis, during the previous semester, he had tried to dissuade me from writing on Lawrence. I managed to make enough of a case for my choice by arguing that I would actually be concentrating on myth and myth-making, but this put him off even more because he despised what he referred to as "the newer criticism."

At any rate, the day of reckoning had arrived. Reluctantly I climbed the dusty, stone steps of Hubbard Hall to Hubie's office, which was also the editorial office for the *New England Quarterly*. I could tell Hubie was there from the smell of his Chesterfields and the sound of his ancient Royal manual typewriter. He turned as I appeared at the door.

"Come in, Mr. Makrides," he said, his lips pressed tightly together. Hubie didn't get up from his desk. He merely pushed his typewriter table to one side and motioned me into a stiff-backed chair opposite him. He was wearing a short-sleeved white shirt, the knot of his red and black rep tie loosened so that he looked like an old-time newspaper reporter. His shirt pocket sagged with its load of red and blue pencils. The brown felt hat was pushed back on his head.

"Well, Lawrence, D. H. Lawrence," he began in the singsong manner he was known for as a popular lecturer to women's clubs in the Bath-Brunswick area. "And what will Mr. Makrides be adding to our knowledge of that controversial writer?" he asked while lighting himself a new cigarette.

"I've decided to focus on a single work," I answered. "*The Plumed Serpent*—"

Before I could say any more, he interrupted me.

"I should say that you've chosen one of Lawrence's most obscure works. And just what will you be doing to enlighten our understanding of such a dark opus?"

At that point I'd barely written two pages on the novel, but I had thought about looking at its mythic aspect. I'd even decided to take as my point of departure Blake's dictum that he would rather create his own system than become enslaved by another man's. This would allow me to discuss Dante's elaboration of Christian cosmology in the *Commedia* and maybe even to speak a little about Vico's sense of myth as *vera narrativa*, along with the example of Joyce's use of the Odysseus myth as a controlling metaphor in *Ulysses*. I began to describe my approach to Hubie whose face remained stony, his fingers stiffly tapping his cigarette ashes into an overfull receptacle on his desk.

Again he interrupted me:

"Don't you think you're being a bit too ambitious, Mr. Makrides? I should think that a close reading of the novel with respect to its place in Lawrence's *oeuvre* might be in order. You could show how it differs, say, from earlier works like *Sons and Lovers* and *The Rainbow*."

"I'd bring that in," I said, feeling the perspiration begin to trickle down through my sideburns. The office was overheated. Above Hubie's desk was a signed photograph of Van Wyck

Brooks. With his steel gray crewcut and piercing eyes he looked like an aging undergraduate. Hubie's desk was stacked with manuscripts of scholarly papers that had been sent to the *Quarterly*, of which Hubie was managing editor. "Redemption in Hawthorne," was the title of one; and I suddenly recalled the meeting of senior English majors at Hubie's house one evening during the past fall. I had been assigned to report on *The Ambassadors*. James bored me to death. I couldn't read the late novels without falling asleep, so I kept putting off the task until the afternoon before I was to give the report. Then I did a speed reading of "The Turn of the Screw," hoping to allay Hubie's criticism with a Freudian interpretation of the story à la Edmund Wilson. My talk was a fiasco. It had been stupid to think that Hubie wouldn't use the opportunity to unleash his most scathing sarcasm on me and, by extension, any other English major who shrank from reading James.

"Rather, I should make it the center of the essay," Hubie said, "keeping in mind that one would like to *see* this commentary as it takes shape. After all, the point of our tutorial is for the major to receive some constructive help during the entire process of writing a substantial critical essay, rather than handing it in just once, as he might a term paper."

"Yes, thank you," I said, wiping the side of my face and not daring to light up as Hubie was doing once again.

"And, finally, let me say this, Mr. Makrides, as we terminate our discussion. You, sir, are the Bertram Louis Smith, Jr. Prize Scholar in English Literature. At least you were elected as such last spring—over some reservations of mine, I might add. Were you not?"

"I was."

"Well, let me note that you are not performing in the manner expected of that member of the class who was chosen as the most promising major in the department, at least as regards this tutorial and the monthly seminars, the most recent of which you were absent from."

"I've been busy with my play," I mumbled.

"Ah, yes, an extracurricular activity." Hubie looked at me as though he had caught me stealing something from his desk.

"It does incorporate a great deal of my thinking about Lawrence's love ethic," I said, attempting to smile.

"In that case maybe you ought to have offered it as a thesis under the guidance of Professor Diehl…as a creative project, so to speak."

"No, I wanted to write *about* Lawrence," I said. "I've been thinking about him for a long time."

"Then let us put pen to paper, Mr. Makrides. Let us make haste because the spring is upon us."

Abruptly he pulled the typewriter table toward himself again. As I got up to leave, he looked at me violently over his plastic-rimmed glasses.

"By the beginning of next month, sir, if not sooner, let me have some pages." Then he began typing again, as if I were no longer present. My hands shook as I left. My back and underarms were drenched with sweat.

✢ The Student One Act Play Contest was scheduled for Friday, March 13. The night before it began to snow. It proved to be the worst storm of the winter. Train service from Boston was canceled, making it impossible for Leslie to come to the perform-ance. Neither could my parents, who were stuck in Gloucester, which was as hard hit by the blizzard as the coast of Maine had been. All day the town and campus crews were out clearing the snow, and by that evening the streets were passable. A large audi-ence of undergraduates and townspeople turned out for the con-test, which had been one of the central events of the winter for some twenty years.

Summer's End was second on the program, preceded by Quoin's play, The Heir. Dell's play was last. I managed to catch a few minutes of The Heir after checking back stage with my cast, where I was enchanted by Mandy in her make-up. Quoins had dropped his usual verse format for a kind of flat Pintoresque prose. The play was about a couple of doting suburban parents, who talk about their only child as if he were a genius. Yet when the son appears it's clear he's autistic and that his parents have created a fantasy about their relationship with him. Quoins played the silent grimacing son, a role in which he was very effective.

From the moment Summer's End began I was enthralled by what Mendel and Mueller had achieved. Errol Garner's shim-mering piano set the scene for an end-of-the-season party against which the action on the verandah of the hotel takes place. The shadows of revelers and dancers could be seen though the French doors behind the principal actors, who sat out front in ancient rockers and wicker chairs, creating an illusion for the audience of watching the action from a harborside garden.

Mandy was a stunning Pat; and in Jessie's Jason I could imagine myself a few years hence, brooding and edgy, as I might have struggled with my decision to return home. St. Pierre's direction was crisper than I had envisioned the action to be, more tense and suspenseful. Mendel's handling of the music was expert. The selections he had chosen from "Cuban Fire" were not overwhelming, but they were ever-present like a pulse beat.

I sat with Murray and Aune, watching my play look and sound far better than it had appeared on the page. The exchanges between Jason and Martha crackled with sexual innuendo. They contrasted powerfully with those between Jason and Pat, in which feeling is withheld to the point of agony. Tears came to my eyes as the two finally admit their love for each other and Jason tells Pat, "Close your eyes...and when you open them summer will have vanished," while the Afro-Cuban strains of Johnny Richards' "Recuerdos" rise to a crescendo in the background and the set slowly fades into darkness.

Dell's play was set in a sweltering Washington, D.C. It dramatized the intensifying attraction between two teenagers on the eve of their senior year in high school. The girl was white, the boy a Negro. There was no music. The set consisted of the girl's front porch on which the couple, who had met at theater camp earlier that summer, sat close together in a creaky old swing. Dell called the play *August Heat* to denote the sense of young people caught in a sexual attraction they feared to act on, while plagued with the thought of returning to their separate schools. He played the part of the boy, Cal, himself.

The audience was mesmerized, not only by the drama of seeing a mixed couple in front of them, but by the action of the play itself. There wasn't one false line. Dell's timing was flawless. When he was awarded first prize, he got a standing ovation. *Summer's End* received second prize. St. Pierre was given the award for best director. And Jessie was voted best actor by the panel of three judges, one of whom was Don Carlo, a New York playwright and alumnus of the College.

✣ Ruth Barry invited everyone back to her house in Bowdoinham for a cast party. Slowly the principals in all three plays made their way over icy roads in a caravan of cars. The snow was piled so high on either side that it appeared we were driving through an arctic tunnel. I rode with Murray and Aune whose Morris Minor station wagon held the slippery road like a Jeep. When we arrived, Ruth's big, white farmhouse with its ells and attached barn was a blaze of warm light and well-tended fires. There was wine and beer, and we all began gorging ourselves on the cheese and dips a neighbor had laid out. By the time everyone had straggled in, Ruth's hallway was littered with boots. Our jumbled coats made the stairway to the second floor impassable.

Dell was the center of attention. First, the photographer for the *Bowdoin Orient* took his picture as he stood in the starched white button-down shirt and neat tweed jacket he'd discarded his costume of T-shirt and jeans for. Then Quoins and I were asked to join Dell. St. Pierre and Jessie came next. We all thanked the set people and the technical directors. Someone had seen Mendel come in, but we couldn't find him. Finally St. Pierre dragged him out of one of the smaller rooms, where he was apparently sitting in the dark on the bench of Ruth's locked antique spinet.

"You know he really does remind me of Glenn Gould." Aune came over to where Mueller and I stood enjoying our first beers. "It's his eyes. They're so intense. And that shock of dark hair."

"Speech!" Ruth shouted, leading Dell to the center of the big reception room.

Dell swallowed.

"I'd just like to thank you all for helping make these plays come to life," he said in his gentle lilt. "And my female lead, Janey Hopkins, who came down from Bates every night to rehearse." We all applauded Janey, who had played Stella in *Streetcar* the previous fall. After graduation, she, too, was headed for a career on the stage in New York.

Aune gave Dell a big hug.

"It was so powerful," she said.

"Really," I said, throwing my arm over his thin shoulders. "If anyone around here's a writer it's you."

"Jason, I loved your *show*, too," Dell grinned.

"Seriously," I said, keeping my arm around Dell, "it took courage to write that play—and to act in it."

"As the only colored person on campus I didn't have much choice." Dell winked at Aune.

Murray, who had been talking with Don Carlo and his wife, came over to shake Dell's hand.

"Don says your play's as good as anything that's running in New York."

"Thanks," Dell said. "I wish my folks could have seen it... I wish they'd take an interest in what I do."

"Aren't they proud of you?" Aune exclaimed.

Dell looked down at the floor.

"Dad thinks there's already too many of us in show business. He's making me go to law school."

"But you're a real artist," Aune protested, reaching out to take his arm. "Your last story in *The Quill* was wonderful."

"She's right," Murray said.

While they talked with Dell I made my way over to Ruth's bookcases, stuffed with interesting first editions of American poetry. Among them I found some handbound volumes of Crocker's lyrics, illustrated with his own blockprints. I'd never liked his verse, finding it largely imitative of Frost; but the blockprints, done in a style reminiscent of Rockwell Kent, held my attention. Oddly, they were of young boys in very tight short pants. The tightness of the pants rounded and accentuated their buttocks. With their chubby, stockinged legs and curly hair they looked almost like little girls.

"You dig those?"

I turned to find a young man with a crew cut so short it made him look bald.

"Ever see that stuff before?"

I closed the book and started to replace it.

"No, no," he said, taking the book from my hand and opening it again. "He gave this to my mother. Here's his autograph."

I knew Crocker's handwriting from having seen his manuscripts in the rare book room at the library. This was indeed from him to Ruth and the language hinted at some intimacy between them.

"Your mother knew Crock?"

"Christ, he was *balling* her," he said, stepping back to light a Lucky. He offered me one, as smoke seeped out of his nostrils. I waved my Pall Mall's at him.

"I'm George," he said.

"I saw you one night at rehearsal. Aren't you at Exeter?"

"I got booted for drinking in my room."

"I thought Crock was married," I said. "Didn't he have a family?"

"My mother wasn't the only person he was after," George said confidentially. "D'you see these boys—"

Slowly he turned the pages while print after print of little boys was revealed, all of them with those round asses and pudgy legs.

"Did you know him?" I asked.

"Yeah," he said flatly. "He tried to queer me."

"Crocker did that?"

"Face it, the guy was a pederast. Here, let's get a beer."

George led me into the kitchen by another door. He opened the refrigerator and removed two bottles of Danish beer.

"Try this," he said.

"So Crock was involved with your mother?" I said, fascinated with this new knowledge of a local icon.

"He used the women to get close to their kids," George said. "But he preferred young boys. They say he picked up the habit at Oxford."

"The way he's idolized at the college, who would ever imagine that?" I said.

"Hey, dark beer!"

Mueller appeared with Mandy close behind him.

"Great set, man," George said, shaking Mueller's hand.

"We were just discussing Kierkegaard," Mandy said. "Bill tells me you're a big existentialist."

"Sartre's one of my heroes," I said.

Her big eyes lit up. "I adore de Beauvoir. Have you read *The Second Sex?*"

Everyone seemed to be crowding into the kitchen. Ruth dragged Dell in to meet George. Murray and Don Carlo started rummaging in the refrigerator. Aune was trying to get Quoins to talk to her about his play. When St. Pierre entered, a cigarette butt in the corner of his mouth, everyone started applauding.

I stood off to one side, unable to get the business about Crocker out of my mind. I knew from Murray and Aune that Ruth and her husband Hank, a potter, had settled in Maine in the 1930s, following in the footsteps of William Zorach and a number of other New York artists and writers. The Barrys had taken up chicken farming as a way of getting through the winters, although both were primarily craftsmen. Hank had been killed in the war, but Ruth still did weaving and her work was exhibited all over the state. She and her friend Dahlov Ipcar, Bill Zorach's daughter, seemed worlds away from Crocker and his precious stuff.

And George. I had seen him cruising around town with a car full of girls. He seemed older than his 18 years. When I went looking for him, I found him sitting with Mendel on the piano bench in the darkened room. They were discussing Art Blakey. Then the party began breaking up. Murray came over to offer me a ride.

"Later, man," George said.

I went off with Murray and Aune. St. Pierre's old Ford brought up the rear on the icy road. Mueller and Mendel were in the car with him.

"You should feel good," Murray said, squinting through the frosted windshield. On both sides of us the snow-heavy trees seemed bent to the road.

"I want to write another play," I said. "I can't wait to get started."

"That's the stuff," he answered. Aune was dozing. The heat suddenly came on strong. And the little car hugged the white road that seemed to lead only to more whiteness and more road beyond until I fell asleep myself.

8

*T*he Kenton band was screaming. June Christy was belting out "Ain't No Misery in Me," as Roonie, face shining like Buddha's, sat in his frayed armchair swigging from a quart of beer. We had driven most of the day to get to New York—St. Pierre, Mueller and I—drinking all the way, stopping occasionally to piss, and finally reaching Greenwich Village during the height of the evening rush hour. Up the stairs to Roonie's 10th Street walkup we piled, stepping on each other's heels in our haste to reach the music that spilled out of the windows and doors of the top floor. It had to be Roonie's place, and we knew it was when he came to the door in his hunting clothes: black and red checked wool shirt, rough tweed pants. His beard was thick and red. He'd exchanged his habitual tortoise-shells for a pair of steel-rimmed spectacles that made him look older than he seemed at 27.

"Come in, you fuckers!" Roonie shouted, pawing us as we fell through the door. "Welcome to the Apple! Goodbye Brunswick, hello Hell!"

We hardly had time to take another piss. And we'd just begun to exchange news and to listen to a cut from the latest Bird memorial album when Roonie was up like a shot from his ratty armchair. He hauled us down the stairs again, out into the twilit city, jammed with people coming home from work or beating it out of their apartments into the bars and cafés that lined the streets.

We sat around a table at the San Remo. At the bar near us there was a group of artists dressed like lumber jacks. Their beards were much fuller than Mueller's and mine, and they were laughing, hunched over their draft beers like the men I'd worked with on the wharves in Gloucester. The women with them wore mostly black: black full skirts or black tight pants. Their hair was long, cascading down their backs or frizzed out around their faces. The only make up some of them used was a charcoal-like eye shadow that made their eyes seem like holes poked in their pale white faces. Many of the patrons had on sandals, some with sockless feet, even though it was cool out, but nothing like the freezing temperatures we'd gladly left behind in Maine.

In fact, there was a sense of warmth all around us in the bar, with its floor of shining white tiles, as Art Blakey's drums rolled out of the juke box and Kenny Dorham's trumpet hit the stratosphere.

"Dig it!" Roonie said, gesturing around him at the abstract paintings on the walls, the cigarette smoke rising above the crowded tables, the intensity of the music. He smiled under his mustache.

"Now tell me," he said, seizing my forearm, "what are you writing?"

I had just started to explain *Sonny's Blues* to him when his roommate Jack appeared, pushing into the booth alongside St. Pierre.

Jack was pre-maturely bald and wore a Navy watch sweater. He studied sculpture on the G. I. Bill. He also wrote poetry and was taking a writing course with May Swenson at The New School. Originally from Seattle, Jack spoke in a quiet, scholarly manner. Never before had I heard an accent like his pleasant nasal twang.

"I was in the Northwest two summers ago, but we never made it to Seattle," St. Pierre said, as they shook hands.

"It's wild." Jack was lighting his pipe. "Just picture a water-front teeming with yellow faces, brown faces, red faces. There are crazy old hotels and fleabag rooming houses where wizened little guys drink Tokay, play cards and talk Wobblie politics. Seattle's the port, too, if you want to go to sea. It's also a frantic music scene. The bop is hard. Cool jazz never made it up the coast from California."

"And the mountains, those imposing mountains!" Roonie broke in. "Forget Katahdin, you haven't seen a mountain until you've seen the Olympic range. I'm gonna drive straight across the top of this country on my way to the Coast. Spend some time in Seattle and Portland. What do you say?" His eyes scanned our faces.

"When are you leaving?" Mueller asked.

"May, June," Roonie said, "whenever."

Roonie and Jack talked animatedly with Mueller. Smoking with half-closed eyes, St. Pierre surveyed the women as they came in. I leaned back in the booth thinking: *Here we are in New York City and we're already talking about Seattle.* I'd never been West of Pittsfield, Massachusetts, or farther south than Plainfield, New Jersey, which I once visited as a child with my grandfather. It was the first time I'd ever seen a Negro. I remember asking the cousins we stayed with why all the colored people seemed to live on the opposite side of the street from them. They couldn't answer my question.

Yet somehow the thought of traveling across the country didn't appeal to me. At the end of freshman year I'd had the opportunity to go out west with St. Pierre to pick peas and work in the Green Giant canneries of Washington and Oregon. He referred to it as his "Steinbeck summer;" and he came back with stories about Mexican workers and whore houses, about drinking with men who couldn't read and who would just as soon kill you as look at you. My sense of travel involved going in the opposite direction, to see the towns along the Piave that Hemingway had described in his Italian war stories, to be in Rapallo where Pound had lived and written, or in Ravenna where Dante had once brooded. In contrast, America seemed a tawdry place to me, a country of little consequence. As much as I loved *On the Road* and *The Dharma Bums*, I was more interested in Kerouac's language and the perceptions of his characters than in the descriptions of the places where Dean and Sal had traveled. But I was paradoxically attracted to the atmosphere of the small Ohio towns in Sherwood Anderson's stories, a sense of wind blowing through cottonwood trees along brown rivers on a hot summer night. Perhaps those images reminded me of my childhood in Gloucester during the last years of the war, when we'd sit up late with our parents on the front porch, catching the refreshing breeze off the water at the end of a sweltering day, the voices of our neighbors floating softly toward us in the dark. Whatever their provenance, they pulled at me more than Jack's evocation of the Cascades. Although I'd often listened to Roonie's tales about his shore leaves in Seattle when he was in the Navy, the drinking, the Oriental women, it all seemed to come out of a Jack London novel. To me, going West meant going backwards, not only in time but in space.

✢ When we arrived at the Village Vanguard, over on 7th Avenue and Sheridan Square, the first set had already begun. Sonny Stitt stood holding his tenor pensively in the blue light while Junior Mance soloed. The waitresses yelled their orders over the music and the heads of the customers; the bartender rattled the glasses. Then Sonny and Ben Riley traded fours. The tune was "Straight No Chaser" and Sonny took it at a breakneck tempo.

"Out of sight!" I yelled at Roonie, who rolled his eyes as he polished off another draft beer. Mueller was drumming on the table with his index fingers, his face enraptured. St. Pierre concentrated fiercely on the swapping of the fours. Then Sonny took the tune out, ending it on a couple of harmonic tones, octaves above the original melody.

"A gas, an unadulterated gas!" Roonie shouted, waving his beer glass at the waitress as the band segued into "Darn that Dream," the entire room still as death.

Out on the street, after the second set, we walked back to Roonie's with our parkas open. The night was balmy compared to Brunswick winter nights. Spring had come officially only a few days before, even though the accumulation of snow from the last storm was piled so high on the center strip of the Maine Turnpike that you couldn't see across to the opposite lane. In the city there wasn't a patch of snow anywhere.

Mueller and St. Pierre crawled into their sleeping bags while Roonie and I had a nightcap, Red Garland's piano softly tinkling "Bye-bye Blackbird" on the hi-fi. At his kitchen table, strewn with poetry chapbooks and a well-thumbed paperback copy of *Atlas Shrugged*, Roonie poured me a brandy. As we lit up, Roonie leaned back in his chair, letting the smoke from his Camel seep out of his nostrils.

"I don't miss that fucking school one iota." He poked his glasses flush with his face. "When it comes time for a degree, I'll be happy to earn it at Berkeley. You should think seriously about making the trip with us."

"I've got my heart set on Europe."

"I'm hip," Roonie said.

"You know I'm going by myself."

Roonie took a sip from his fingerprinted glass.

"He who travels farthest, travels alone."

"It's probably going to wreck things between Leslie and me," I said.

"If you're tight nothing'll come between you." Roonie tapped a fresh cigarette on the table top and lit up again. "Besides, you need to get away by yourself. I didn't have that choice. It was either the service or the slammer. I thought I'd chosen the lesser of two evils until I got to Korea."

"You should write about that," I said.

"Eventually I will." He spoke while exhaling. "All I can think about now is that North Beach scene."

"No one at Bowdoin had your feel for literature. Your Shakespeare papers were the best in the class. You'd make a great teacher, even if you never write a word."

Roonie smiled reflectively, his ruddy face lighting up.

"'*And gladly wolde he lerne, and gladly teche.*'"

"Seriously," I said. "We miss you in Lou's class, and especially in Loren's Lit Crit. I'm sick of the aestheticism of guys like Quoins."

Roonie chuckled.

"I transferred from NYU to Bowdoin because I thought that by holing up in some shitassed monastery I'd really be able to study. After a week with those baby-faced preppies, talking interminably about the boarding schools they attended or their parents' summer places at Northeast Harbor, I knew I'd made the wrong choice. It was hard enough transiting from Korea to NYU. What took the cake was watching those fuckheads tossing waterbombs out of the dormitory windows or barfing on their dates at the fraternity house!"

He shook his head in disbelief. Then he looked me in the face, his flushed complexion highlighting the pores in his nose.

"Experience is my school, Jason. I felt that way in the service and I'm more certain of it now that I'm back in the city. I've promised never to say no to anything that presents itself to me, no matter how strange or terrifying. I didn't have the room to move in Brunswick. Why do you suppose I blew a hole in the wall of the TD house? Not because I was drunk, which I was, but because I felt imprisoned in that place. Why did Frank go to Cuba? People can only take so much confinement."

Roonie hunkered down on his elbows across the table from me. He put his face close to mine, his deep, breathy voice shaking with feeling.

"From what little I've seen of it, this is the sickest society on the face of the earth. I promised myself if I got out of Korea alive I'd never be held back by rules or regulations. I vowed to make my own laws to live by, testing them though my senses, through the limits of my own body and mind. I don't want anyone telling me how to live my life. In turn, I won't preach to others. My ultimate necessity is to choose to be what I am."

Leaning back in his chair, he ran his fingers down both cheeks and through the red curls of his beard.

"Let's get some shuteye," he said, his voice trailing off. "There's another big day in store for us tomorrow." Then he grabbed my forearms with both of his huge pink hands. "I've missed you, old Greek. I'm glad you finally made it to the Apple."

✝ When we hit the streets at noon the next day, the sun was so bright we couldn't see straight.

"Shit, man, it's insane," St. Pierre said, blinking in the blinding light.

We walked over to Washington Square Park to find it teeming with people. Musicians played fiddles and guitars, singing the blues and old labor songs. Artists displayed paintings propped against benches and trees. Some were drawing on the pavement with colored chalk. A group that called itself the Student Peace Union was chanting, "Ban the bomb! Ban the bomb." Kids ran among the legs of adults, their long-haired and sandal-clad mothers yelling after them as they sat talking and knitting on the concrete and wooden benches.

Roonie milled with the others, stopping to talk to Ted Joans, a brightly dressed Negro with a black beret on his head, who was selling his poetry by the sheet. Another guy was handing out leaflets that encouraged people not to enter bomb shelters during the upcoming air raid drills.

"To run from the bomb is to embrace the concept of nuclear war," he was saying. "Refuse to capitulate to Cold War terrorism."

"Don't you love it?" Mueller shouted, as he forged ahead of St. Pierre and me, tossing his brown leather jacket over his shoulder.

I turned to St. Pierre, who was standing fascinated by a woman all in green, who sang without accompaniment.

"Bill's in his element," I laughed, shaking my head, as I waited for Henri to catch up to me.

He stood still for a moment, his black curly hair uncombed, dark face mesmerized by the woman who was singing her heart out.

"This is the way I want to live. Don't you see, Jason?" He rushed ahead of me now, stopping to watch a tall, skinny, gray-bearded and gray-haired man chalking a nude on the blacktop. Beyond him a group of painters stood critiquing a friend's monotypes that were hanging from a steel-mesh fence.

Roonie waved us under the arches and across the square to a coffee house where we ordered *espresso* and *brioche*.

"Human beings are made to live out of doors," he said, gesturing out beyond the big windows next to us. "We've lost the entire concept of the *agora* in this country. Why do you think people flock to the few places where it's still practiced?"

"I wouldn't want it all day long," Mueller said. "But just to know it was there, to see people drawn to the streets."

"Someday you'll visit Hong Kong," Roonie said. "You'll see an Oriental market that will make you speechless."

I sipped the rich, sweet coffee, inhaling its fumes. The prospect from the coffee house window seemed miles away and centuries apart from the view out of Clayton's Food Shop in Brunswick.

✠ The next morning St. Pierre went to his audition at the Actor's Studio. I accompanied him uptown so I could visit the Museum of Modern Art. It was practically empty as I showed my student card and got in free. Getting off the escalator on the second floor, I made way into the wonderfully lighted galleries to see the Cezannes first. The paintings were everything I had hoped for. I knew what Cezanne had meant to Hemingway, especially after reading Lillian Ross's profile of Hemingway in *The New Yorker*. Yet when I encountered him in the flesh, it was clear not only what Cezanne had given Hemingway but what Picasso and Braque had learned from Cezanne.

I'd never gotten around to taking a course in art history. On my own I read Herbert Read on Cubism and Clive Bell on the post-impressionists. After a couple of summers of trying to review art for the Gloucester Daily Times and nearly four years of poring over reproductions in the college library, I could trust my instincts a little better. But I wasn't prepared for what I saw as I moved awe-struck from Cezanne to Picasso and Braque and then to Matisse, all in the space of a few-minute's walk. Here was the "Demoiselles d'Avignon" and the works that had led up to it, including the portrait of Gertrude Stein. Here were the Matisse interiors that seemed more daring than anything being painted today, except maybe for the work of Pollock or Kline.

Suddenly I was transfixed by the achievement of European modernism. These were the images of the world I'd felt closest to since my discovery of them in high school. This was the vision I sought as a fourteen-year-old, who yearned for something less conventional than what my teachers had tried to give me of art or literature. This is what I went searching for at the Sawyer Free Library, unearthing only a volume of Amy Lowell or a poem by Yeats, a picture book of poor reproductions by Gauguin, which led me finally to the Museum of Fine Arts in Boston and to the Fogg Museum at Harvard, where I began truly to look at paintings.

Tears in my eyes, I walked through MOMA'S vast rooms marveling at the paintings of Kandinsky and Tcheltichew. I envisioned the places where they had been painted, the studios in Paris or St. Petersburg, and I dreamed of a time when there was the excitement of new horizons, when new writing flourished, new music, new language, not the stupid sameness I saw around me, reflected and intensified by TV.

Later, when St. Pierre and I were sitting at the bar of the Cedar Tavern, I tried to explain to him my affinity for those images, that very way of seeing the world so newly, even though it had been nearly 50 years before our time. But I could only stammer.

Henri was full of his own day.

"They had me sit in a room that was dark except for a circle of light," he reported. "I was a person who'd just learned that his fiancé had been raped and murdered. First I had to react soundlessly and then I had to vocalize. It was the hardest thing I've ever been required to do."

As St. Pierre spoke, I pictured his audition as the analogue to my discoveries at the museum. The scripts for what was to be done didn't exist. The aim was to take human expression beyond what had been inherited, beyond old habits and stale images. And the objective was to discover a new interiority and exteriorize it.

"I want to study at the Studio so *badly*."

As I listened to St. Pierre, I was taking in the conversation to my left.

"'No ideas but in *things*,'" a man who looked like a poet was quoting to his companion. "Have you dug what Williams was putting down? Do you know how revolutionary that is?"

"For the first time in my life I knew what I really wanted," St. Pierre said. "I finally knew who I was. Even if I don't get in, I'm coming to the city to study acting."

"I'm hip," the poet's companion said. "But there's Whitman's native diction to take into account…"

✢   That night, our last in the city, Roonie and Jack threw a party. A bunch of their friends and neighbors showed up. At first we all crowded into the kitchen, conversing wildly, interrupting each other, couples spilling over into the big front room that faced the street and finally into the hallway itself outside the apartment. People drank beer and wine. The record player was going full tilt. Sarah Vaughn was scat singing "Shulia Bop." There was a smell of burnt leaves coming out of the bathroom that I was certain must be dope. And everyone was yelling at once.

Jack's girlfriend was six feet tall and blond. She had green make-up under her eyes that transformed her entire face into an iridescent mask. Roonie told me that they spent half of their nights together at her place over near the Bowery. I could imagine Leslie and me living that way, sleeping in the same bed at night, waking up together on brilliant spring mornings, throwing parties like this.

Alicia worked uptown as a publisher's reader. She came from Minnesota.

"What made you move here?" I asked.

She smiled in a way that made me feel she had to answer that question a lot.

"I heard it was the place to be," she said in a friendly tone.

Jack put his arm around her shoulder.

"Alicia went to Carleton College. It's probably not unlike Bowdoin."

"Small, you mean."

"That, of course," she said, "but just not alive." She turned to kiss Jack and it broke my heart to see them there, Jack in his blue jeans and workshirt, Alicia in a long black skirt and Mexican blouse, silver bracelets on both arms, her lips so red.

Halfway through the night Hillary blew in with two friends from Bennington. St. Pierre was ecstatic to see her and they immediately disappeared into the bedroom. The other girls, Zoe and Babs, were smooth skinned and tall like Hillary although they wore no makeup. They seemed utterly at home at a party like this as they rummaged around for water glasses to fill with the cheap red wine everybody was drinking.

It turned out they were each studying myth, literature and criticism with Stanley Edgar Hyman whose book, *The Armed Vision*, I owned but hadn't read. As we talked, leaning first against the kitchen wall and then finding seats in the living room, I realized how much I missed the presence of women at Bowdoin. Babs, who wore black horn rims and had wonderfully long fingernails, jumped in aggressively.

"Lawrence," she said. "Save me from that romantic view of sexuality! I suppose you approve of it. You know, the woman submits completely to the man who dominates her, giving her back her feminine essence as mirrored in him."

Zoe laughed.

"Actually I adored *Women in Love*," she said. "It's such a homosexual novel."

"I'm concentrating on *The Plumed Serpent*," I explained, feeling overwhelmed.

"Mr. Hyman says it's not one of his strongest books," Zoe remarked. "Besides there's some really ominous proto-fascism in it."

"Lawrence was a terrible authoritarian," Babs added.

"Don't you think he was criticizing the tendency?" I asked.

"He was the very embodiment of it," she replied, pushing her long dark hair away from her face. "Could I have a cigarette?"

I offered them both a Pall Mall, lighting us all up with my Zippo as I tried to hide the Bowdoin shield on it. I found myself drawn to both women yet somehow intimidated by their beauty and their sophistication. I felt like such an idiot in the face of their articulateness, their knowledge of literature that seemed far more advanced than mine—or was it just that they'd learned how to say the right things?

Frank Sinatra was singing "Come Fly with Me." Zoe rolled her eyes. Quickly someone changed the record to Dave Lambert. Then the lights blinked off and on for an instant. As Jack made his way to the center of the living room, the guests parted to create a path for him. He was holding a paperback copy of *The Long Goodbye.*

"People," he said as the talk died down, "A moment of silence, a moment of remembrance. A great writer has gone, one of the golden poets of the American night."

Jack opened the book and began to read:

"*'When I got home I mixed a stiff one and stood by the open window in the living room and sipped it and listened to the groundswell of the traffic on Laurel Canyon Boulevard and looked at the glare of the big angry city hanging over the shoulder of the hills through which the boulevard had been cut. Far off the banshee wail of police or fire sirens rose and fell, never for long completely silent. Twenty-four hours a day somebody is running, somebody else is trying to catch him. Out there in the night of a thousand crimes people were dying, being maimed, cut by flying glass, crushed against steering wheels or under heavy tires. People were being beaten, robbed, strangled, raped and murdered. People were hungry, sick; bored, desperate with loneliness or remorse or fear, angry, cruel, feverish, shaken by sobs. A city no worse than others, a city rich and vigorous and full of pride, a city lost and beaten and full of emptiness.*

"'It all depends on where you sit and what your own private score is. I didn't have one. I didn't care. I finished the drink and went to bed... No feelings at all was exactly right. I was as hollow and empty as the spaces between the stars.'"

There were gasps and cries of "Yeah, man," and "I hear you," as Jack handed his glass to someone, who filled it to the brim with red wine.

"Drink to Raymond Chandler, who died in La Jolla today." Jack raised the glass. "Drink to an authentic artist!"

"To Chandler!" Roonie said, his face red with drink, his eyes brimming with tears. "To the earliest angel-headed hipster, who drank himself to death in that loneliness we call America!"

I was listening to Sarah singing "Detour," when I felt a hand on my shoulder. Hillary was smiling.

"Where's Leslie," she whispered, her hair askew, her green eyes burning.

"Oh," I said, "she doesn't have break this week."

St. Pierre came up behind her.

"We're going to another party. I'll be here by morning for the drive back."

"That's what you think!" Hillary said. She turned to me. "Say hi to Leslie for me. Tell her I'll look her up when I'm in Cambridge." She paused, her lips parted, her astounding face brightening. "Henri says you're going to Europe in September."

"Yes," I said, "Italy."

She looked intensely into my eyes.

"You'd better take Leslie. That is, if you don't want to lose her."

9

When I got back to Brunswick there was a dusting of new snow on the ground, a presage of winter's return. On the mail table in the downstairs hallway I found a small package from Leslie. Rushing up to my room, I tore the wrapping off to discover a white cardboard jewelry box. On a bed of cotton beneath its cover lay my fraternity pin. I sat heavily on the bed and began to read the note which accompanied it:

"Dear Jason, I wanted to give you this pin back during Winter Houseparties, but I didn't have the heart. I couldn't stand to hurt you. Yet here I am doing it anyway.

"The fact is that returning your pin doesn't mean I don't love you any more. It just means that one of us has to call a spade a spade and put this relationship on a different footing, the one you began to put it on when you decided to go to Europe.

"You say you love me, and part of me believes what you say. Yet you act in another way. Practically speaking, you *could* go off to Italy. I do have two more years before I get my degree, and if I go to summer school I could even get it sooner. A year apart wouldn't kill us; it might even do us some good. It will do you a lot of good. That's my head talking to me. My heart says something else. I feel that deep down you really want to get away from me. I feel that once you are in Italy I won't exist. Oh, you'll write me long, loving Lawrencian letters like you always do. But I will know that you will be sleeping with someone else and your letters will be written out of guilt. I won't even be real to you by then.

"I also believe that Europe will change you, and once that change has been wrought there won't be any place for me in your life. My intuition tells me that you have the capacity for escape, for exile. My fear is that a taste of Europe will be like a drop of elixir, dissolving your life up to then, your memory of us. I imagine you becoming a man without a country. I picture you never returning. I see you changing, losing your American identity, taking on another one, another language; and I just don't want to be hurt by it.

"I guess what I'm trying to tell you is that I love you, have loved you, more than I could even admit to myself. Or maybe I'm fooling myself—it's hard to tell. All the dreams I had of us together in graduate school, in our own little house, with children—dreams of your someday writing a big, wonderful book…

all those dreams don't feel the same any more. I don't know what I feel. A lot of the time I just feel like screaming, 'You bastard, why are you destroying our love!' But maybe I am the one who is destroying it. Maybe it's all my fault.

"So here is the pin I accepted that meant we were engaged to be engaged, that I would only be with you; the pin that would show everyone I met that I had already been spoken for.

"I can't do anything else right now but give it back to you. I know it has to be this way and I'm sorry to be hurting you, if indeed I *am* hurting you.

"I hope your trip to New York was fun. I miss seeing Roonie. I miss driving around in the big maroon Caddie. But then, I'm going to miss a lot of other things about us, too... Be well.

"Love (I mean it),

"Leslie"

✝ The room I had looked forward to reclaiming felt grim and bleak. There was no heat. I could see my breath take shape on the cold air. I wanted immediately to run over to the Union and phone Leslie. I wanted to beg her to reconsider. I got up and started to zip my parka again. But then I flopped back on the bed. It was late. My duffel bag lay on the floor beside me. My sleeping bag was still downstairs in the entryway. I felt grimy after the drive. My stomach ached from the greasy cheeseburgers we'd wolfed down at Ho-Jo's on the Maine Turnpike. My head spun from all the beer we drank. I felt like I'd lost everything I ever had.

Lying back on the bed I went over Leslie's words, now indelibly etched in my memory. I began to answer them. I argued with her, tried to convince her that it was silly to throw away what we had merely because I was leaving the country. Besides, that wouldn't happen for another six months. There was a lot we could do in the mean time, a lot we could be for each other.

Then I offered in my head to take her with me. I proposed that we go together. But as I moved toward my typewriter table; as I stretched my arm out to snap on the gooseneck lamp, I knew that if I traveled at all to Italy I wanted to be alone. And that was the crux of my dilemma. I wanted Leslie, but I also wanted to be free of her, at least for as long as I was away from her. I wanted to do whatever I needed to do, but I expected to have her there for me when I got back. I didn't even want to think about her being with someone else. If she continued to wear my pin I wouldn't worry about it, yet I would be able to live a life apart from her.

I knew it wasn't right. What I was asking, indeed demanding from her, was fidelity while I would be free to be unfaithful. She had put her finger on it, in the unerring way she always seemed to divine the meaning of a poem or story. She had exposed the contradiction at the heart of my thinking, even though I hadn't directly revealed it to her. She had read my mind and the feeling of having been found out gave me as much pain as getting my fraternity pin back.

Slowly I got up and tossed my parka on the arm chair. I stripped down to my underwear and put my flannel pajamas on over it. Then I went into the bathroom to wash. I let the slowly warming water flow over my hands and wrists. Soon I splashed it on my face. My beard needed trimming. I didn't like the way I looked with my bloodshot eyes, the whites tinted with yellow in the weak light of the tiny bathroom. I brushed my teeth and took a long piss. Thinking about Leslie, just having her face in my mind, gave me a hard-on. Then I thought about Babs and Zoe, the two girls from Bennington who had come to Roonie's with Hillary. Of course I'd be free now to see anyone I wanted. Maybe I could go with St. Pierre when he drove out to Bennington. Maybe some Bennington girl would wave her bra at me; certainly Leslie never did.

But, oh, I had taken hers off and I had tasted the flesh of her breasts and felt the hardness of her nipples in my mouth. I couldn't possibly touch another woman after what we shared. There was only one woman for me, and now she was gone. I had pushed her away from me.

I padded back into my bedroom in my smelly stocking feet. The uncarpeted floor was freezing in the hallway, but I could feel the heat beginning to come out of the grate in my room. I went to the closet to reach for my woolen bathrobe. I thought again to start a letter, but it weighed on me, the task of it, so heavily that I crawled into bed. I reached over and turned the light out. The yellow glow from the streetlamps on Federal Street made stripes on the floor. I could hear the engine of a trailer truck passing on the Bath Road, pipes banging in the other wing of the house. I could smell the heat coming. I closed my eyes.

Images of Washington Square Park swam into view, pictures of Roonie drinking in his battered armchair, of Jack's girl Alicia with her green eye shadow; of the red and blue stagelights in the Village Vanguard transforming Sonny's golden tenor saxophone into silver. I heard the cascade of notes against the hard ticking of the drum stick on the ride cymbal, the pianist's comping: rich bebop chords ringing like bells in my head, the bass's steady "ding, dong, dong, dong, dong." I was lost in the music. It seemed to leave my head and fill the space of the dark room. It carried me beyond the room, away from my thoughts of Leslie, until there was just the music and nothing else and I must have fallen into a deep sleep after days and nights of no sleep at all.

✝ The next afternoon Murray and I were sitting in the window at Clayton's, two coffees steaming in front of us. I'd confided that I needed to talk. Then I had rushed impatiently into the coffee shop ahead of him, while Murray obligingly taped a "back in ten minutes" note to the bookstore door.

I told him everything in a tumble, even showing him Leslie's letter, pressing it on him, although he seemed reluctant to read it. I talked like a madman, repeating myself, trying to justify my decisions, asking him what I should do.

Murray was patient in his response. He said he understood how I felt about being rejected. He agreed that it did seem odd that Leslie had broken up with me without warning, without even the opportunity for discussion. He suggested that maybe the lost opportunity hurt more than Leslie's having returned my pin. Then he told me there would be many other women in my life.

"You don't believe it now," he said gently. "You don't want to believe it, but it will be so." He added that only alone could I become the writer I wanted to be.

"Only by yourself can you travel the full length of that journey," he repeated. "It's hard because you exchange the comfort of friends and lovers for something Hemingway used to claim you can only experience when you're alone."

Murray left me to get back to the store. Darkness was falling, although I could see the last glow of the sunlight on the church steeple. It was getting close to dinnertime. I sipped the dregs of my cold coffee, feeling some comfort from Murray's words, but I couldn't wait to call Leslie.

Once I was downstairs in the Union, I had to confront the usual after dinner rush to the payphones. Guys were calling home or chatting happily with their girlfriends. I stood waiting nervously. What would I say? How would I begin? Did I have enough change for a long call?

When it was my turn and I'd closed the folding glass door against the noise in the corridor, I realized that Leslie must be home on spring break. My hands shaking, I dialed her parents in Gloucester. When the person-to-person call went through, her mother's voice commented dryly that she wasn't in. I told the operator I'd call back later and hung up. My chest was heaving; perspiration ran down my face in the hot cubicle. As I opened the door I could see the line of people waiting outside. I didn't want to look at anyone. Soon I had to take my shift at the library and I didn't even want to do that. Leslie's parents went to bed early, so I couldn't call her when I finished work. And where was Leslie anyway? Whom could she possibly be out with in Gloucester?

I called twice more early in the week, got no response once and then a curt remark from her mother that Leslie was out yet again. It was useless leaving a message because there was no phone where Leslie could reach me. I tried calling her dorm in Cambridge but no one answered. Finally I mailed a letter to her in Gloucester. It was a long one and I hated the way it sounded. I told her I'd try calling her again after break. "I *must* speak with you," I wrote. "It's driving me crazy not to be able to talk this thing out."

When I woke up at noon on Saturday, I found a note from Aune on my mail table. She wanted me to pick her up that night at seven. They were showing Olivier's *Hamlet* at Smith Auditorium. Murray was going to baby-sit. I knew he'd probably put Aune up to it. Earlier that week I'd sensed the concern in his voice.

Aune wore her purple cape. Everyone stared at us when we entered the auditorium. Aune's face flushed.

"It will be all over campus," she whispered. "You've taken up with a married woman!"

"Fuck them!" I said, putting my head defiantly close to hers. "The faculty wives have nothing better to gossip about anyway."

Olivier's interpretation was embarrassingly Oedipal. During the bedroom scene, after Hamlet has mistakenly killed Polonius, there was such intensity between Hamlet and his mother Gertrude that I cringed in the dark.

"*Mamma mia!*" Aune gasped.

Someone's wife turned around and shushed us. I leaned forward as if to mouth a retort, but Aune put her soft hand on mine. For the first time that night I thought about Leslie.

Later, as we sat over wine in the Stowe House lounge, fraternity songs intruding on the quiet from the pub below, Aune encouraged me to talk about Leslie's letter.

"I don't mean to butt into your emotional life." Aune had a way of enunciating each word perfectly, yet in a manner that was entirely natural.

"You're not." I felt relieved to have the opportunity to let go.

"Murray was worried about you getting that letter out of the blue. You really didn't need that, now did you?"

"I thought Leslie and I had a great time during Houseparties. We didn't fight, we seemed quite close."

Aune took one of my Pall Malls.

"Murray's going to kill me, coming home with tobacco on my breath." She inhaled deeply, closing her eyes serenely.

"Sometimes when we think everything is going well there's an ominous message hidden under the surface. Of course, we generally deny it."

"Leslie hasn't been happy about my going to Europe. And we probably haven't talked enough about it, *really* talked."

"Argued?"

"That, too. But I hate it so."

"We don't argue enough, any of us," Aune said. "Murray and I are just learning how to have a knock down drag 'em out and still love and respect each other. And that's after four marriages between us!"

A couple of my former TD brothers walked past our table. They looked embarrassed to see me there with Aune. I motioned to the waitress to bring us another round. This time I ordered bourbon for myself.

"Oh, my," Aune said smiling.

"It's my hard times drink," I laughed.

"Well, don't let them get too hard."

I shook my head.

"Look, Jason," Aune began. "There's no medicine for this kind of pain. Talking a conflict through helps, but what if the other person doesn't want to? And it sounds as though Leslie doesn't, at least at this point."

"So what do I do?"

"Well, nothing." Aune turned her cigarette tip until the silver rind of ash had descended completely into the glass ashtray between us. "I mean, you get on with your life as hard as it may seem. Each day feels a little better, each day you get a little stronger. After a while the pain recedes and you're in control again."

✛ The next day I went to the library to gather the books I would need to begin work seriously on my thesis. I knew that my conference with Hubie was coming up and that I would have to produce more than an outline of my paper to avoid his wrath. I also wanted to lose myself in something. I had tried to work on *Sonny's Blues,* but it reminded me too much of Leslie and me. Set in Gloucester, the play was taking shape around our relationship even though I hadn't originally planned it that way. Sonny, the trumpet player, who returns to his hometown and to his mother's house, after a time of hard drinking and failure on the road, was modeled after many musicians whose lives I had read about. Also, he wasn't unlike the protagonist in *Summer's End.* And Marie, the girl Sonny had left behind, his high school sweetheart now a librarian, was reminiscent of Leslie. The more I worked on the play, especially as I approached a scene in which Sonny and Marie would be reunited for the first time since he had abandoned her years before, the harder it was to take my mind off Leslie. I still hadn't heard from her, and each day that went by without a response made it more difficult for me to contemplate calling her. Consequently, I had done nothing.

In the stacks I located all three volumes of Edward Nehl's composite biography of Lawrence. The chapters on Lawrence's life in New Mexico seemed a gold mine for my own work. Then I came across Witter Bynner's *Journey with Genius*, the Santa Fe poet's personal account of his relationship with Lawrence and Frieda and their joint trip to Mexico, which became part of the first chapter of *The Plumed Serpent*. Next I found *Dark Sun*, Graham Hough's ground-breaking critical study of Lawrence, with much on the Mexican novel. There were also Lawrence's posthumous papers, collected in the 1936 edition of *Phoenix*, which contained some wonderful essays on New Mexico and the American Indian; and of course an illustrated first edition of *Mornings in Mexico*. The last checkout date on it was 1951.

I carried the pile of books back to my room and lined them up on my desk. Just being able to see the titles on their spines reassured me. Then I set to work. I dipped first into Nehls. His transcribed oral comments of arts patron Mabel Dodge Luhan, along with the words of Lady Dorothy Brett, the deaf, aristocratic painter who had followed the Lawrences to New Mexico, seemed particularly insightful. They helped me to construct a picture of Lawrence at the time of his life when, wracked with illness and hating his weakness, he somehow found the strength to envision what would become his penultimate novel, his great myth of man's renewal in the New World.

Inspired by Erich Fromm's discussion in *The Forgotten Language* of the relationship between dreams and myths, I began to draft my introduction to the paper. First, I chose an epigraph from the *Commedia*, in which Dante speaks of having begun to grasp the sense of form that knits the whole world together. Then

I quoted Blake's assertion that he must create his own system of myths or "be enslaved by another man's." From these twin beacons I proceeded to a discussion of Yeats' occult system in *A Vision* and thence to Lawrence's own burgeoning mythic vision, compact of what he'd learned from anthropologists about the animism of indigenous ritual and what he saw of its practice among the Taos Pueblo peoples—all in a landscape he described as "so open, so big, free, empty, and even aboriginal...the great space to live in."

I wrote until it was time to try Leslie again. As I set out once more for the Union, I felt I had something of my own against which to balance the emptiness that washed over me.

"She's not here. I think she's at the library with Karl," one of her dormmates said when I asked for Leslie. I felt suddenly sick as I replaced the receiver on the hook and sat back in the stifling booth, its glass panes covered with greasy fingerprints.

Who was Karl, and what kind of relationship did she have with him that they were at the library together? I had never heard of Leslie being at the library with anyone.

"They could be doing a presentation together," I said out loud to myself. "They could just be friends...classmates."

When I saw someone who wanted to make a call staring oddly at me, I kicked open the folding door of the booth and stepped out. I felt dizzy. The last thing I wanted to do was work that night, but I got myself a coffee to go and headed out the front door of the Union for the library.

It was a quiet night; all the worse because I couldn't take my mind off the news that Leslie was at Widener with someone else.

When I finally managed to reach her, just after midnight, Leslie's voice sounded strained. Mine was just a croak.

"Who's Karl?" I managed to bark out.

"A friend," she answered. "He's a graduate student I met in my Contemporary Phil class."

"What were you doing at the library?"

"Oh," she hesitated, "we're working on our papers together."

"I never heard of you doing anything like that," I said.

"I've never had occasion to tell you. Besides, I can study with whomever I want."

"Yeah, especially after breaking up with me!"

"It's not the way you think it is," Leslie said.

"Then what way is it?"

"Jason, we have a lot to talk about and this isn't the time or the place."

"Just what *is* the time and place," I shouted. "You send me back my pin. You write me a letter dumping me. Now you drive me crazy with this news that you're studying with some graduate student. Who is he? How *old* is he?"

"What does it matter, Jason?"

"I want to know. I have a *right* to know!" I heard my voice echo in the booth.

"Of course you do," she said calmly. "I'm going to tell you all about it. I was planning to do it anyway."

Slowly she explained to me that she had met Karl at the beginning of the new semester. He was 28. When Leslie discovered that his parents had a cottage in Rockport, she had told him about working there as a waitress during the summer. One

135

thing led to another and they began having coffee together after class.

"He's interested in a lot of the same things you are," Leslie said. "He loves Sartre, and Dostoevsky is one of his favorite novelists. He writes, too. He says he's got a desk full of manuscripts."

"What kind of manuscripts?"

"Fiction," she said.

"Is he any *good*?"

"I think so. But that's just one person's opinion."

"So he hasn't published."

"Only in the *Advocate*," she said.

Suddenly I didn't want to be talking about whether this guy had published or who the fuck he was anyway.

"What about you and me?" I asked.

"You and I... Well, I miss you."

"You aren't acting that way."

"Karl's been very helpful," she said. "He's an understanding person."

"You mean you've told him all about us?"

"I told him that I returned your pin because one day he didn't see me wearing it."

"So he jumped right in," I said. "He pressed his advantage."

"Jason, please try to understand. Sending your pin back and my friendship with Karl are two separate things."

"It doesn't appear that way to me," I insisted. "I think you dumped me for him. And I think it was cruel of you not to tell me about it right away. Here we were together at Houseparties and you didn't have the kindness to tell the person you claimed to love that you'd met someone else?"

"I hardly knew him, Jason. And it didn't happen that way at all. I've been thinking about us ever since you told me you were going to Italy. What I wrote you in the letter is exactly how I felt. Karl is a friend."

"But you've been out with him. You've been on dates with him. You were with him when I called you in Gloucester."

"Yes, I was," she said. "He took his spring break in Rockport."

"At his parents' house," I said. "Were they home?"

"No."

"You were alone with him in his house?"

"Yes," she said, her voice rising in irritation. "We just sat by the fire and talked. We drank some wine, if you want to know the truth."

"I called you several times and each time your mother said you were out, so you must have done a lot of sitting by the fire."

"Jason, this is silly," she said. "Karl came into my life at a time when I wasn't expecting it. He's someone I can talk with about a lot of things, not just about my emotions. He's mature, he was in the service. I need someone like that right now—"

"*You* need someone! What about me? I counted on you. I still love you."

Leslie's voice softened and I could hear her beginning to cry.

"Jason, it's so complicated. I want to talk about it with you. I want to help you, but I just can't do it now." She was sobbing.

"Look," I broke in, "I'll come to Boston this weekend. We'll get everything straightened out."

"Jason, no," she said. "It's too soon."

"What are we going to do?" I shouted.

"Write me," she said. "I'll reply. I promise I will."

"And Karl," I said.

"What about Karl?"

"Will you still see him?"

"Yes," she said. "I don't know."

"Yes or no?" I yelled.

The custodian walked by, signaling that it was time to close the Union. And there was the call to pay for.

"Jason, I've got to get off the phone. Someone needs to make a call."

With that we said goodbye. Slowly I fed all my quarters into the slot. Then I bundled up and walked back to my room, my head spinning with the conversation as I played and re-played it endlessly in the dark.

✝ "Consider it a favor," St. Pierre said. "Consider yourself free now."

We were sitting at our usual table in the window at Clayton's. Classes were out for the day and Maine Street was empty of traffic. I had stayed up most of the night retyping the introduction to my senior thesis so I could read it in Loren's class that afternoon. We were examining the role of myth in modernist literature and Loren had asked me to share my work-in-progress with the group. I looked upon the reading as an opportunity to get some response. Quoins said he thought the essay was pretentious; everyone else liked it and encouraged me to press ahead with my thesis that Lawrence was creating his own myth of regeneration in the novel.

"Free to do what?" I asked St. Pierre.

"For Christ's sake, Jason! I don't have to lecture you on freedom."

"Seriously," I said. "Explain how I'm suddenly free when the woman I love has ditched me. I don't feel free at all. I feel like shit!"

"How you feel has nothing to do with your existential condition," St. Pierre said. "Separate the emotional effects of the act from its actual consequences. By breaking up with you Leslie has given you the freedom to sleep with any woman you want."

"Leslie and I don't *sleep* together!"

"In a manner of speaking," he said. "You're attached by mutual agreement, or you were. You made a contract to be faithful to one another. Since one of you has broken that contract, you, no matter how you feel about the rupture, can now proceed to enter into other contracts of whatever duration you choose."

I took one of Henri's Luckies. He lit me up, pushing his chair back against the wall. I could tell by the flash in his eyes that he relished our discussion.

"I hear you," I replied. "But sleeping with someone else, even going out with anyone, is the farthest thing from my mind. I just feel paralyzed."

"You'll get over it," Henri said. "Besides, you were going to have to deal with it sooner or later. How could you have gone to Europe without breaking up?"

"I never gave it a thought."

"Now you have to. Freeing herself, Leslie has liberated you, whether you like it or not."

I sipped my cold coffee. Outside it wasn't as dark as usual. Gradually the days were lengthening. I heard Murray slam the front door of Fairfield's. He waved to us on his way home. I had no one to go home to; no one who loved me anymore.

"But this guy Karl," I said to St. Pierre. "It breaks my balls to think of Leslie with someone else. Why did she do it? Do you suppose she was trying to get back at me? All I did was tell her I'd decided to go to Europe. From that day on she started acting weirdly. Now she sticks it up my ass."

St. Pierre stubbed out his cigarette. He brought his small, dark hands up to the table, placing his fingertips together. His hair was getting longer, black curls tumbling around the collar of his blue workshirt. I could see the nicotine stains on his slender fingers.

"If I know Leslie she probably feels as badly about this as you do," he said. "Maybe her way of dealing with it was to start another relationship. Who can say? Maybe she's dulling the pain by escaping. Frankly, he doesn't seem like a bad guy. A little on the old side, but, heck, 28 isn't all that ancient."

"Thanks a shitload," I said. "Here I am asking for your sympathy and you tell me I've got to love this guy who's probably fucking my girlfriend this very minute."

"Don't do this to yourself, Jason." St. Pierre grabbed me by the shoulder. "Leslie isn't fucking anyone. If she wasn't fucking you, she's not going to be fucking Karl."

"It wasn't for not trying," I said ruefully. "And look who's talking."

"I admit I'm lucky," St. Pierre said.

I walked back with him to the Zeta house. Among the shadowy trees on the campus I smelled something fresh, just a breath of air from the sea perhaps, a hint of spring in what still felt like winter's depth. As we walked, Henri put his arm around my shoulders. I reciprocated. We said nothing as we moved under the still, leafless trees, past the chapel and library. When we shook hands in front of the Zeta house, I felt tears in my eyes.

10

$\mathcal{O}$n my way over to the conference with Hubie I was feeling more confident about my thesis, a copy of which I'd left at his office the afternoon before. Jeff, my Italian professor, had also asked to see the draft. After class on the *Purgatorio* that afternoon, he told me how much he liked it, adding that I shouldn't doubt my ability to do scholarly work simply because I preferred to write fiction.

"Critical work involves the imagination, too," Jeff said. "A perfect example is the excitement Francis Fergusson generates in

Dante's Drama of the Mind. I think we often make false distinctions between different kinds of intellectual work. Lawrence was a superb critic, don't you agree?"

Jeff had coarse, dark hair that fell over his ears. After years of speaking French with his native-born wife, his English was slightly accented. He added that my discussion of Dante was sharp and apposite to my thesis. Leaving Italian class in Sills Hall, I walked anxiously to the library, where I found Hubie with a smile on his face.

"Now we're in business, Mr. Makrides." He motioned me to sit down on the other side of his desk. "I think you're on the right track. You've laid down the terms of your argument, often elegantly I must admit. Next comes the crucial step."

Hubie lit a cigarette and nodded his permission for me to do likewise.

"What's wanted now is a close reading of the novel," he suggested, "demonstrating exactly how you believe Lawrence has constructed his myth. A third section or chapter might discuss the novel in the context of his earlier work. There you could also address how it anticipated, *Lady Chatterley's Lover*, since we are about to have that novel in unabridged form, although this library owns a copy of the original Florence edition of 1928."

"I've seen it in the Rare Book Room." I was afraid to tell Hubie I'd skimmed a pirated edition Roonie had picked up in Japan.

"Ah, yes."

Hubie removed his glasses. Then he wiped his eyes and his lips with a crisp linen handkerchief, which he continued to hold, passing it back and forth between his left and right hands.

"I'm not insensitive to your generation's renewed interest in Lawrence," he said, inhaling sharply as if to clear his nostrils of some obstruction. "As a younger man I, too, admired Lawrence. I read his later works as they appeared and I found much of value in them. Mrs. Braun and I traveled one summer to Taos. I must say that the landscape held my attention as few others have. It is sublime in many ways and, at the same time, primordial, just as you describe Lawrence painting it."

"I never thought about that part of America before," I began haltingly. Hubie was one of those people I felt I could never say the right thing to.

"It is quite breathtaking. You must see it sometime, although I gather you are headed in the direction of our forebears, that is, our European ones, if we are to respect Lawrence's recognition of those Red Men who preceded us to this continent."

I smiled, hoping soon to be dismissed. But Hubie warmed to his argument.

"I was younger when I first read the man," he said, "and I have taught him time and again. It's the preaching that disturbs me now, the stridency of tone and temperament. Lawrence does seem so awfully to *insist*, to wish to instruct."

Hubie paused and looked directly at me, a look that was not unfriendly, indeed warm.

"James once wrote a younger disciple what I consider to be the most useful, if not the best characterization of the narrative art, indeed of life itself. 'There are no fortunes to be told,' he maintained. 'There is no advice to be given.' That for me is the supreme definition. For the novel is not a handbook. It does not tell us *how* to live; it merely shows us examples of living as such.

And the great achievement of realists like James—not withstanding his concentration on consciousness, especially in the late novels—was his adherence to that school of writing which regards the imitation of reality as its principal task and goal. For you see, the Master had no need to preach or to teach, such as Lawrence was driven to do. He merely wrote about life as he observed it, leaving it up to his readers to discover what they might."

"But I find James hard to read," I said, trying not to betray my impatience.

"Yes, yes," Hubie replied, almost gently, "it *is* the undergraduate complaint. Yet how can you all admire Cozzens, who is nothing but an imitator?"

"I can't stand Cozzens," I said. "His diction is so anachronistic."

As I walked back to my room, chapel bells sounded the close of another academic day. Carefully I memorized those words of James, resolving to look up their context. My head churned with new ideas. I rushed ahead to get them down on paper before dinner. Then I thought about Leslie and the old, empty, lost feeling returned, the terrible hurt I couldn't seem to write away, talk away, *think* away.

✣ The next afternoon I was back at work on my thesis, mild April air coming in the window. Just then I heard a dry knock on the door. George Barry stood there with a cigarette between his thin lips.

"Nice pad," he said without removing the butt from his mouth.

I motioned him toward my arm chair, but he chose the bed behind me. George leaned back to touch his head to the wall, the pointed toes of his black boots transcribing minute circles in the air.

"What's up?" I asked, surprised to find him visiting me.

"Wanna go out Saturday? There's a girl who's dying to meet you."

"Meet *me*?" I laughed.

"Yeah, she's a friend of my girlfriend's."

"A high school girl?"

George nodded.

"How old is she?"

"She's a senior," George said.

I turned from my typewriter to get a Pall Mall.

"I've got a girlfriend in Cambridge."

George smiled slyly.

"Cambridge is a long way away."

I lit up. George bummed one of mine, lighting it for himself. He grabbed my not so clean pillow and jammed it behind his head.

"I'm intrigued," I said. "What made you think of me? I mean, how does she know who I am?"

"She saw your play. Two of her friends were the waitresses in it. When you went up to get your prize, she had a good look at you. She dug your long hair and your beard."

"But George, a high school girl?" I shook my head in disbelief.

"What do you care? I'll drive, you pick up the booze. We'll catch a flick and go parking."

"Parking?"

"Hey, man, if a chick wants a date she puts out."

✠ The anticipation of this blind date seemed to counteract the guilt I felt over the very thought of seeing someone else. I longed for Leslie, even though it was she who had broken up with me. In my heart I still considered her my girlfriend, so I felt I hadn't lied to George in telling him I was committed. I still loved Leslie, or my hurt caused me to cleave to that love, to want it back, to want *her* back. Yet the idea of a date with a girl, who George told me was good looking, made me feel less hurt and discarded. It made me feel as if I could make a new start. It was an opportunity to get back at Leslie with her graduate school boyfriend. But how could I let my friends know I was going on a date with a high school girl, a townie at that?

✠ Mary didn't resemble my stereotype of a high school girl with a poodle cut and Peter Pan blouse. She had black hair with red highlights in it, and she wore it short, waved on the sides and parted in the middle. It barely covered her ears, coming together in a DA in the back. She was wearing a long, tight grey skirt and blue suede shoes with a fringed tongue that covered the lacing.

George didn't make much of an introduction as he picked me up in front of my house. I got into the steamy interior of his mother's old Pontiac beach wagon and found myself sitting in the back seat next to a quiet girl, who looked older than her age. Sandy, George's date, sat jammed up against him in the big front seat. After a while she turned to me, spinning her blond pony tail around.

"Jason, Mary," she said.

I nodded, feeling my hands go clammy. Mary smiled. The car was overheated. George let me out at Mike's where I bought two six-packs of Miller's. Then we headed out along the Bath Road to the drive-in.

As soon as the movie started, I cracked four beers and George and Sandy disappeared from view. The tinny sound of the speaker hanging in the window of the driver's seat drowned out any conversation between front and back. I took off my parka and sat sipping my beer. Mary concentrated on the flick, which was about a group of teenagers on a beach confronted by a werewolf in their midst. I couldn't believe what I had agreed to do.

Trying to break the ice, I finally turned to Mary.

"Do people actually *like* this stuff?"

"I guess so," she said, her eyes on the screen.

"What do you think of it?"

She shrugged.

"I mean, do you and your friends go to this kind of movie a lot?"

"We're doing it now," she said.

"I suppose we are," I answered, reaching for another beer.

When I offered her a Pall Mall, she pulled out her own Winston's. Opening my window a crack, I lit us both up. We smoked. The film went on—rock n'roll dancing, girls in two piece bathing suits, guys with slicked down hair, a halting plot involving teenage necrophilia.

I stole a look at Mary in the pearly light reflected from the screen. I was trying to recall if I'd ever seen her before. She had high cheek bones, a slightly curved nose, round chin. Her eyes looked almost Oriental. As she brought the cigarette to her lips, I marveled at her womanly hands. She seemed different from the local high school girls, who tried to imitate the dress or mannerisms of the dates they'd seen on campus. But for someone who supposedly wanted to meet me, she didn't seem too outgoing. I wondered if I should make the first move.

"They've disappeared." I gestured at the front seat as I chuckled softly.

She shrugged, flicking her cigarette butt out of the window.

Then she turned her marvelous eyes toward me. Amazed at my forwardness, I reached my arm around her. Mary snuggled against my shoulder. For the first time I smelled her lightly perfumed skin, her hair imbued with cigarette smoke. She was a stranger, but the motions I initiated with her were ones I'd done with Leslie so often and so unconsciously that my body took over.

Mary turned her face up to mine and I kissed her on the lips, tasting the beer and cigarettes and then her lipstick, a little like raspberries. The voices from the speaker crackled; the windows were so steamed up I could barely see the cars around us. She pressed her body against mine as I ran my hands down her back and over her hips. Slowly she slipped her tongue between my lips as if to invite mine into her mouth. I let my own tongue go, wanting suddenly to kiss her hard.

"Here, lie down," she said softly, stretching herself out along the seat to face me so that I could slide down comfortably alongside her. Her coat was off and I had one arm around and under her, feeling the softness of her sweater. With my right hand I touched her face as I kissed her, touched her shoulders, her back. I thought I could have touched her breasts. My instinct told me that I might have touched her any way I wanted, but I concentrated on our kissing. And she kissed me back deeply and strongly. We continued to kiss and to play with each other's tongues and lips. Mary shifted her solid hips and I pulled her more tightly against me, my eyes closed, hearing the sound track of the film, like voices from outer space. I drifted into and out of being with her, being with Leslie, being anywhere, until I felt the engine starting and heard the motors of all the other cars around us reluctantly gunning into action.

Mary and I sat up. In the front seat George and Sandy looked sleepy and disheveled. Sandy was fidgeting with some buttons. It was nearly midnight. We dropped Mary off first. I wanted to walk her to the door, but she jumped out of the car as if nothing had happened between us. George took me home next.

"Catch you later," he said. As I got out of the car and walked up the stairs to my room, I could hardly believe what I'd done. Dropping off to sleep, all I could feel was Mary's small, sharp, probing tongue in my mouth. Sometime during the night I had a wet dream.

✝ Mary Legault was French Canadian. She was also part Mic-mac. "*Metisse*," was the expression she used. I hadn't heard the word before, but she said it denoted a mixture of French and Indian blood. She explained this to me one afternoon at her house on Page Street, a couple of doors down from Lucy's Cash Market. George and I had gone over to find her mother's rumpus room full of Mary's high school friends drinking screwdrivers and watching old flicks on TV. I already knew Claire and Jahna from my play. Mary introduced me to a small blond girl dressed in black with her hair in a pixie cut. Her name was Annegret. I immediately remembered her as the girl with amazing breasts I'd discovered studying by herself one night at the library. Her mother was a painter, she said, and her father taught languages at Yarmouth Academy.

These friends gathered after school each day at Mary's. Her mother was a hair dresser, who came home from work late, leaving the house unattended. Mary had a brother stationed with the army in Germany. Her older sister, Lucille, was a junior at Orono.

Their father had flown the coop years ago, as she put it.

"I've been on my own a long time," Mary commented without emotion.

The rumpus room was in the basement of the green, asbestos-shingled house, but the kids spread out into the upper floors, some of them listening to records on the hi-fi upstairs, others just talking in the bedrooms. It was like a continuous house party with no chaperons. The girls knew George from before he went to Exeter, and they were all friends with Sandy. A few boys came and went. Mostly it was the girls who hung out together, smoking and talking, practicing dances, reading magazines and watching TV. And drinking, of course. That first afternoon I noticed that they put away a lot of vodka without showing it.

When George and Sandy disappeared upstairs I tried to get Mary to do likewise, but she sat stiffly in a Naugahyde lounger, smoking her Winstons and watching a western on TV. I started discussing e.e. cummings with Annegret, who had heard him read that fall at Westbrook Junior College. She told me she'd applied to Swarthmore to study art. Claire and Jahna wanted to go to Wellesley together, although they'd also applied separately to Smith and Barnard. Their eyes widened when I told them I was headed for Italy in the fall.

Mary said she'd probably go to Orono like her sister, although she'd also applied to Gorham State College. She said she didn't know what she wanted to do. When she left the room briefly, Annegret told me that Mary was one of the smartest kids in the class but that she didn't like people to know about her good grades.

"Does she have a steady boyfriend?" I asked Annegret.

She pursed her lips as if to say it was forbidden to tell.

✢ That night Murray was holding a *soiree* at the bookstore. He'd invited Lou to read as a gesture of good will toward the faculty and because Lou had a following among the women in Brunswick, where he was on the Episcopal vestry. But the evening would be capped by a drum performance by Mendel and Mueller, who had been practicing for it each afternoon in the basement of Gibson Hall. Mary showed up with Annegret, who was all eyes when the drumming began. Lou, of course, had read well. There was no question that he was a pro, even though his rhymed verse seemed utterly dated. While Lou was reading, Annegret shot sarcastic looks at me over the heads of the sizeable crowd. Mary, who told me she had trouble understanding poetry, sat looking bored. But she perked up as soon as Mendel started rapping his expensive bongos with rim shot like blows and Mueller kept a base-like rhythm going on the deeper congo drum.

Even Lou, who'd never heard drumming like this, paid attention as the two M's got into some amazing polyrhythms, slapping and popping until the room was filled with so much sound you thought there was an Afro-Cuban band playing right there with Machito and Diz and Chano Pozo on drums, only your imagination made up the melody, aided by the layers of drum rhythms, marvelously rich and varied. Dressed in T-shirts, white duck pants and barefoot, the drummers improvised endlessly, hypnotizing the audience. Slowly the embers died in the fireplace, until Murray stood up in the smokey, darkened room to call it an evening.

After the performance Annegret went dashing up to Mendel, who was still in a daze, his black curls damp with perspiration, moisture beaded on his upper lip. I couldn't make out what she was saying to him in the confusion of people leaving, but Mary gave them a knowing look as we left. She pulled on my arm to make me stop as we approached her house. Before I could even kiss her, she dashed up the front steps and in the door. As I walked back to Federal street, the drums reverberating in my head, I felt as though I were entering a new life, one that amazed me as much for what it appeared to offer as it did for its unexpectedness.

✢ That Saturday night I borrowed St. Pierre's Ford and drove to Portland with Mary. *La Strada* was playing at the Fine Arts on Congress Street. I'd seen the film before with Leslie. It was one of a string of amazing movies, like *Bicycle Thief* and *Bitter Rice,* that made me want to go to Italy. Once again Anthony Quinn's portrayal of Zampano, the carnival strong-man, and Giulietta Masina's performance as the girl he buys from her parents, rapes and ultimately discovers he loves, brought tears to my eyes. Not only did I want to be where such films were made, I wanted to share in the atmosphere of innovation they seemed to project. Mary, however, seemed unmoved. She watched attentively as I translated what Italian the subtitles missed. She smiled at certain comments I made. But in the end I had no sense that she had connected with the film.

Later, when we stopped for Chinese food on the way out of the city, I asked her what she thought of the film.

She shrugged. "It was okay, I guess."

"I apologize for taking you. I thought you might enjoy something different."

"Carnivals," she said, tapping her Winston on its box lid.

Back in Brunswick, I drove the car out to Mere Point and parked by the water near an abandoned summer cottage. We could hear the groan of a distant foghorn. With the car well heated from our drive out of the city, we took our coats off and I moved the front seat back so we could lie down on it. Mary came immediately into my arms, lying on top of me at first so that I could feel her pelvis rocking on mine. I reached up the back of her legs and under her skirt, slipping my hands into her panties as we kissed. She moaned softly, gyrating her hips. After sliding my hands up under her sweater, I unhooked her bra. But before I could free her breasts she moved to get up. I thought she was pulling away from me. Instead, she began to unbuckle my belt. She unzipped my fly and just as I expected her to move back on top of me she pulled on my arm for me to sit up. Then Mary bent over to fumble in her shoulder bag. I smelled something like perfume or soap in the near dark of the car, but before I could ask her what she was doing she covered my mouth with a wet kiss. I felt her spreading something cool on my erect penis. She stopped to spit in the palm of her hand and she began to masturbate me. It was cold cream she was using and the icy, slippery sensation drove me wild. I let out a cry and Mary kissed me again, moving her hand, her fingers, slowly up and down the shaft of my penis, faster, then slower, until I was so tense with anticipation that I could hardly catch my breath. I came all over the dash board, on the windshield, too, and then I started to laugh.

"*Too* much!"

"You liked that?" Mary asked.

"It's unbelievable."

My head was still swimming in the white light of my orgasm as I tried to wipe off the dash board with a bunch of Kleenex Mary had extracted from her bag. We laughed together at my ineptitude, jism smeared all over the place.

✣ When I confessed to St. Pierre what I'd done in his car and with whom, he couldn't stop smiling.

"Don't be so shy about it," he said. "It's the best thing you could do for yourself. And what about Mendel? Did you ever think you'd see him in love? Can you believe the body Annegret's got? Wouldn't you like to get your hands on those bazoobies?"

Still, during the many afternoons I spent at her house with Mary and her friends, I couldn't seem to get her alone. She was always reserved, sitting with her screwdriver or a whiskey and soda, while Claire and Jahna talked excitedly about college. Now we were joined by Annegret and Mendel, who would slip over from the physics lab. Off by themselves, they listened to the esoteric records he brought, conversing softly, their heads close together, eyes brimming with pleasure at their discovery of each other.

There was so much I wanted to say to Mary. I wanted to tell her about myself; I wanted to get to know her. Leslie and I had been able to talk about practically anything, especially after sessions of heavy petting, which seemed to bring us closer together. But Mary remained aloof. Rather than frustrating me, her behavior made me want all the more to be with her. And when I wasn't with her I thought continually about her hips, the marvelous firmness of her breasts, the way her fingers had felt when she was playing with me——the crazy act of using cold cream to jerk me off.

Afternoons when I excused myself from the party to work on my thesis, I could only lie on the bed and masturbate, dreaming afterwards of Mary's coppery skin, or of Leslie's freckled shoulders, until I had brought both Leslie and Mary together in my fantasies to such a degree that I couldn't picture them separately. It was then that I wanted to write to Leslie. I felt that some floodgate had opened within me and that I loved her and wanted her more than ever. But I felt equally that she was far away from me, or I from her, and all I had now was taciturn Mary, whose Asian eyes and inscrutable silences drove me wild with desire.

I tried to put some of this down in writing. But I was too reticent, even as I sat at the typewriter by myself, to see on paper a description of what I'd thought or done. How could I tell Leslie what I let Mary do to me? All I wanted was more of it, more of Mary, and of Leslie, too.

Slowly, however, in stolen afternoons and late nights I returned to work on Lawrence. As soon as I'd completed my analysis of the novel, I was in a quandary as to how to proceed with the paper. Instead of discussing his work in general, I wanted to write about Lawrence himself, for I continued to identify with his quest to transcend ordinary relationships, mundane sexuality, in a spiritual fusion of both. I thought of Rimbaud's desire to achieve that vatic state—"*se fait voyant par un long, immense et raisonné dereglement de tous les sens*"—in which he'd been able to write *Illuminations* and then, just as ecstatically, give up poetry. My critical sense told me that a thesis was not the proper place for such an investigation. The kind of writing, indeed the kind of living I felt I would have to do in order to explore the farther reaches of my own consciousness, could not be done in an academic setting. I was not a poet; I'd given up the writing of verse after my freshman year. I might have been able to make a symbolist play like *Axel* out of such struggles, although I was more comfortable with the realism of *Sonny's Blues,* which I was also eager to get back to. More properly, I could imagine myself writing a novel or a series of novels about this quest, but not here, not while the immediate task of completing a senior thesis in order finally to graduate, to liberate myself from this prisonhouse of college, hung over me.

Soon I realized that I was struggling with yet another level of conflict. There was already the conflict between the critical and the imaginative that I'd begun to discuss with Jeff, the one that seemed to undermine all my work as a student of literature. I was continually torn between my love of books and the demands imposed upon me as a scholar, who was compelled to write analytically about them, and my deeper desire simply to express myself, to write anything that came to my mind, to use writing as a mode of exploring myself and the world around me.

I had been drawn to Lawrence initially because he seemed to be such a writer. Everything he wrote—novels, verse, essays, travelogues, philosophy—was an expression of his quest to achieve a kind of intellectual and spiritual integrity, to transcend what he called "the shrieking failure of modern life." But the more I read of Lawrence, indeed the more I read *about* the man, the more I found him veering toward areas of experience, the sacred and the mythic, that I could not comfortably follow him into. For my own quest was existential. I cared about the here and now and how one mediated one's way through the daily imperatives of living. That's what I wrote about; it's what I *thought* about—how to experience each day, how to shape a life knowing that at a certain point there was no God, no ultimate reality, and therefore no transcendence, only death. Rimbaud seemed already to have discovered that, once he'd reached what he referred to as "the other side of despair." Perhaps it was the reason he gave up art and embraced life in all its unknowable risks and enticements—gun running, trading in human flesh, losing himself in Abyssinia—and never writing or needing to write again. Could I do the same?

✝ That Saturday night Mary and I drove out to Bailey's Island with George and Sandy. There was a party at the summer cottage of someone's parents. When we arrived, the cars were jammed together on the lawn and all the way down the unpaved road. I could already hear music from inside the house mingling with the shouts of dancers. As we entered the cottage that smelled musty from having been closed all winter, I was tense. I wondered who would be there. I recognized no one among the dozens of high school students and their dates. And nobody seemed to remark my presence as we carried our bags of vodka and orange juice into the bare kitchen.

Sandy and Mary seemed to know everyone. No introductions were made. We mixed some drinks and then the girls wanted to dance to Johnny Mathis. Couples wandered into the living room from darkened bedrooms while others disappeared into those bedrooms. The bar was in the kitchen where the remaining guests congregated, smoking and talking. I entered the room awkwardly, wishing I had invited St. Pierre or Mendel to the party. Mary and Sandy stayed with me while George circulated.

Claire and Jahna arrived with dates, both of them rushing up to us.

"We both got into Wellesley!" they shouted ecstatically.

"Let's celebrate," I said. "Pretty soon we'll all be kissing this town goodbye."

While we talked and danced, other kids come up to stand around. Soon I found myself the center of attention as I described what it felt like to arrive in Brunswick four years earlier. Then the party went silent. Everyone turned to watch two guys in motorcycle jackets and engineer's boots enter through the kitchen door, followed by a group of girls with slicked down hair and tight skirts.

"Oh, oh," someone said. "It's Mickey and his crowd."

My heart sank as I turned to see one of the guys who'd taunted us on our way back from Murray's that night, the pug-faced kid with the bowed legs. Hopefully he wouldn't recognize me.

"I say we split," George said.

Stopping first to help themselves to beers, the group headed into the living room. The dancers, who had been frozen in their steps on the floor, parted so they could enter. No one spoke at first. Then someone put a Buddy Holly record on and the dancing started up again.

Relieved, I stepped back into the darker corner of the living room, edging my way past the dancers to mix Mary and me another screwdriver. Those who weren't dancing crowded into the kitchen, abandoning the dance floor to the crashers. Claire and Jahna slipped quietly outside with their dates. And when I turned to confer with George, I found the pug-faced kid making his way toward me, followed by a girl I recognized from Ernie's Drive-In.

"Shouldn't you be back at the frat house?" he said.

I faced him, hands shaking in the pockets of my black chinos.

"I don't belong to a fraternity."

"Whattaya doin' hanging around with high school girls?" There was a tone of disgust in his voice.

"These are my friends."

"No girls your age around, you gotta rob the cradle?"

"I could ask you the same thing."

"I could ask you to shut your fucking mouth," he said.

"You're the one who started the conversation."

I looked out of the corner of my eye to see Mary clutching at George's arm. Sandy stood next to him. No one seemed to be dancing any longer.

"I started it," he said, sticking his face up near mine, "and I'll finish it."

"That's a pretty one-sided conversation." I was amazed at what was coming out of my mouth.

"You making fun of me?"

"I'm not making fun of anyone."

"Just keep it that way."

He started to turn away from me, but I watched his fists clench and I saw his shoulders tighten.

"Let's go outside and settle this by ourselves," I said.

"All right wise guy." He turned to face me fully. He was a head or so shorter and compactly built, even though his legs were curved outward to the point of deformity. He limped in his scuffed black boots with their turned over heels.

Once we were outdoors in our shirtsleeves, the cold, damp air off the water made me feel more alert—or was it the adrenaline I felt coursing through my body? I didn't know what would happen next, so I stood poised to react to Mickey's first move.

He seemed befuddled by my apparent calm, halted in his initial aggressiveness.

"So whattaya wanna do, wise guy?"

"It's up to you," I replied as unsarcastically as I could. I caught sight of some faces watching us out of the kitchen window. Otherwise the house was silent.

"I could beat the shit outta you in two minutes flat." Mickey sniffed through his flattened nose.

"Try it," I answered softly.

"Why don't *you.*"

"You're the aggressive one."

"Talk, talk, talk," he sneered.

I took a deep breath.

"What are you so bullshit about, Mickey? We don't even know each other?"

"You college guys got no business with our girls."

"They're not *yours*," I said calmly. "They're free to date anybody."

"Say that again, motherfucker, and I'll knock those pretty teeth in."

"What's the point of fighting," I said. "I haven't done anything to you."

"You bastards come into town, you think you own the place."

"What about you?" I said. "I was walking down Maine Street minding my own business one night and you and your friends started insulting us. You called a friend of mine a nigger. What did we do to deserve that?"

"I thought you looked familiar," Mickey said.

"I've been in Brunswick for nearly four years."

"Some of us are stuck here for life."

"You can leave any time you want," I said.

"Where you gonna go without a education? I tried for the service but with these legs of mine..."

"Mickey, for God's sake. I come from a small town."

"Don't tell me your parents don't have dough. I see everybody driving around in these sports cars."

"My father owns a luncheonette. I'm here on scholarship."

"At least your old man works," Mickey said ruefully. "Mine got laid off when the mill closed and he ain't had a job since."

Suddenly I knew we wouldn't be fighting. The realization came over me with great relief. I had wanted to smash Mickey in the face, if I could ever have done it, to get back at him for that night on Maine Street, for all the other insults and obscenities he and his friends had hurled at Bowdoin students over the years. I had pictured myself banging his head on the kitchen floor for every one of us he abused, watching the blood come, the surrender in his little, pig-like eyes. But I didn't feel angry anymore. The fear went out of me, too, replaced by sorrow and an immense feeling of compassion. Mickey was every one of those classmates of mine at Gloucester High School, who were condemned to menial jobs and a life of immobility. No wonder he was so angry; no wonder the kids I'd known like him, who hung around the Cape Ann Diner all night, made wise cracks at me and my friends when we came in with our dates. What did they have to look forward to?

I held my hand out.

"My name's Jason," I said. "Let's be friends."

"You mean that?"

"Of course I do."

"Okay, buddy," he said. "No hard feelings."

After Mickey and I had re-entered the kitchen, arms around each other, the party started up again. I shook hands with Jimmy, Mickey's companion, and then I met Debbie and Janine. The two girls were still in high school, but the boys, who were my age, had dropped out. I mixed them all screwdrivers.

As we talked and drank I could still feel the tension in my body. My hands shook, too. Mary stood close to me, looking up into my face with a kind of awe. But all I wanted to do was get away by myself. Mickey wouldn't let me. He kept engaging me in conversation as if I were some long lost friend of his. He sought my advice; he assumed a confidential manner, slapping me on the back as if he wanted everyone to see that we were intimate now. Finally, just before midnight, when the girls had to be home, we managed to escape. As we hurried out the door, I caught a quick look at Mickey rocking back and forth on his bowed legs and chuckling soundlessly.

After we dropped the girls off, George and I sat talking in the car in front of my house.

"What did you do to him?" George asked me, as the windshield fogged up in front of us.

"I talked to him," I said. "I just found myself trying to explain to him who I was."

"Man, I thought he was going to kill you."

"I'm still shaking from it. Part of me really wanted to get back at him. Then I just looked at him and I saw how pathetic it was for us to be fighting. We could've been in high school together. I could be Mickey instead of me."

"I'm hip," George said.

As I got out of the car, my breath hung like smoke in the damp night air. Slowly I approached the back steps of the house, my head still whirling from the screwdrivers and from the near miss of having to fight Mickey.

11

The narrow country lane ran between orchards and fields whose shrubs and fruit trees were just beginning to turn green with new leaves. Ahead of us St. Pierre and Mueller were silhouetted against the last orange light of afternoon. Murray and I took up the rear as he described the mating dance of two woodcocks he'd been observing each night. It was the first Sunday in May and the air was fresh and sweet. I'd gotten up late, still shaky from drinking the night before. All the way out to Richmond to meet Murray and Aune, I attempted to describe my encounter with Mickey to Mueller and St. Pierre. St. Pierre insisted that I should have responded to Mickey's challenge.

"The only language those assholes understand is violence." He gripped the steering wheel as though wrestling with it. "I'd have beaten him to a pulp."

Mueller disagreed.

"What's to be gained by perpetuating the cycle? Jason got him talking. I see that as positive."

"Just think of that night on Maine Street," St. Pierre shot back angrily. "Remember how powerless *we* felt?"

Mueller only stroked his goatee.

"Henri, my man, this is only the beginning. If we feel powerless now, wait till we get out in the real world!"

At that, we had all fallen silent.

The Aarons had purchased their hundred and five acre farm with the help of a Veteran's Administration loan. Back at the house, Aune was preparing dinner as the boys ran from room to room in their excitement. But Murray was anxious to show us his find while there was still some daylight.

"I've wanted to grow things ever since I used to visit Louis Bromfield's farm near Oberlin," Murray said. "This year I'll start with a vegetable garden, so we can live partly off the land."

I took a deep breath of the clean air.

"My God, it's delicious." I was finally beginning to feel the tension of the night before drain out of me.

"It will be your home as well as ours."

Murray patted me solidly on the back. Already he had showed us the loft in the barn he hoped to convert into a guest room. The space adjacent to it would make a summer studio for

Aune, who was ecstatic over their discovery of the solid, white Cape Cod farmhouse with its dark green blinds and an L to the rear containing a good-sized shed.

Richmond was about ten miles northwest of Brunswick, farther inland and sparsely inhabited. It struck me immediately as a livable place, though a bit remote for my own taste. Aune said they'd move in as soon as they could, working all summer to make the house comfortable for winter. Murray would continue to manage Fairfield's, but he hoped by fall to have negotiated an advance for a novel he wanted to write about American expatriates in post-war Europe. When the advance came through he'd quit the bookstore and write full-time again. He and Aune talked of joining me in Italy while he worked on his book. Aune was scheduled to have a show that summer in Ogunquit. Hopefully it would lead to one in New York in the fall. As they discussed their plans, I half wished I weren't leaving for Europe. I had a sudden flash of Leslie and me in the coziness of this house, the smell of woodsmoke on the sharp winter air. Just thinking about it brought back the old feeling of loss and regret.

"Hey, guys, look at this!"

Murray led us through what once must have been a beautiful orchard marked off by a wall of lichen-covered boulders.

"A little pruning," he explained hopefully, "and we'll have some Cortlands for the farmer's market in Bowdoinham next September. And look at these pear trees!" He danced merrily through the stubble of weeds and grass still winter-yellow in places.

Back at the house St. Pierre helped himself to one of the hot toddies Aune was serving in mugs. There was a salad all prepared, steaming bread from the massive black iron stove in the kitchen, and *pasta* on its way. Already I could smell the *sugo*, an odd intruder in the severity of the house's interior with its low-ceilinged rooms and small-paned windows.

"You're our first guests," Aune said, offering a toast as she tucked a plaid flannel shirt into the back of her jeans. "I hope you won't be our last."

"Are you kidding," St. Pierre said. "You couldn't keep me away from here. My grandmother had a farm like this just outside of Gardiner."

"The truth is you'll all be leaving next month." Aune turned her mouth down.

"I won't believe it till I see it," I said.

Chris and his older brother Will tumbled into the room pulling St. Pierre away. Mueller sat reflectively by the fire, his head in his hands.

"And what about you?" Aune asked.

"Me?" he said, as if awakened from some reverie. "Who knows?"

✣   The next morning I found a note under my door telling me to report immediately to the president's office. I dressed quickly, slicking my unwashed hair down with water and splashing some aftershave lotion under my arms in place of deodorant. On the way over to Massachusetts Hall I wondered what I'd done to be called in. My grades were okay, my term papers had all been submitted, and I didn't owe the school any money. I'd only cut a few classes this semester, so I probably wasn't in any kind of academic or disciplinary trouble. Was it Mary then? Maybe her mother had complained about Mendel and me hanging around the house drinking, or about Mary going out with me. But the president's daughter Claire had been with us, too!

It could have been some news from home. Maybe Dad had suffered another heart attack. No, my parents would call the Waddells immediately if anything went wrong in Gloucester.

All the way over to the campus I was troubled by the call, never suspecting that it might be something fairly routine. After all, I was on good terms with the administration. Or so I thought.

As I took a seat in the waiting room, I felt the palms of my hands sweating. Quickly I wiped them on my rumpled chinos, expecting that I'd have to shake hands with Carter when he came out. His secretary said he'd only be a minute. She had a serious look on her face, but it didn't appear ominous, I thought, as I thumbed through a copy of the *Bowdoin Alumnus* I'd be receiving as soon as I graduated in June...if I was graduating.

That was a preposterous thought! It reminded me of being in elementary school, when each year in June, on the last day of school, we'd get our report cards and learn if we had been promoted to the next grade. My marks were always excellent. There was never a question about my going ahead, as we called it. Yet I was always afraid I'd be handed my card only to find out that I had actually stayed back.

Alice, the president's secretary, continued typing quietly in her alcove. I was the only student in the room. Outside I heard the chapel bell signaling the end of noon classes. I worried that the president would think it rude of me to have come late. As I looked around the room I knew so well after these four years—

at the framed engravings of the campus during its early years, the cups and trophies of athletic and academic contests—I wondered again why Carter had summoned me.

Soon I would be saying goodbye to all this. I would be in a city of old stones, far from the college with its Georgian brick buildings and stately maples, the bells demarking the academic day: first classes, chapel, end of classes, vespers.

I remembered back to when I'd first entered this building. I had been accepted at Bowdoin without ever visiting the campus, having applied on impulse because I read that Nathaniel Hawthorne once matriculated here. Some of my high school teachers had encouraged me to go to Harvard. But the idea of a university as vast as Harvard terrified me. What I envisioned was a small school in a small town like Gloucester, although after my first Maine winter I came to regret my decision.

I recalled that first day in mid-September. I was standing outside my new room on the bottom floor of Appleton Hall while some fraternity brothers carried my bags in. At first I thought it was a courtesy. Then I discovered it was merely part of the process of rushing incoming freshmen. I couldn't imagine what I was doing in Brunswick, Maine, which I'd never seen before, or on a campus that initially appeared as large as Harvard Yard. My father was standing near me. When he didn't think I could hear him, Dad had taken one of the Kappa Sigma brothers aside and asked him to keep an eye on me. "He's a good boy," he said, wondering, I suppose, what those rushers were planning to do to me. "Be nice to him."

I was mortified. My mother read the look in my eyes and gave me a little smile of hoped for understanding, a smile that said, "Don't hurt your father's feelings. He means well." Ordinarily I might have interrupted my father as he spoke what I suddenly heard as incorrect English, a foreigner's English that would embarrass me no end if these new companions of mine listened to any more of it. I'd have begged him not to interfere. But, remarkably, I understood his purpose. He was telling me he loved me and would miss me; telling me that he had misgivings about his ability to take care of me now that I was going to be so far away. He was indicating to me his concern that in losing me he had not been an adequate father. Somehow I intuited this, even in my mortification. So I said nothing. And when it came time for us to say goodbye, I kissed him. I kissed my father on the lips and told him for the first time that I loved him.

That moment flashed through my mind as I awaited the president. It was my first real experience at Bowdoin, the first occasion I had something to *feel* about, and I tried to address it in my opening theme in Sean Minturn's English 1 class. I attempted to describe the initial moments of my encounter with the College. I began with the green stripes of the wallpaper in my room, stripes which I described from the vantage point of the chair behind my desk as growing up those walls. I described the sounds of the arriving students on the staircase outside my room, classmates I was afraid to meet. Then I described the campus as seen from the big window next to my desk in that corner room. It was a window that afforded me a panoramic view of the quad, from Hubbard Hall library and the Walker Art Museum all the way over to the chapel. I wrote about my anxiety as the fraternity brothers carried my bags into my new room, then about the empty room as I entered it. I introduced my roommate and my entry mates, among whom was St. Pierre. I wrote about my earliest minutes, my first day at Bowdoin, but I left out the part about my father. By omitting how I'd felt about my father I had falsified the account. Even though Sean gave me an A– on the paper, my first grade at Bowdoin, I knew the paper wasn't complete. In fact, Sean, who had been the best of my writing teachers and a real mentor that first year, had commented at the end of the essay that he felt I was withholding something from my account. "Don't be afraid to speak even the unspeakable," he had noted in red ink in the margin of my essay. "That's why we write."

I had concluded that essay with a few sentences about signing the ancient matriculation book in the president's office. It was something each entering freshman was required to do. First, you had a brief get-acquainted visit with the president. Then you were invited to sit at a small writing table that had belonged to Nathaniel Hawthorne. There you added your name to the long list of men who had entered the College since its doors first opened to eight candidates for admission on September 3, 1802, with only President McKeen and another professor as instructors.

I recalled so well my first meeting with Carter Alexander III, recently inaugurated as Bowdoin's ninth president. "It's my freshman year, too," he said, his blue eyes smiling as he towered over me. Carter was a tall and thin but stately physicist, who had been chosen to guide the College into the new world of the coming space age. And it was Carter with whom I was to stand two Octobers hence on the observatory roof of Searles Hall as a group of us scanned the night sky, looking overhead for the fiery tracks of Sputnik, the sign that indeed the new age had been born.

So Carter had initiated a rapport with me that continued over the four years of my undergraduate career. We met at numberless receptions. I interviewed him during my stint as a reporter for the Bowdoin Orient. I had gone to him for funds to keep *The Quill* running. I'd even sat with him and his wife at concerts. And he'd complimented me for *Summer's End* in a way that made me feel he had not come to see my play merely because his daughter Claire had a walk-on part in it.

I was deep in thought when Alice announced that he would see me now. As I entered his office, part of me still in the world of my reveries, Carter rose behind his desk with a grave look on his open face. We shook hands, my palms still sweaty. Suddenly I thought I could smell my own perspiration underneath the sickly perfume of the aftershave lotion.

"I've got some bad news for you, Jason," he said, seating himself again behind his desk. He shook his head as if to inhibit his speech. I could feel my hands trembling.

"Frank Crow's father called me yesterday." Carter spoke haltingly. "Frank was killed in Cuba."

I sat staring ahead of me. I hadn't thought about Frank for a long time. I felt my eyes begin to fill up.

"The family is having a small memorial service at Cape Elizabeth next Sunday. They wonder if you would say a few words."

I barely listened to what the president was telling me. His phrases, when I did catch them, didn't register. All I could think of was Frank in that outlandish haircut of his. It couldn't be true. And why was the news coming so late? There must be some mistake. I was about to interrupt Carter, when I saw his composure break. His own voice cracked.

"Jason, I can't tell you how it happened. Doctor Crow just had the news confirmed by the Cuban emissary at the UN. They were awaiting more details."

Carter paused.

"I know you saw a lot of Frank. I'm truly sorry."

As I walked across the campus to the Union, I felt a sense of unreality about me as though I'd walked out of a film that still held me in its thrall, the way a Western would when I was a kid. I'd have just emerged from the dark of the Strand Theater in Gloucester on a late Saturday afternoon into the violet light of winter, not knowing if I was in my home town or in some frontier settlement in Texas, gunshots still echoing in my ears along with the music of the finale. But now there was no music, no shots and no finale, just an emptiness where before there had been the sharpness of a new day attenuated by the anxiety of wondering what the president wanted me for.

✝ Dr. Franklin Crow was an older version of Frank. He had the same crew cut, except that his hair was a just a shock of gray. In place of Frank's clear plastic glasses, his were steel-rimmed. His soft Brahman voice was what Frank's might have become had he lived to grow older. I'd driven down in silence with St. Pierre, Mendel and Mueller. Dell asked to come too. We had little trouble finding the Bayview Unitarian Church. There were about 100 people in the sanctuary as we made our way unconducted to the pews. Carter and his wife sat in the front row. Schrebner, whose hawk-nosed profile was immediately recognizable, sat next to them with Ilsa, his wife, who wore her gray-black hair in a severe Dutch cut. Behind them sat some brothers from the TD house and a couple of Frank's classmates, who were now in grad school. No music was played and Dr. Crow was dressed plainly in a rough gray tweed sport jacket and loose charcoal flannels. It was the way Frank often appeared.

He approached the pulpit and began to speak.

"You will all want to know something about Frank," he said, clearing his throat. "Let me share with you what I've learned."

Dr. Crow told about how, during the summer before, Frank had made contact with the New York office of the 26th of July Movement.

They were mostly Frank's age, he explained, young people who had come to the United States to study after Batista had shut down the University of Havana in 1957. "It was their job to raise money for the revolution and to counter propaganda from Batista by presenting the revolutionaries to Americans as democratic."

"The movement did not recruit members or mercenaries directly," he continued. "But somehow Frank found out that the Fidelistas were assembling and training expeditionary forces near Mexico City and he made his way there. From Mexico the group Frank had joined sailed to Cuba where they were smuggled into the country. Frank was assigned to a guerrilla company that would be making its way from the Sierra Maestra northwest to the Sierra Cristal. He was given the *nom de guerre* of *El Cuervo*. Apparently his comrades in arms thought that along with his name in English his voice sounded like that of the bird's, especially when he spoke Spanish, which they admired."

Dr. Crow smiled momentarily as the light from the long windows reflected off the circular lenses of his eyeglasses. In the front row was a thin, youngish woman in a brown woolen dress, who must have been Frank's mother. Next to her was a blond girl with freckles. She was obviously the sister Frank had spoken of.

"There was another movement of troops coming East from the Pinar del Rio," Dr. Crow continued. They would converge with both the Fidelistas and the independent revolutionaries for the occupation of Havana. Frank was traveling with a platoon that had been intercepted by Cuban regulars near Las Villas. Separated from their company, they were isolated. Several were killed. Frank might have been slightly wounded at that time, he reported. At any rate, they were soon captured by the Batista forces and taken to a small village in the jungle.

He paused.

"There was an interrogation. Some reports say that the survivors were tortured. As an American, Frank was thought to be a CIA agent. He may well have been brutally treated to extract information he obviously didn't have. His imperfect Spanish might have been a problem. This was in mid-December, as far as I can ascertain."

Dr. Crow continued to speak calmly.

"They took Frank out to the edge of the village, along with several other prisoners, and they shot him."

Then his voice broke.

"The bodies," he said, choking back a sob, "the bodies were thrown into a ditch. The Cuban authorities have no idea of its location. They only know of Frank's presence because of the commander of the company his squad belonged to. He remembered that Frank had been with the group that was intercepted and cut off from the main body of the troops. Of course, they kept no records because of the underground nature of the operation. Frank never told anyone who he was or where he came from. He was simply called *El Cuervo*."

Dr. Crow went on to describe how Frank's family, having heard nothing from him after his departure for Mexico City in October, contacted both the U.S. State Department and Castro's government as soon as Fidel had assumed leadership in Havana. It had taken a long time to get any information because of the chaotic nature of the revolution and the extreme secrecy under which its operations were carried out. Finally, when Fidel had come to the UN in New York in April, Dr. Crow had been able to meet with him through an intermediary in the U.S. delegation. Castro had promised to do everything in his power to find out about Frank. True to his word, he had reported back with the necessary information, following up with a wire to Dr. Crow in which he expressed deep regret over the loss of his son, only hoping that the family might take some solace, as he himself did, from the fact that Frank had died in the struggle for freedom. Dr. Crow read from the wire before sitting down.

There was silence in the sanctuary. The plain white walls, devoid of religious images, seemed to focus one's attention on the matter at hand. There being no body, no flowers, no music, indeed no apparent mourning, I found myself all the more able to picture Frank's last hours as his father had described them. As I rose to speak I could see Frank before me, dressed not in the fatigues of the soldier but in the clothing that made him so familiar to those of us who knew him.

No one motioned to me to take the lectern. But the silence in the white, empty space, the light from the narrow, many-paned windows, seemed to leave us all to our own promptings.

I had prepared a few paragraphs. However, once I'd heard Dr. Crow's remarks, I realized how inadequate mine were. I decided to trust my own immediate thoughts.

"I've never had a friend who died," I began. "And I don't quite know what to say or how to mark the occasion. The only funeral I remember is that of my grandfather, the spring before I came to college."

I looked around the room. Frank's mother's resolute gaze met mine. Mueller and St. Pierre nodded as if to encourage me.

"It was a Greek funeral," I continued, "with a priest in black robes and the thick perfume of incense. At the funeral home my grandfather was laid out in a casket in a dark blue pin-striped suit. It was the first time I'd ever seen a dead person and I couldn't take my eyes off his waxen face. At the cemetery, where my grandfather had tended his lot for ten years before he was buried in it, we all tossed clods of earth into the open grave. When they closed the casket finally and were lowering it into the ground, my grandmother, who had shown perfect composure all through the ceremony, said quietly in Greek, '*Fiyeh 'o geros,*'

'The old man is going away.' And of course he was. We all watched him enter the earth.

"It's hard for me to imagine that of Frank. None of us who knew him, if we really did, had the opportunity to follow him through the last weeks of his life as I was able to do with my grandfather in his illness, to watch him fail and finally slip into a coma. I know we are not speaking of decline or illness when we speak of Frank, but it would somehow make it easier for me if I had that concrete condition to go by."

I closed my eyes and took a deep breath. My hands shook no longer. Dr. Crow was smiling. Frank's sister seemed attentive to my words.

"The Frank I remember," I said, "the Frank I want to remember, is the Frank who used to come over to my room on Federal Street late at night and sit in my only chair. Chainsmoking Camels, he would talk about Sartre and freedom, about how it terrified people to grapple with the responsibility which accompanied the very freedom that forced us to choose how we might live. All I can say is that I imagine Frank had enough of talking, although I never had enough of his. All I can say, or imagine, is that Frank went to Cuba to demonstrate by his very act that freedom is not to be imagined abstractly but to be torn from the hands of those who would maim and mangle it."

"Ours is not a very political generation," I went on. "We came to college to prepare ourselves not for a life of learning how to change the world, but for one of earning a good living in the world as we found it. If we are ever going to become political, I suspect that it will not be in the conventional way of ballots and elections, but more like the way Frank had the courage to choose, the way of direct action. It is hard for me to imagine someone as gentle as Frank carrying a deadly weapon; it is also hard for me to imagine his death in a war we Americans knew or seemed to care so little about. But I respect Frank for his choices. I thought I would always have him for a friend, a kindly conscience with a funny hair cut and worn out Navy oxfords, his fingers stained by nicotine. I thought I would hear his raspy voice in my room or,

181

years later, over the phone going on about Kierkegaard's leap of faith. Now that I won't have his company or his guidance any longer, I know that I will miss him all the more. Goodbye my friend. For all of us here today, *Ave atque vale.*"

When I sat down I could hear someone sobbing softly. St. Pierre grabbed my hand and Mueller gave me a stern affirmative shake of his tonsured head. Then one of Frank's instructors from St. Paul's, someone, I gathered, who had known the family well, began to speak with great emotion about Frank's prep school days. I listened attentively to stories of a Frank in the making, a Frank I could also picture, although I was now learning that Frank also excelled in lacrosse.

As the speaker made his way back to the uncushioned pews where we all sat, I heard some commotion in the rear of the sanctuary followed by firm, slow footsteps. The footsteps came up the center aisle between the pews. Those of us in front turned to see the hulk of a man dressed in a baggy, dark brown, three-piece tweed suit. His reddish hair and beard obscured his shirt collar. And his bird boots, into which the unkempt trousers were stuffed, made rubbing noises on the polished wooden floor. As he turned at the lectern to face the congregation, I saw that it was Roonie. Smiling grimly, he removed his steel-rimmed glasses and wiped them with a red bandana, extracted from the breast pocket of his suit coat.

"Each man has only one genuine vocation," Roonie began, in the quiet but sonorous voice I heard him use when he played the part of Doc in *Mr. Roberts.* "That vocation is to find the way to himself, as Hesse tells us in *Demian.* A man might end up a poet or a madman, a prophet or a criminal. That's not his affair.

Ultimately it is of no concern. His task is to discover his own destiny, not an arbitrary one, and live it out wholly and resolutely within himself."

"Everything else is only a would-be existence," Roonie said, taking a breath, "an attempt at evasion, a flight back to the ideas of the crowd, to conformity and the fear of one's own inwardness and individuality."

"I knew Frank but little," Roonie continued with a look of loss on his face. "But that little I knew was not because Frank gave little. It was because I could not receive more. Nevertheless, Frank was the truest person I ever met. In discovering his own destiny and trying to live it out, even if it meant dying in the process, he gave the rest of us an example we will hold to for the rest of our lives."

✝ Back at the family home in Cape Elizabeth, I had a chance to speak with Frank's parents. They seemed pleased we had come. Mrs. Crow said it meant a great deal to learn about Frank's impact on the people around him. She had often feared that he led too introverted a life. Roonie reassured her that he had played many a game of bridge with Frank at the TD house and that Frank was as admired for his bidding expertise as he was for his philosophical depth.

As we stood drinking tea out of bone china cups, I asked Dr. Crow if Frank had ever confided in him about going to Cuba.

"Yes," he said, smiling, "we had some long talks about his wish to participate in the revolution. I was afraid for him. But when I was a student at Union Theological Seminary some of my friends had joined the Abraham Lincoln Brigade to fight with the

Republicans in Spain. I had yearned to go too, but something kept me from it, perhaps a lack of vision or courage, it's hard to say. At any rate, when Frank told me of his desire I encouraged him. I'm not sorry I did."

He looked down so that I would not meet his eyes that were now welling up with tears. Mrs. Crow came up to him and touched his arm softly. We said our goodbyes, each of them standing in the door as if looking out beyond the big yellow house within view of the ocean for something they could not quite catch sight of.

In Portland, we met at the Cathay Gardens for Chinese food. It was four o'clock and Roonie wanted to make New York by midnight. He had the maroon Cadillac, which would have been the occasion for jokes and banter, but no one was in the mood for levity. We exchanged some desultory talk about Frank. Mueller and Roonie discussed Roonie's impending departure for the coast. St. Pierre was unusually silent. Dell, who was dressed in his natty manner, seemed on edge, as if he wanted to be somewhere else.

Regretfully we said goodbye. No one even proffered the final beer for the road. We walked Roonie to his car. He tossed his jacket and vest into the back seat, pulled off his red and blue striped tie and got behind the wheel in his shirtsleeves, wheezing from the swiftness of the effort.

"Catch you cats on the coast," he said.

As we watched Roonie drive out of sight down Congress Street, Dell announced that he was staying in Portland to see a film. The rest of us climbed into St. Pierre's Ford and headed for Brunswick. Silently we smoked, shaking our heads, each to himself, as though engaged in mute conversations. It was dark when St. Pierre left me off at the corner of Federal and Bath. I had an hour to change and relax before heading over to the basement of Sills Hall where, at 8 p.m., they were holding the Brown Extemporaneous Essay competition for members of the senior class.

At first I had been reluctant to participate because I never felt that I wrote well or coherently under pressure. When St. Pierre, who wasn't going to compete, asked me pointedly if I were going to enter, I said no. Then I thought it might be an interesting challenge. I had won the Hawthorne Prize for fiction the year before and it had given me a powerful sense of accomplishment. The more I thought about the Brown competition, the more I got excited about entering. But that night, all I could think of was Frank. In front of me I could see Dr. Crow, as if his image had displaced Frank's in my memory. And I felt a sense of almost physical pain in my very being, a sense of loss I could only relate to Frank's death.

I noticed just a handful of participants when I arrived at Sills. Quoins gave me an odd look as if I hadn't been expected. Grierson, who taught the 18th century, monitored the competition. On the front blackboard he had chalked a quotation: "War is the health of the state." We were to write about it in any way we wished for ninety minutes only. When he passed out some blue books, it seemed as if I were sitting for a final exam. But, oddly, I felt energized. Perhaps it came from having expressed myself about Frank's death, or meeting his parents and knowing they appreciated our presence at the memorial. Maybe it was because seeing Roonie I knew that I, too, would soon begin my own journeying.

Whatever the reason—it could even have been Quoins's presence; I wanted to beat that self-assured bastard—I started writing without first making notes or even outlining my essay. The quotation was from Randolph Bourne; I recognized it immediately. Reading Dos Passos's *USA* the year before, I had come across a reference to the deformed war resister and social critic, which motivated me to devour everything by Bourne I could find in the library, including his brilliant anti-war papers. But as I moved from an analysis of the quotation into the body of my essay, I began to think about Frank. It was almost as if he were speaking through me, not about war but about the human condition. For some reason Carlo Levi's *Paura della Libertà*, one of the first contemporary books I'd actually tried to read in Italian, came to mind as well. And suddenly I knew what I was going to write about. Not about war itself or how our leaders dragged us into it (often to save their own skins, while enriching munitions manufacturers who would profit by it, thereby boosting the economy), but about the fear of freedom that Levi said underlies our capitulation to the warmongering of our leaders.

I wrote furiously, quoting from Levi and from Erich Fromm. But mostly I wrote as if I were writing for Frank, *to* Frank, as if I were writing beyond the contest or the campus, speaking to him in the jungle I imagine he died in. I pictured Frank's body in green fatigues decomposing in the moist earth of the steaming jungle, slowly becoming part of the land itself.

"The wars our leaders entrap us into fighting for them, in the name of abstractions like liberty and justice, are not the wars that foster the health of the state and the human person in a community of persons," I wrote. "The real wars are the internal struggles to know ourselves and become ourselves, struggles that are such a threat to the state that they must be contained and suppressed. And one way of suppressing them, one way of diverting the internal energies from those essential confrontations, is to create political and economic wars in which the young are sent to fight and die falsely, without reason or sense; wars whose true purpose is disguised by the leaders of embattled nations or factions."

While noting that there may indeed be just wars, such as our Revolution or the Second War to free Europe of fascism, or, indeed, the Cuban people's insurrection Frank had given his life in, I spoke of how Randolph Bourne understood the true meaning of war, its use as a means of controlling one's own people while sending the young to die in a foreign land for an absurd reason. I added a few sentences about the Cold War, undeclared and with no overt casualties, yet nevertheless a further manner of control in which the fear of communist "subversion" instilled in our population motivated us to support the development of ever more sophisticated weaponry. This, in turn, created anxiety in the hearts of our supposed enemies in the Soviet Union, causing them, in response, to expand the capabilities of their own war machine in a deadly contest of mutual terror.

With ten minutes to go, I summarized my points, my hand aching from the tension with which I gripped the ballpoint pen. Grierson called time. I was the first up with my bluebooks, two of them, filled with closely packed prose. I was up and out of the door; and as I hit the night air in my shirtsleeves I felt a great sense of liberation, a sense of having done something important in the way that I knew how to do things, by writing and writing alone. I fairly flew over to the Union for a coffee that I suspected would only stimulate me more. But I didn't care. I was glad I had entered the contest, glad I had been given the opportunity to say what I might not otherwise have been able to express. That was my true farewell to Frank.

✝ The next day at noon I met St. Pierre and Mueller at Clayton's. They told me it was all over campus that Dell had been beaten up in Portland the night before. He'd been rushed first to Deering Hospital in the city, but now he was back in the infirmary.

"A couple of sailors knocked him unconscious," St. Pierre reported.

"But *why*?" I shouted.

"Why do you think?" Mueller answered.

"You don't just go up to a person and cream him because he's a Negro. Dell was all dressed up. He didn't look like some vagrant!"

"That's apparently what happened." St. Pierre scowled.

"Where, where?" I screamed.

"Down in the Old Port," St. Pierre replied, "outside of a bar. They beat him senseless and left him lying on the sidewalk."

"What was Dell doing there?"

"Beats the shit out of me," Mueller said, as the bell called us to lunch.

Once my Dante class was over that afternoon I stopped at Coe Infirmary. It was still light out, although the shades were drawn in Dell's room. The nurse said I could go in but he might be sleeping. He'd been sedated. She said he had a concussion and some facial lacerations that looked terrible but that otherwise he was healing.

As I entered the room which smelled of iodoform, Dell smiled behind the bandage that covered what looked like a broken nose.

"I couldn't believe it," I said. "What happened? We should have taken you home with us."

"No, no," Dell protested hoarsely. "It's not what you think it was."

His voice sounded resigned.

"It was and it wasn't," he went on. "I mean, Jason... Look, sit down. There's something you have to know. I've wanted to share it with you for a long time. I've always thought you'd be the one person to understand."

"What are you saying, Dell?"

"Light me a cigarette, will you please. I'm not supposed to smoke, but I need a cigarette for this one."

I looked around for the nurse as I applied a match to one of my Pall Mall's and drew on it for Dell. Then I handed it to him.

"Remember my play, Jason?" Dell sucked hungrily on the cigarette. "Remember the couple in it."

"The girl and the boy. It was so powerful the way you shaped those characters."

"They were real," Dell said, as he exhaled pleasurefully, the cigarette dangling between his long brown fingers. "They *are* real. Only they aren't a boy and a girl, Jason. It's two boys, and one of them is me."

I could feel my mouth open in surprise.

"What do you mean?"

"I mean that I'm attracted to men. The play told about something that happened to me. I was trying to get it out in the open. I wanted my friends to find out about it, but no one got it."

I was smoking and my hands were shaking. I didn't care if the nurse came in or not. Dell continued calmly.

"The other night I did what I often do in Portland or Boston. I cruised a young sailor."

"You *what?*"

"I saw a good looking white boy and I tried to put the make on him. I sat down next to him in a bar. I'd had a few drinks. I started talking to him. At first he wasn't responsive, but then he opened up a little. We were the same age. I might have touched his arm, just a small gesture of friendship or communication. I can't really remember. Then he was on his feet shouting. He accused me of grabbing him, of trying to make a pass at him. His buddy came running over. I tried to get up from the barstool and leave. They followed me outside and began hitting me. The two of them started calling me a fucking faggot and pounding on me. I don't remember anything else."

"Dell!"

"I've been this way since high school, Jason, and I can't stand to hold it back any longer. I thought about changing. I've even tried to go out with girls, but it just doesn't work. I prefer men. I mean, I love women. But it's men I want to be with. I'm especially attracted to white men. I like them to be uneducated."

As Dell spoke the light fell outside. Only the lamps in the corridor illuminated the room with its single hospital bed. He was sitting up now, his face like an African mask. But it was a different Dell who spoke. It wasn't the Dell of Larry's Lit Crit class or the Dell who bantered so wittily with Lou in creative writing. I had the feeling I was listening to a Dell who was much older than I, a Dell who had seen and done things I only knew about through jokes and gossip, through novels like Gore Vidal's *The City and the Pillar*, which I'd slipped out of the library to read in one day, taking it back late the next night so that no one would discover me with such a book. But the narrative of the young, handsome athlete Jim, who falls in love with his high school buddy Bob and attempts to relive their one and only moment of intimacy in frantic love making with a host of actors and sailors, cast a spell over me. I couldn't put the novel down. It aroused me and I became frightened of that arousal. I got the novel out of my room as soon as I'd finished it, never speaking about it to anyone.

"Do you hear me, Jason?"

Dell's voice returned to me as if from a dream.

"Yes," I said, "I was just thinking—"

"Jason, forgive me. I know it's a blow for you. But I couldn't go on without you knowing. I'm leaving Bowdoin as soon as they let me out of here. I'll move to New York. I just can't stand being on campus. Already I feel that everyone knows, that all eyes will be on me."

"But no one will know," I said. "They assume you were attacked because of your color and because you were in a rough part of town."

"Somewhere I didn't belong?"

"Yes," I said.

"But isn't that just it, Jason? I *am* everywhere I don't belong. *Everywhere* I go I'm an outcast."

✢ The next afternoon I stopped by Mary's on my way home from Lou's class. Without Dell there had been no humorous exchanges, just the same old reading and dull critique of it. Quoins had been especially obnoxious. He was writing fiction now. It seemed as syrupy as his verse plays, but I didn't have the heart to go after him. All I could think of was Frank and now Dell. Mueller, whom I'd confided to about Dell, sat smoking dreamily. We didn't even walk out of class together.

Mary let me in and we went down to the TV room. She was alone and we acted awkwardly at first. I told her a little about Frank and she suggested we have a drink. I mixed us some screwdrivers at the bar and we sat together on the couch in front of the dead screen of the TV.

Mary announced that she'd been accepted at Orono. I reacted with pleasure, but the news seemed to have no effect on her.

"Aren't you glad to be getting out of here?" I asked her.

She shook her head non-commitally.

"What's the difference between Brunswick and Orono?"

"It's the campus," I said. "You'll meet some new people."

"Big deal," she said, taking a long drink out of her highball glass. The wetness stayed on her dark lips.

"Most people would be overjoyed going to college. What's wrong with you?"

"I've seen my sister at Orono. You go there, you go to class. At night you sit around drinking beer and eating pizza. I can do that here. I can get a job here and make some money, buy a car if I want."

I listened to the flatness of her voice, a sense of near futility in it.

"You can earn more money if you graduate from college," I said.

"I know that, *stupid*."

"Of course you do," I said. "I'm only trying to encourage you to move on to something new."

"You can say that. You're going to Europe."

"But I came here first. Bowdoin helped me get there."

"I don't really care where I go," she said, "or what I do. Here, let's freshen up our drinks."

I settled myself in the Barcalounger, placing my drink on an end table. Mary came over and sat in my lap. I tasted her cigarettes in our first kiss. Then it was just lipstick and orange juice. Mary kissed me passionately, sticking her tongue in my mouth and running it all over my teeth. I pulled her closer to me feeling the hardness of her hips against my stomach. We kissed and we bit each other's lips gently.

"Let's lie down," I whispered. "I want to hold you."

I thought we would move over to the couch, but Mary took me by the hand and led me up the basement stairs to the first floor and then up another flight to her bedroom. It smelled of perfume and face powder. In the dim light I could see a Teddy Bear between the pillows of the double bed. The dresser was littered with framed photographs of her girlfriends. On the wall at an angle to her mirror she had tacked a Brunswick High School pennant.

As we stood in the middle of the floor, I started to unbutton Mary's white blouse. My throat tightened and my hands shook.

"I want to see you naked," I said.

Mary let me take her blouse off. I felt it falling onto the braided rug we stood on. She kicked her shoes off and I unzipped the back of her long tight skirt, down to her buttocks. As we kissed she began slowly to unbutton my shirt. I loosened my belt buckle so she could lower my pants. I had such a hard-on that it stuck out of the opening in my boxer shorts. When she felt it against her, she said, "Oh," and laughed.

We stood in our underwear. Mary's bra was white and she had on a pair of red plaid panties. I put my hands down inside the back of them to feel her warm skin. Then I reached up and unhooked her bra. As I was letting it fall it caught on my penis and we both laughed again. She pulled my undershirt off and then I knelt as I slipped her panties slowly down her legs, all the way to her ankles. She stepped out of them and began pulling my shorts off.

"You are so beautiful," I whispered hoarsely, as the two of us stood looking at each other in the fading light of her bedroom. Then we were lying across her bed and kissing. Slowly I kissed her breasts, then her stomach, letting my tongue circle around in her navel. I kissed the hair between her legs and she made a sound as if to stop me. We edged our way over to the pillows. Pulling the covers off we got under them and started hugging. At first I thought my head was going to explode. But as we hugged and kissed and touched each other I became calmer. Slowly I started to caress Mary, touching her nipples and then going all the way down her back to her buttocks, which felt so smooth and wonderful.

When I put my hand between her legs and tried to slip my fingers into her vagina, she held her hand down there to stop me.

"No," she said.

"I've got a rubber in my wallet," I whispered. "Let me get it."

"Get the cold cream on my dresser. Wait—" she said.

I reached over for it in the near darkness, expecting she'd do what she did that night in St. Pierre's car. Instead, she turned her back to me. Taking the jar she spread some cream down between her buttocks and then she rolled over on her stomach.

"Do it this way," she said, as she urged me up on my knees, the covers slipping away from us. "Put some cream on yourself first."

I did as she directed, my excitement almost more than I could bear. I kneeled between her legs as she guided me down to the place where she had spread the cream.

"Yes," she said, "put it in there. Go ahead, don't be afraid."

I began slowly to push myself into her.

"Am I hurting you?'

"No," she said, "keep going."

It felt strange as I entered her more deeply. The penetration was tight yet pleasureful. As I entered she raised herself on her knees, too, and began to move her hips.

"Keep going," she urged me, "yes, yes."

I began to thrust in and out slowly and then with a more steady rhythm. As I moved I looked down at her long back and at the roundness of her buttocks in the last of the light. My excitement was so intense I thought I would collapse on top of her.

"Go ahead, Jason, come, come!"

I kept pumping until I felt the beginning of an orgasm that rippled all the way up my back. My head ached and I ejaculated with a gasp of pleasure as I lay on top of her, the two of us covered with perspiration.

Mary took me into the bathroom where we stood washing ourselves off with soapy face cloths. It felt like we'd known each other forever. Then Mary sat on the toilet and peed, a quiet look of satisfaction on her face. As we dressed I asked her why she wouldn't let me touch her vagina, why we couldn't make love the regular way.

"I promised my mother," she said softly, as I held her once again. "I promised her I'd stay a virgin until I got married."

On the way back to my room in complete darkness I felt like singing. After having perspired so much, the air was delicious. All I could think of was the feeling of entering Mary that way, the look of her body as she kneeled under me moaning. I just wanted to lie on my bed and think of what we'd done. I wanted to go all over it again in detail in my own mind. I didn't care about dinner. I was furious I had to go to work at the library.

As I turned up the driveway, I saw St. Pierre sitting on the outside steps under the porch light.

"Henri," I said joyfully, "what's up?"

Glumly he waved a letter in the air.

"Hillary flushed me. She's in love with one of her professors. She says it's all over between us."

12

It was Friday, May 15, the beginning of the biggest social event of the year. St. Pierre and I sat in the front window of Clayton's, sipping black coffee and watching other guys' dates arrive for Ivy Weekend. I had my thumb in the new Grove Press edition of *Lady Chatterley's Lover*, but my attention was split between Lawrence and the sight of all those women pouring in by train and by car.

Nothing had seemed to go right since we heard about Frank's death. St. Pierre was beside himself after getting Hillary's "Dear John" letter. He couldn't concentrate on his senior thesis. Instead of spending the weekend working to complete it, as I had determined to do with my own, he was headed for Boston. Mueller was drinking heavily and cutting classes. The Dean warned him that he was about to rival Nathaniel Hawthorne's dismal record of absences, but Mueller only took it as a compliment.

I missed Leslie terribly, although I was afraid to write her, believing that she'd only be impatient with me. To make matters worse, Mary had pulled away from me, too. Ever since we'd gone to bed that afternoon it was harder for us to talk, or even to be alone, because her house was always full of kids drinking and necking. When I called to tell her that I'd borrow St. Pierre's car so we could go for a ride, she'd make excuses. I suspected she was frightened we'd gone too far. George had gotten Sandy pregnant and skipped town after he learned that Sandy's parents were gearing up for a shotgun wedding.

Through all this, Mendel and Annegret remained inseparable. They sat kissing on the steps of the Walker Art Museum, or they drank screwdrivers on a blanket under the campus trees, oblivious to the rest of us. It had been weeks since Mendel had invited anyone over to listen to music. No one knew the status of his thesis. St. Pierre heard that Annegret's parents weren't pleased with the relationship but could do nothing short of locking their daughter up to keep her from seeing Mendel.

"They're babes in the wood," St. Pierre commented irritably. "It's the first relationship either one of them has ever had. Why don't people leave them alone?"

"Her parents are probably worried she'll get pregnant like Sandy did."

"Take my word for it, they're not fucking. It's a very innocent relationship."

"Say the two jades." I laughed.

"At this point I'd take anything." St. Pierre pushed his chair back. "I'm splitting. Who knows, I may even get laid in the city. Sure you don't wanna make it?"

"Count me out." I held my book up.

"A little date with Mary Five Fingers?"

"Ten on the typewriter, you bastard!"

But work didn't go well on my thesis. The deeper I read in *Lady Chatterley*, the more I thought about Leslie and me, and the guiltier I felt about having gone so far with Mary. That wasn't the way it was supposed to be with Mary or anyone else. I didn't deny that the sex had been exciting. Every time I thought about being inside Mary, or about the way she looked as she stood by her bed in the dim light wearing only her red plaid panties, I couldn't keep myself from wanting to repeat what we'd done. But I had dreamed of going all the way with Leslie. It was she I had first wanted to make love with, to feel close to after the act. Yet, I liked Mary. I had the feeling we could share a particular kind of relationship. Getting closer to Mary had made me realize that it was possible to be intimate with more than one woman, to love them both, but in different ways. I felt that I could draw Mary out, help her overcome her reticence about college. Perhaps I could even get her to admit she was a good student. There was something inscrutable about Mary and I wanted to discover it. As for Leslie and me, all I could conclude was that I'd ruined everything by deciding to go away in September.

I thought about Mary and Leslie as I tried to write that last chapter. I revisited Lawrence's major novels, carefully reviewing the notes I'd taken when I read them all with Loren the year before. I wanted to place *The Plumed Serpent* in the context of *Sons and Lovers, Women in Love* and *Lady Chatterley's Lover* with respect to Lawrence's "love ethic," as Mark Spilka called it. But I also wanted to say something about *The Man Who Died* as Lawrence's spiritual *summa*, comparing its Christian symbolism of resurrection to the visionary myth of regeneration Lawrence had created in the Mexican novel.

However, a statement in Graham Hough's *Dark Sun*, describing Lawrence's actual experience in the landscape of the New World among Mexicans and Indians, troubled me. Hough contended that in the American Southwest Lawrence had achieved "his glimpse into the abyss, hesitated on the brink, and ultimately turned back appalled." That insight, I felt, might explain the unsatisfactory conclusion of the Mexican novel. For, in the end, Kate, who had been the wife of an Irish revolutionary and a sexual rebel herself, ultimately acquiesces to Don Cipriano by marrying him and agreeing to subordinate her very being to his and to the new religion of Quetzalcoatl that Cipriano and his lieutenant Don Ramon are promulgating. All this, in the face of Ramon's obvious authoritarianism, the cruelty of the cult's rituals, and the violence with which it was insinuating itself into Mexican life!

Was that what Lawrence had concluded? Did the novelist really believe the true relation between men and women was subordination, especially of the woman to the man, just as the fundamental religion entailed surrender of the believer to the myth, the force of the belief? Was this the core of his philosophy? And if it was, what did it have to say about the way we should live among what Lawrence called the "ruins" of modern industrial society?

Subordination, surrender, passivity... That was not what the thinkers who meant the most to me offered. Neither Sartre nor Camus preached quietism. And surely the "tenderness" that Lawrence ultimately sought as the crux of the sexual relation wasn't achieved by mere surrender. On the contrary, it seemed to me that the person who surrendered would always carry anger as a result of giving in, of subordinating either the self or one's beliefs to those of the partner. How, then, could there be a complete tenderness between men and women if the relationship was attained at the expense of one of the parties to it? And what, in the end, had Mellors and Connie achieved? Hadn't Connie given in to the gamekeeper, deferring her orgasmic pleasure to his? Wasn't her pregnancy, the fact that she became the vessel of his seed—his force, his *will*—the symbol of his domination over her? And in the final chapter, when they separate, pledging ultimately to reunite and emigrate to a farm in Canada, isn't it Connie who is left by herself to give birth and nurture their child?

These questions disturbed me as I tried to draft the final chapter of my thesis. I wanted desperately to discuss them with someone before writing any further. I also realized that I had boxed myself into an approach to Lawrence and his novel, his very thinking, that I was ill-equipped to understand because of my own lack of experience. What did I know of sexual love, or of human relationships, considering the sketchy nature of my own? Reading the extended scenes of foreplay and intercourse in *Lady Chatterley's Lover,* I felt myself to be the very babe in the woods that St. Pierre had called Mendel and Annegret.

What I really wanted to write about, to delve into, was Lawrence's own psychology, his very being. I felt that unless I understood his life, his brief but "savage pilgrimage" through the time and space of the first decades of this century, I could not possibly comprehend his novels or write about them with any cogency. In fact, it wasn't even Lawrence the man I needed to learn more about, it was the *artist* in him. And in learning about Lawrence as artist I really hoped to gain some insight into what was vexing me. Unfortunately, I had no time for this investigation; my thesis was due in a week. A discussion with Frank would have been helpful, not to speak of one of the long, ruminative talks Leslie and I had been having for years. But Frank and I would never speak again, and I was beginning to wonder about Leslie and me.

As I left the room periodically to clear my head, all around me were the signs of Ivy Weekend. During walks I took on the periphery of the campus, along paths near Sills Drive and up College Street to avoid the happy couples strolling hand in hand or kissing under trees, I began to think of what lay ahead for me now that the die was cast and I was soon to graduate and leave for Italy—*if* I completed my thesis. The evening air was soft. The days were lengthening in the extended light of May. I could hear children playing as I walked; hear, too, the bells of an ice cream wagon in the distance. Kids rode their bikes, parents worked in their yards or dug their gardens. A new life was beginning, a life I'd paid scant attention to, a warmth I'd hardly noticed as I walked with my head down, wrapped in my own thoughts.

How nice it would have been to be walking with Leslie as we often did on party weekends. Just a year ago it had been so warm during Ivy Weekend that we'd been able to wear Bermudas and drive over to Popham Beach with St. Pierre and Mueller. Leslie and I had wandered off into the dunes to hug and kiss and make plans for the summer that was soon to engulf us. Little did we know that it would be our last one as a couple. Little did *I* know that I would lose Leslie to someone else, or that she would act first to leave me because she felt I was abandoning her.

I reflected on our days together, on what our shared dreams of marriage and graduate school had been. Now they were over. I was truly alone. I would graduate alone and leave for Europe alone. Worse than that, come summer I would be alone in Gloucester while Leslie was seeing someone else, in the very town where our love had taken root.

I walked on Friday and again on Saturday, in the afternoon and late at night. As I listened to the sounds of Billy May's orchestra coming from the gym—the screech of the trumpets, the swoop and dip of the saxophones—I could picture the dancers, drunk in each other's arms. Only a year before Leslie and I had danced to Count Basie in that very spot, listening raptly to Frank Foster's tenor saxophone solos, just as I was now hearing Sam Donahue's. We had swooned to "April in Paris" and to Joe Williams singing "Gee Baby, Ain't I Good to You," both of us smiling knowingly about what we thought were the song's hidden meanings.

But that was over now and I walked alone in the dark past the dancing couples, listening to the giggles of those who had run out to drink secretly under the trees or to kiss in the private dark; to make furtive love in cars or motel rooms on the Bath Road as Leslie and I would never do.

I walked through the campus like an *eminence gris*, a ghost of past Ivies and forgotten fall and winter weekends. I circled the stadium imagining I could hear the roar of the crowd after another Bowdoin touchdown. How often had Leslie and I attended the ritual football games, not so much to cheer at those infrequent hometeam scores as to be seen among the crowd of students and their dates, she in her racoon coat, I in my Arctic parka, a pipe sticking out from under its fur-lined hood, drinks in our gloved hands, our faces aglow with the cold and the wind and the love we felt and wanted everyone else to acknowledge.

All that was gone now, and I was alone near the empty stadium, walking by myself past the baseball fields and the track, the field house still seeming to echo with the shouts of the players as they dressed or showered after play. Our love had disappeared along with those fall and winter weekends. What remained to me was a sobering final spring in college.

On those walks I began to observe the elm-lined streets set with Victorian cottages and smaller white frame houses, realizing that I had never paid attention to their architecture before. I imagined myself going off to teach at the nearby college from an apartment in one of those houses. I tried to picture what it would be like coming home in the afternoon for a cup of tea followed by a relaxing walk to town for groceries and a bottle of wine. Evenings I might spend grading papers; and on the days I did not teach I would write.

What I would do precisely in those imagined hours seemed suddenly less insistent. The primary image in my fantasies was of the quiet street, whether on a fall afternoon with the leaves in rough piles and a bright sky, or on a spring evening such as this, with the voices of neighborhood children in the distance, the bell of that ice cream wagon. It was the street itself that I pictured, and the house that I might live in, the house I could walk down that street to and from; and a feeling of quiet joy came over me as I imagined myself on such a street in some college town.

A few weeks before, I had found in the mail an invitation from the Graduate School of Letters at the University of Indiana to apply for a teaching fellowship in English. Disdainfully I had tossed the letter aside, picturing myself not in the American hinterlands but in Italy, the cradle of civilization. Suddenly there appeared to me a new possibility. I had a vision of a path I might pursue after I returned from Europe. I could come back here and teach, in a small college like Bowdoin, in a small New England or Mid-western town. All this was not lost to me. That which had suddenly become so precious as I was about to lose it—the long afternoons in the library, the peace and quiet of my room as I read late into the night—I could recapture, initially as a graduate student and then perhaps as an instructor. I could teach the things I loved to students who might care to learn them. I could live by myself and write. Yes, I could live alone, be alone, create alone...

✣ On Monday I received a letter from Carter telling me that I was one of a number of semi-finalists chosen by the faculty to give a commencement address. I would have to prepare a draft of my talk to be read in a week before a panel of judges. The request floored me. It was an honor, of course. But how could I draft a speech while trying to finish my thesis? What would I say?

When I returned to my room after picking up the mail, I looked at the Lawrence manuscript spread out all over my bed.

At that moment I knew what I would write about. I would use the commencement address to say what I couldn't articulate in the thesis. I would write about the artist!

That afternoon, as soon as Dante class was over, I returned to my room and sat down at the Smith Corona. I cleared a space around it on the typing table next to my desk, snapped on the gooseneck lamp and started to work. What I had been hearing in my head were the words of Yeats: "Turning and turning in the widening gyre/ The falcon can not hear the falconer;/ Things fall apart; the centre cannot hold;/ Mere anarchy is loosed upon the world..."

I decided to call my address "The Artist in the Modern World." I would take Lawrence as my model, without identifying him, and I would define what I thought were both the duty and the role of the artist in our own time.

As I wrote, there were no more fantasies of elm-lined streets or quiet college towns. What I heard was the clamor of great cities as I pictured myself in Paris and in Rome, London and Firenze. I saw myself in the places where the Modernist revolution had erupted, in Paris where Pound had insisted that poetry must have the quality and concision of prose; in Zurich where Joyce had worked on *Finnegan's Wake*. But beneath the drama of their days I saw other figures take shape. I tried to imagine what forces converge to form a creative person. What constitutes the soul of an artist, I asked myself—what is the essence of art itself?

Just as I'd plunged into my work I had a visit from Aune, who insisted I accompany her immediately to the Walker Art Museum, where there was a traveling exhibit of the last quarter century of American painting.

"This is part of your education, too," she said excitedly as we crossed the campus together.

It was a mid-week afternoon and the gallery was empty. Aune swept from painting to painting, her purple cape swirling around her. She wore sandals with pink socks and her sandy hair frizzed out from her face as though blown by the wind.

"Oh, now look at this," she gestured, as an immense Jackson Pollock canvas loomed above us. "And this, Jason. It's just overwhelming!"

Aune rushed ahead to stand in front of one of de Kooning's women. I, too, was immediately attracted to the Abstract Expressionist paintings in the show, especially Franz Kline's "The Bridge." But the exhibit also contained the first paintings by Edward Hopper I'd seen in the flesh. One in particular, "Early Morning," mesmerized me. That empty street, the redbrick buildings above it, the barber shop with the red and white barber pole in front of it, was intensely familiar to me. As I contemplated the painting, I suddenly recognized where it might have been painted—in Gloucester, in the West End of Main Street. Whether or not that was so, I at least knew that Hopper had summered in Gloucester during the 1920s and 30s.

Aune urged me on.

"Here's a Marsden Hartley." She pointed to a bold painting called "Log-Jam, Penobscot Bay." It was of immense, stripped trees being swept down a boiling river. Next to it was a portrait of Abraham Lincoln, also by Hartley. I asked Aune who the artist was.

"Hartley was amazing. A powerful artist, a troubled man," Aune said, catching her breath. "He was also a fine poet. Bill

Zorach knew him in Robinhood in the 1930s. He was born here in Lewiston, traveled all over Europe and the U.S."

Before I could really focus my attention on the two paintings, another caught my attention. It was of red mountains in New Mexico. Another Hartley! Next to it were two more images of New Mexico, one of an adobe chapel in Ranchos de Taos by Georgia O'Keeffe and another of Indian Country mesas by Stuart Davis, who had once painted in Gloucester with John Sloan, in a small red cottage on East Main Street not far from my own house on Rocky Neck.

Having circled the show, Aune and I separated, returning to the paintings we each liked best. Although she was primarily a figurative painter, Aune was enthralled by the abstract work, especially by the one large shimmering painting of red, yellow and orange rectangles by Mark Rothko, another new artist for me. I stayed with the Hartleys and the O'Keeffes, although I was terribly drawn to Edward Hopper. The second Hopper painting in the exhibit was called "The House by the Railroad." It was of a large Victorian mansion with a mansard roof. I was certain the model for that house was on Washington Street in Gloucester, just before you reached the Boston and Maine Railroad station.

Later, over tea at Clayton's, I listened to Aune talk about the paintings.

"We do have a tradition here." Her hand shook with emotion as she raised the cup to her pale lips. "I've spent so much time in Europe I forget how wonderfully Americans can paint. I can't wait to get down to work again!"

I walked back to my room in a daze. I knew I would return to those paintings many times. No one seemed to have captured the character of Maine quite like Hartley. Next to his strong canvases of the Penobscot River and Georgetown, Andrew Wyeth's paintings seemed staged and effete. The Hoppers, whether or not they had been painted in Gloucester, had given me new respect for my hometown. If Gloucester had inspired artists of the caliber of Hopper, Stuart Davis and John Sloan, I should be more careful about denigrating it as a place to have come from. Above all, it was the images of the American Southwest that remained in my head. Reading Lawrence's essays about Santa Fe and Taos had awakened a yearning in me to experience what he'd discovered in the magical spaces of that high desert and mesa country, a yearning I didn't know I possessed, or, more rightfully, that possessed me.

For two days I secluded myself. Working first on my thesis, I blocked out all distractions until I had a clean enough copy to rush over to the typist's. I wrote and I wrote, finally concluding:

"The novel closes, but not abruptly. Things are left unsaid and the whole construct seems always to hover above the reader like some bright, throbbing phoenix, nervous and in constant tension, never really coming to rest.

"As with most of Lawrence's novels, *The Plumed Serpent* did not mark a stasis in the writer's thoughts and ideals. It was merely a further synthesis, for Lawrence did not rest with that novel as his final statement of a human and ethical vision. In *The Man Who Died* he exchanged Quetzalcoatl for Christ, Mexico for Nazareth, and the synthetic rituals of Don Roman for the plainer ones of Isis. But again, Lawrence did not linger over this later novella, published in 1929, a year before his death. His 'savage pilgrimage' continued. His encounter with the death culture of the Etruscans fueled *Apocalypse*, the spiritual summation which he worked on until hospitalized, his last testament, a final attempt at making himself understood. Sickness finally stopped him, as it often does the visionary. Although the spirit is alive and willing, the flesh is often weak."

Once the thesis was at the typist's, I went to work on my commencement address. Quoting Yeats, I spoke first of the contradictory age we found ourselves in, "an age of stasis and kinesis, of restless movement and confused stability." I spoke of the protagonist in the drama of existence, Man himself, "who lives in an antagonistic world, which he himself has in part created." But I went on to qualify that my topic would not be all men, it would be only one, "the man who interests me and excites me and provokes me and angers me and drives me often to despair; the man who sometimes sees all, and sometimes sees nothing; the man who would see all but for the looking into himself too much sees nothing; the man who looks not enough into himself and therefore sees little elsewhere; the man who can give us sublime moments of created beauty or who can make us shiver in horror and anguish. That man is the artist, and for us, the artist in the modern world."

I felt good about the address. I had poured my heart into it. Everything I couldn't express in my thesis I had begun to articulate in the speech. I read it in the basement of Sills before a panel of judges, one of whom was Hubie, the campus orator *par excellence*. My delivery hadn't been very good, but I was still pleased with the content. When they posted the names of the three finalists on the chapel bulletin board the next morning, I was thrilled to see my name among them. It didn't matter that Quoins had been selected too. We were now supposed to work with Professor Chassen, the speech teacher, to revise and shape our talks. He would also be coaching us in their delivery.

With that behind me, I began preparing for my major orals at which I would also have to defend my thesis. The days grew longer and I got up early in the morning to have as much time as possible to study. Opening the windows of my room, I let the warm air in, laden with the perfume of lilacs. My notes and papers were spread out all over the floor and on my bed and desk. The work of four long years was painfully visible to me. I knew I could never encompass the history of English literature, much less remember the names of all the major writers, or a salient fact I might be asked about a minor poet like Lovelace. But I'd mastered those writers and poets I was attracted to—my adored Romantics, the late Yeats. *Please*, I thought to myself, *don't ask me about the Augustans!* Then there were the beginnings of our literature to review, those Anglo-Saxon gems like "The Seafarer" that Pound had so brilliantly translated.

As I thumbed through the pages of the many anthologies and textbooks I had accumulated during my four years as an English major, I came across one of the poems that had meant so much to Leslie and me: 'O Westron wind/When wilt thou blow?/ And the small rain come down./ Christ, that my love were in my arms,/ And I in my bed again!"

Reading the lyric over and over, I recalled how we used to recite it to each other in Gloucester as we walked arm in arm by the ocean. A terrible feeling of remorse came over me. I stood in the middle of the room, tears streaming down my face, a soft breeze puffing my curtains out. It was the last day before my exam, but I couldn't study. All I could think of was being with Leslie.

✝ From four to six each evening it was happy hour at the Eliot Lounge on Massachusetts Avenue. Every drink in the house was forty-five cents. The stools around the circular bar were filled with patrons sipping their cocktails. In the middle of the circle, on a raised bandstand, a tenor saxophonist, accompanied by a trio of piano, bass and drums, was playing "Come Rain or Come Shine," with a breathy, Ben Webster vibrato. Leslie sat across the table from me still looking stunned after my sudden appearance at her dorm in Cambridge.

She seemed more beautiful than ever. My heart soared as I re-experienced her hazel eyes, the clearness of her complexion, the deep gold of her lustrous hair. It was growing longer and longer and she wore it in such a way as to frame her face. Leslie's hands held mine across the table; her eyes sought my own as I tried to tell her everything that had happened, beginning with Mary and going on to the news of Frank's death. I described my afternoons with Mary and her friends, told her about the run-in with Mickey at the party. I talked to her about Mendel and Annegret, about how Hillary had flushed St. Pierre. And I confessed to her about what Mary and I had done that afternoon in her bedroom.

Leslie listened sympathetically as I explained about Dell's beating and what he'd revealed to me afterwards. The story of Frank's death brought pain to her eyes. But when I told her about my relationship with Mary, she seemed to be trying to catch her breath. For an instant her eyes closed and she withdrew her hands from mine. When they returned they seemed cold to the touch.

"Forgive me," I cried. "I couldn't live another minute without telling you everything. You're the only person who understands me."

"Jason, don't get yourself into a state."

Leslie spoke gently, urging me to take up the glass of bourbon that lay untouched in front of me.

"I understand," she said calmly, although I could read the sadness in her eyes in the dim light of the lounge. "It means a lot to me that you can tell me these things. I feel so sorry for you, for losing Frank. And poor Dell on top of that! Oddly, I always felt he was tormented by something underneath that sophisticated facade. Now I suppose he'll just drift in the city."

"You don't know how much this means to me," I started to say.

"It's my fault, Jason. I pushed you to do what you did. If it wasn't with Mary, it would have been with someone else. I'm just sorry that we didn't have our own chance."

"But I've hurt you," I blurted out. "Can you ever forgive me?"

"Jason, I hurt *you*. You're just hurting me back."

"But that's no way for two people who love...who *said* they loved each other."

Leslie smiled wanly, reaching for one of my Pall Malls. The saxophonist, who had begun playing "Angel Eyes," lowered his horn and stepped up to the microphone.

"No, it isn't," she went on softly. "But people don't always do what's right. I should never have hurt you the way I did."

"*So drink up all you people*," the tenorman sang.

"*Order anything you see,*

"Drink up you happy people
"The drink and the last laugh's on me..."

"Can't we try again?" I said with desperation.

"Things have been done, Jason. Decisions have been made."

"Decisions can be reversed!" I was nearly shouting.

"But you and I are the first people to argue that once the die is cast there can be no turning back."

"It's just a pose and I'm tired of it. I want to say what I feel even though it isn't what I think."

Leslie reached out again to cover my hands with hers.

"Jason, don't violate yourself for me. You know what you need to do. I had to stand away from that. I didn't choose the best way to do it and I'm deeply sorry I hurt you. But the decision is made. You may think you'd like to change your mind, but when you get off by yourself you'll know you were doing what you really wanted to do."

"I can always go to Europe," I said, "we can go together—"

"It won't be the same and you know it."

"How can I be certain?"

"You can't, but that's the indeterminacy of our lives. The Karls and the Marys will come and go. Trust me. But those things we're impelled to do most deeply, the things that have nothing to do with other people but with ourselves, they can't be violated."

"So you're saying there's no turning back for us, that we can't try again."

"Jason, I'm just saying that you know what you have to do and I have to let you do it."

"It sounds so final!"

"Not final, Jason, just necessary, *contingent*. Call it what you will. It doesn't mean I don't care for you and that I won't miss you or think about you a lot."

Leslie started to get up.

"I'd like to walk," she said, looking suddenly worn out.

We walked up Commonwealth Avenue, stopping at the Dugout for more drinks and a pizza. We talked and talked until I had drained the last of my confessions out of myself and Leslie had told me everything about herself and Karl.

"It's funny," she said. "One of the first things he asked me was if I were a virgin. I told him yes, I was. He said he thought I seemed virginal. Maybe I am in a manner of speaking."

"Are you sleeping together?" My voice trembled as I asked.

Leslie shook her head gravely.

"No, Jason. We aren't."

Catching the "T" to Harvard Square, we rushed to get Leslie back to her dorm on Garden Street by midnight, "the witching hour," as she called it. Jammed in among couples making out, we stood hugging in front of the doorway. I could smell the soap I was so accustomed to on her face. Softly we kissed each other on the lips. Then Leslie stepped away from me.

"Don't punish yourself, Jason. And good luck with your orals. I know you'll do fine."

I didn't look back as I walked quickly in the direction of Harvard Square, where I took the subway to North Station. There was no train to Portland until morning. Self-consciously I sat in the depot on a wooden bench among the vagrants and late travelers, reliving our conversations, imagining myself bereft of all the people I'd loved, cast adrift in Europe—waiting in a distant country for an unknown train whose destination was uncertain.

When I woke up with a start in the grainy light of early morning, I discovered that I'd missed the milk train north. I limped into the men's room and splashed some cold water on my face. All around me it smelled of urine. I felt like a bum on the morning after a bender. Grabbing a cup of coffee and a donut from the lunch counter, I ran out into the street to begin hitching a ride to Brunswick. It was already nine o'clock. I had to be in Sills Hall for my oral examination at two. I was so anxious about not making it on time that my hand shook the coffee right out of the cup and onto the sidewalk.

Once I was headed into the tunnel with a St. Johnsbury trucker whose destination was Portsmouth, I felt better. We exchanged pleasantries, but as the strip of submarine sandwich and pizza places flashed past on Route 1 north, I started to drift off to sleep, re-experiencing the agony of my impulsive train trip south the day before, the brown and green landscape giving way to suburbs and cities. All I could recall was thinking, *You'll never take this ride again. You'll never see these places from the windows of the Boston and Maine.*

The trucker woke me up in the Howard Johnson's parking lot in Portsmouth. We ate a couple of cheeseburgers and each of us gulped down a milkshake. He wished me luck on my exam as he pulled his big rig full of fifty-five gallon drums back onto the highway.

I got onto Route 95 and started walking with my thumb out when a fat guy in an Olds 98 pulled over and motioned me in. His name was Rolly, he said, thumping his stomach. As he slapped the automatic shift into high gear, I caught him eyeing my rumpled tweed jacket and uncombed beard.

"Had yourself a little romp?"

"I was in Boston with my girlfriend."

"Get anything?"

At first I didn't catch what he said.

"You hitch all that distance, I figure you're gonna see some action."

Rolly had an expectant grin on his face. Reflected in the front mirror I saw a rack of women's dresses stretched across the rear of the car.

"Bonny Belle's my line. I don't sell anything I haven't tried on the little ladies myself. I cover the big stores and the small ones, Porteous, Benoit's. All the college towns."

"You must be familiar with the Bates girls," I said.

"The Lewiston cuties in their kilts and kneesocks! Those plump little legs drive me to distraction."

As he grinned, the pink of his face extended all the way up to the crown of his bald head.

"So tell me, how'd it go?"

"In Boston?"

"Where else?"

"We just sat talking in a bar."

"What'cha do after?"

"She lives in a dorm."

"Smart kid like you oughtta be able to find some place to shack up."

I was beginning to feel uncomfortable. His dashboard clock read twelve-thirty as we approached the several exits for Portland, leaving me an hour and a half to go before my orals. If we made the Brunswick turnoff by one o'clock at the latest, I'd be able to shower and get over to Sills with a couple of minutes to spare. But Rolly was slowing down to 50 MPH.

"What's she like?" he asked.

"My girlfriend?"

"Who d'you think?"

"She's smart."

"A looker?"

"I'd say she's attractive."

"B-cup or C?"

"I don't know."

"You would if you had yourself a handful."

Rolly was slapping his hands rhythmically against his thighs, as the car gathered speed.

"She wear panties?"

"Of course."

"What color?"

"Plaid?"

His face lit up, fingers dancing on the steering while. Then he slowed the car down.

"Oh, God, what color plaid?"

"Red," I answered, sneaking another look at the clock.

"Bet you got into them."

"Actually..."

"No secrets between friends!"

He accelerated the car again. As it surged wildly ahead I wanted to tell him to let me out, but Rolly was my only hope of making the exam on time.

"What's her name?"

"Jacqueline," I said.

"Oh, jack me, Jackie!" Rolly's body bounced in the car seat as he sang.

I could see Exit 9 just ahead.

"This is where I get out," I said anxiously.

"What a story, what tale," he shouted. "I could take you all the way to Bang-whore to hear the rest. Quick, quick, d'you go down on her?"

"That's kind of private."

"Bashful boy," he crooned. "Sips the nectar of the gods and won't tell a soul."

"Look, Rolly, please. I've got an exam in less than an hour. If I don't make it I don't graduate."

He gunned the engine.

"Far be it for old Rolly to keep a man from his degree."

With that he veered off the Maine Turnpike and headed for the Brunswick-Bath toll booth.

"I don't mind a little detour," he shouted above the sound of the overworking engine. "We'll do the good samaritan number. Get you right to the college door."

It was one-twenty when we entered Brunswick.

"Drop me here," I insisted, as he turned off Pleasant Street and approached the campus.

Practically falling out of the car, I thanked him.

"Keep that old tongue wagging! Spank those hard little bottoms!"

He was shouting out the window at me, as he spun the big blue and white Olds around in traffic and headed north. I raced

219

across Maine and up School Street to my room. Tearing my clothes off, I threw myself into the shower. Still wet, I stumbled back into the room where I pulled on my last clean shirt and combed my hair into place.

✛ It was exactly 2 p.m. when I got to the exam room in Sills. As I approached the door, I could hear Hubie's voice.

"It's hardly a coherent essay," he was telling someone.

I knocked.

"Ah, yes, Mr. Makrides." Hubie broke off what he was saying.

Loren and Lou were seated at a table with Hubie. Lou winked while Loren waved me into a chair in front of them.

"I was telling my colleagues how disappointed I am with your thesis," Hubie began.

"Your introductory chapter is, of course, exemplary," he went on. "But the second and third chapters leave much to be desired." He paused to light up a cigarette as Lou rolled his eyes impatiently.

"They're, how shall I say?" Hubie continued. "Perhaps unintegrated is the word I'm looking for."

"I did have trouble concluding the essay."

Hubie interrupted me. I felt the palms of my hands getting wet.

"It's really three essays," he said, "one on myth, one which gives us a close reading of the novel under discussion, and a final one which ought to integrate the concerns of the first two while summarizing your thesis."

"I rather like the third chapter," Lou interjected. "It points to further work on Lawrence, opening up a number of approaches to the relationship between art and life."

"But, Professor Diehl," Hubie insisted. "The purpose of this exercise is to assist the candidate in undertaking a coherent investigation of an original subject."

"I think he's done that." Loren drew on his unlighted pipe. "Each essay has its own interest and there is a subtle inter-relationship among them. I'll admit those lines could be more carefully articulated. Nevertheless, there's some fine critical thinking here."

I listened to Loren and Hubie debating the merits of my thesis as the hour allotted for my oral passed. Then Lou broke in, asking me a question about Lawrence's relationship to the Modernist movement. I jumped to respond, ecstatic that it wasn't about the eighteenth century. Loren followed up with a related question about Lawrence and Joyce as technicians of the novel. Hubie, who may have felt that Lou and Loren were keeping me in safe territory, asked me to discuss briefly Shakespeare's use of analogy in the major plays. Having read a draft of St. Pierre's thesis on *Hamlet,* I suggested Francis Fergusson's essay on the play's action as a jumping off point to discuss how the drama was structured around analogous relationships. For example, those between Hamlet and Claudius, his step-father and the killer of his real father, and Laertes and *his* father. In this case, Hamlet's accidental murder of Polonius served as an ironic commentary on his tormented eventual killing of Claudius, the two bereaved sons ultimately fighting to the death.

Apparently pleased with my response, Hubie asked me a further question on the period, a comparison of similes from plays by Shakespeare, Webster and Marlowe. Loren followed up with one on the Romantic revival of interest in Shakespeare, while Lou asked me to characterize Eliot's view of the Bard. At five to three, Hubie noted there should be at least one question on the earliest period of English literature. He asked me to quote some lines in the original from any Old English poem and briefly gloss them. I chose "The Wanderer." Reciting the five or so lines I'd memorized in my sophomore year, I translated them and commented upon the poet's use of the kenning. Lou congratulated me, and Loren commented on what he felt was the apparent range of my interests. But when Hubie gave me a satisfied look, I knew I was home free.

I rushed back to my room and fell into bed with relief. Two hours later a knock on my room door woke me out of a sound sleep.

"I'm fucked," St. Pierre said as I let him in. "I couldn't answer a thing!"

He had gone in at 4 p.m., drawing Hubie, Grierson and Bennett, who was a medievalist, for an examining panel.

"Jesus, I didn't get one question on the 20th century."

"What happened?"

"I just didn't prepare," he said. "I've been going through hell. I've got to talk to you. I came over last night but you weren't in."

"I went to see Leslie. I almost didn't make it back in time. I hitched a ride with some salesman who turned out to be a voyeur!"

"Jason, listen. What I'm going to tell you is just between the two of us."

"Naturally," I said.

Accepting one of my Pall Malls, St. Pierre sat on the messy bed.

"This is the end for me," he confided, cupping his dark face with his small hands. "It's worse than anything that's ever happened."

"Tell me," I urged him. "It can't be all that bad."

"I'm going crazy, Jason. I can't keep my mind on anything. Ever since Hillary flushed me I haven't been able to study. I've been up all night pacing the floor. I think I'm sick—"

"Ridiculous!"

"No, really. You remember that night last November at the Stowe House? It was your birthday and we went over to celebrate your first legal drink. There were those Navy wives at the bar. Remember? And they put us down?"

"Those two? Sure! Drunk out of their gourds, slobbering into their daiquiris. I think they were furious we didn't move in on them. We were so naive we didn't even think to make a play!"

"Do you remember the blond one, the big one?" St. Pierre asked.

"She was the one with the filthy mouth. The manager finally asked them to leave. We were mortified. But what's that got to do with anything?"

St. Pierre lowered his eyes from my face.

"I met her in the record store the other day. She recognized me and we started to talk. She invited me over for a drink, some fucking trailer out there on the Bath Road. Said her husband was away on a mission. I don't know why, but I went. I was feeling horny. We had a couple of drinks, listened to some bullshit Jackie Gleason music. She wanted me to go to bed with her. I guess I wanted to. But when we got undressed and into bed… Goddamn room was like a closet, dirty underwear piled all over the chairs! It stunk of her perfume. When we got into bed and started, you know, fooling around, I couldn't get it up—"

"So what?"

"No! No!" St. Pierre cried. "She got furious. Instead of fondling me the way Hillary used to, she jumped out of bed and stood over me naked. Her boobs hung down to her stomach. She started to scream at me. 'Pretty boy, you think you're so tough! You got a cock like a baby!' I didn't know what to do, so I got up and took my clothes. I ran out the door, right into the middle of all those mobile homes. I was just running around in circles carrying my clothes. I got dressed in the woods. Then I ran like hell down the Bath Road, back to the campus. I was supposed to study but I couldn't. I haven't been able to do anything since."

St. Pierre began to sob.

"Jason, it was so humiliating!"

"Henri, Henri." I got up to sit next to him on the bed. Feeling him gasp and shake, I put my arm around his shoulders.

"I always knew there was something wrong with me," he cried.

"Don't be silly," I said. "How could you possibly feel desire for someone like that? You were just lonely. I've felt that way myself."

"I swear, Jason. That did me in. I can't even jerk off anymore. Now I know I'm queer!"

I held St. Pierre tightly, trying to comfort him with words that seemed to have no effect. Together we lay on my bed in the quiet room. Finally, when I heard him breathing rhythmically in sleep, I got up and covered him with a blanket. Sitting in my chair in the dark, I began to understand how Dell felt. Maybe it wasn't so different to love men.

13

By May 30th I had finished the major oral and six hours of written exams in English. There was no exam in Lou's course, and Loren had accepted the first chapter of my senior thesis as my final paper in Lit Crit. All that stood between me and my degree was the Italian exam, which I prepared for with relish, dreaming of walking the same cobblestoned streets of Florence that Dante had traversed.

Between periods of translating from the *Purgatorio* and the *Paradiso* I worked to shape my commencement address. With Professor Chasson's help I refined the language and practiced my delivery. He insisted that the speakers memorize their "parts," as he called them. But I wanted to keep mine fluid because I seemed to get new ideas every time I sat down with the manuscript.

I continued my walks, alone and in the hush of evening. Once, passing Schrebner's yellow cottage on Bowdoin Street, I saw him sitting quietly on the porch with Ilsa. Inviting me to join them, Ilsa offered me a glass of lemonade. The drink was cool and tart and I sipped it slowly while they asked me about my plans for September. Ilsa warmly offered her opinion that Europe would be a good experience for me, but Schrebner seemed to withhold his encouragement.

"Must you go, Meester Makrides? Why can you not find a haven in this country where you may study and write to your heart's content?"

"But Anton," Ilsa insisted, "Jason wants to see some other part of the world."

Schrebner only shook his balding head. As I accompanied him back to his office in the dark, he said gently, "Have your *wanderjahr*, then, but come back to us." His bicycle tires whispered on the gravel as we crossed the campus together. When we had reached Schrebner's office, I confessed to him that I often wondered what he did there late at night. With an uncharacteristic twinkle in his otherwise mournful brown eyes, Schrebner replied, "Oh, I vork, I *theenk*. While the College sleeps I am awake!"

✝ Still preoccupied with my address, I stopped in almost daily to revisit the American paintings at the Walker Art Museum. Never had I been so taken by a group of canvases. Studying them inspired me to sharpen my comments on the role of the artist, to re-think the positions I had taken in my speech. It seemed ironic that just as I was about to free myself from my own country I had been moved beyond words by the work of some of her most native artists. The paintings by Edward Hopper and Marsden Hartley continued to cast a spell over me. Each contributed to a vision of an America I had never before imagined.

Hartley's raw power attracted me to the Maine landscape I'd paid scant attention to during my four years in Brunswick, while Hopper's bleak vision of an empty Main Street and his two stark interiors, "Hotel Window" and "Room in New York," seemed to dramatize an existential despair I had only guessed at beneath the surface of American life. I asked myself why I was leaving for Europe just as I had begun to get a handle on my own culture. Henry James was right, being an American seemed indeed a complex fate.

I thought about Lawrence, too; about how I'd really botched my thesis by starting to work on it late and setting myself too broad a topic. After all, what did I know about myth? I also thought about the American writers I had been reading for the past two years—Kerouac, Ginsburg, Corso. Absorbed as I was in the Hartley and Hopper paintings, the words of the Beats seemed to wear thin. Murray had predicted that I would outgrow them, not because they didn't have important things to say, but because, he assured me, I would eventually find my own voice. As I worked over my address, I began to hear myself speaking the way I used to write to Leslie. It was a more supple voice, not so riddled with academic jargon. It felt relaxed, personal. In it I heard again the local intonation that Professor Chasson had tried to help me overcome in freshman speech class, the same broad A's and dropped R's he warned me about now as he heard me rehearsing my delivery.

But this was the way I'd always talked. I suppose my pronunciation retained something of the nasal twang of Gloucester, along with what I had assimilated after four years of listening to the flat speech of coastal Maine. No doubt the bit of theater I'd done in my first two years in college helped me project more properly. Nonetheless, one still had to sound unaffected, natural. And that was the voice I began to hear as I revised and practiced delivering my address.

Then it was all over. I took my Italian exam on Friday, June 5th. Commencement would take place the following Saturday. That Friday night there was a huge party at the Zeta house, celebrating the end of classes and exams. Mueller and I joined St. Pierre in his room after dinner, where we started drinking beer out of jumbo quarts and listening to Art Blakey and the Jazz Messengers. There was a festive air about the house as the Zeta brothers rushed up and down the stairs in their skivvies, faces flushed with alcohol.

By dark the campus was in an uproar. There were lights burning in all the dorms. Everywhere students shouted and sang. Cars tore up and down Sills Drive and College Street, speeding past the Moulton Union with occupants screaming out of the windows, tossing beer cans and swearing at everybody they saw.

When we went down to the Zeta kitchen to make ourselves some ham sandwiches, we heard a commotion outside in the driveway. Hurrying to the window, we saw a group of brothers vigorously rocking an old white DeSoto back and forth. We ran outside to see what was happening.

"She'll fuck you,

"She'll suck you,

"She'll blow your guts out!" the brothers were singing while they rocked the car from side to side.

"What's going on?" St. Pierre asked, as we approached the group.

"Hosmer's in there getting head," one of the brothers yelled. Then he threw his shoulder against the vehicle that tipped and swayed like a carnival car.

"Head from a date?" St. Pierre shouted back.

"It's some slut he picked up at Ernie's."

As the car settled back normally on its tires, the brothers started pulling on the door handles.

"Come out, come out, wherever you are!" they started chanting. Only the front porch light illuminated the scene, as the brothers yanked urgently on the door handles.

"Here they are, here they come!" one shouted. "I got dibs."

St. Pierre and I stood holding our Miller's quarts. On impulse I rushed over to the car. Putting my thumb over the mouth of the bottle, I began furiously to shake it. As the door opened I let the beer squirt into the dark interior of the car in an enormous cascade of foam and liquid.

Someone shouted with surprise and anger from within the car and a pair of legs, barefoot and in white shorts, started to get out of the back seat. Hosmer was a lineback from Upstate New York, well over six feet tall. He leaped out of the car swinging and cursing.

"Who the fuck did that?"

The other brothers all closed in around him, pouring beer on his crew cut head. As he disappeared in the huddle, the car was

229

momentarily abandoned. Mueller and St. Pierre joined the brothers around Hosmer. Still holding my quart of beer, I watched a copperskinned girl climb hesitantly out of the car. She was wearing a skimpy black dress and her hair and face were wet. Slowly her frightened eyes met mine. It was Mary.

Just then Mueller ran over.

"Quick, Jason, Mendel's in a bad way."

He grabbed at my arm. I watched St. Pierre running into the house. Mary looked as though she was going to call out to me. But Mueller pulled on my arm again and I ran off with him, pitching my empty quart violently into the driveway where I heard it shatter as I entered the house.

Mendel had locked himself in his room. St. Pierre stood banging on the door.

"Annegret's parents threw him out of the house tonight," Mueller explained, breathing hard. "They told him not to show his face there again."

"Let us in, for Christ's sake!" St. Pierre shouted.

"Bob's been drinking," Mueller said. "He's just crazy. He could do anything."

The door opened and Mendel stood framed by the light behind him. His hair was wild, his eyes red. St. Pierre rushed to his side.

"What happened?" he asked.

Mendel didn't respond. His gaze dropped to the floor. He began shaking all over.

"Talk to us," Mueller said, as we entered the room behind St. Pierre, who helped Mendel over to his messy bed.

Mumbling, Mendel told us that Annegret had warned him her parents were giving her a hard time about the relationship. They felt she was too young to be seeing him. They were afraid it would interfere with her plans for college. They also objected to the fact that he was Jewish. During the past several weeks they had tried to break the friendship up, insisting that Annegret not encourage Mendel's attentions. They were afraid the couple was sleeping together, especially when Annegret would sneak out at night after her parents were in bed.

But Annegret paid little heed to her parents. She encouraged Mendel to continue visiting. When he'd gone over that night as usual, her father was standing on the front porch. He'd been a gymnast in Munich and he was blond and physically imposing. Apparently he planted himself between Mendel and the door. As Mendel approached he started shouting that Mendel was corrupting his daughter, that the relationship was creating a scandal for the family. Mendel had tried to explain to him how he felt about Annegret, when the mother came out and started shouting for Mendel to leave or they'd call the police. Mendel could hear Annegret sobbing in the living room. "I'll kill myself, I'll kill myself!" But there seemed no way of reaching her.

St. Pierre said we should all get in the car and make a run for Annegret's house.

"Let's case the scene," he suggested, helping Mendel to stand up from the bed where he was sitting despondently.

We piled into St. Pierre's car and drove over to the bungalow on Magean Street. All the lights were out. St. Pierre cut the engine and we sat in the dark trying to figure out what to do next.

"I don't want them to hurt her," Mendel said. "Her father's crazy enough to tie her to the bed."

St. Pierre started the car again, pressing softly on the gas pedal.

"Time for some air," he said, heading out of Magean Street and turning right toward the Mere Point Road. Mueller handed us each a can of beer. After we cracked them, he began passing a fifth of blended whiskey around.

"Oh, shit, boilermakers!" St. Pierre shouted, as we raced past old farm houses and open land. We stopped close to the water, all of us tumbling out to sit on an old stone wall and drink. Mendel seemed drunk already. I lit a cigarette. My head was spinning.

"It's fucking insane," Mueller was saying. "What right do those assholes have to dictate to their daughter?"

St. Pierre agreed. Below us lay the inlet that lead out to Casco Bay. Although the night was clear with a million stars overhead, you could still hear the fog bells in the distance. St. Pierre picked up a stone and threw it soundlessly far out into the water. Mueller followed. We passed the whiskey around again. Turning to ask Mendel if he wanted a swig from the bottle, I saw that he wasn't with us.

"Mendel's gone," I said.

"Don't leave him alone!" St. Pierre headed up toward the road.

"There he is over there," Mueller said. "What's he doing?"

We saw what looked like a flash of light in an upland field.

"He's setting a fire!"

St. Pierre began to run, Mueller and I following him.

"Spread out," I shouted. "Let's try to surround him."

Ahead of us there was a sheet of flames. Mendel stood tossing matches. Then he began running away from us.

"I'll get the fire," I said.

"Grab the blanket in the car," St. Pierre yelled over his shoulder.

Just as I was about to turn I felt something cutting into my thighs and I fell backwards. I reached out to find my pants torn. There was blood on my legs. From the ground I could make out a low barbed wire fence. I limped back to the car and grabbed the old army blanket St. Pierre used for making out. Racing to the fire, I leaped over the fence and threw the blanket down on the flames. Ahead of me Mueller was stamping out a couple of smaller blazes. St. Pierre had Mendel down on the ground and was trying to comfort him.

My thighs were throbbing with pain, but I knew I had to keep the fire from rekindling. It was a big field and the grass was dry. Mueller came over to help me. I felt faint from the exertion of smothering the flames.

"I did something to my legs," I said. "Watch out for the barbed wire fence over there."

Mueller took the blanket from me as I lay on my back, my head reeling from the beer and the whiskey. To keep myself from vomiting I closed my eyes and concentrated on my thighs.

St. Pierre helped Mendel, who was sobbing uncontrollably, back into the car. We made a beeline for the Zeta house, where I took a look at my legs in the glaring light of the second floor bathroom. My pants were ripped to shreds. Halfway down and across my thighs there were two lacerations. The bleeding had stopped, but the cuts were deeper than surface scratches. I washed them out with soap and water, figuring I'd have them checked at the infirmary in the morning. Taking some gauze pads from the Zeta first-aid closet, I taped them over the cuts.

Mendel was sleeping now in his own bed. St. Pierre volunteered to spend the night with him. As Mueller and I left the house, the party was still going strong. In my torn pants I limped across the campus, past the Union that was closed and the dorms where the undergraduates were packing to leave the next day. We watched them as they tossed cartons though windows and doors, piling old furniture outside to be carted away by the Grounds and Buildings staff. Then we both stopped under the lighted windows of Schrebner's office, where we could see the shadow of his movements on the wall.

"The last time I saw Schrebner he urged me to stay in school," Mueller reflected. "I'll never forget the look on his face. 'The creative, not the destructive, Meester Mueller. A leetle less Dionysos, a leetle more Apollo!'"

Mueller accompanied me to the porch at 83 Federal Street where we shook hands. He was leaving early in the morning to join Roonie in New York. Together they would begin their drive to the Coast.

"I told the Dean I wasn't coming back in September," Mueller said. "Without you guys I couldn't cut this place."

"It's finally over," I said, feeling weak on my legs.

The porchlight gave Mueller's skin a yellow cast.

"When you get back from Italy we'll still be out there. I figure I can finish up at Berkeley. I'm sick of justifying everything I care about to these idiots."

I leaned against the porch railing listening to him. The pain from the cuts in my thighs came and went.

Silently we smoked a last cigarette together, and I watched Mueller saunter off across Federal Street, heading up the Bath Road on his way back to the ARU house. As his shaved head disappeared, I wondered when I'd ever see him again.

It was balmy, the first really warm night of the month. I hated to go up to my room. But I was exhausted. Now that Mueller was gone and everything had quieted down, the encounter with Mary came back to me. I saw her frightened eyes, the look of shame in her face, as she got out of the car in front of the Zeta house and recognized me, her dress up above her knees. She had tried to speak; she looked at me imploringly. As angry as I was about her apparent betrayal, I was still sorry that I'd walked away from her.

✝ When my parents arrived on the afternoon before Commencement, the first person out of the car was Leslie. She rushed toward me looking radiant in a white linen skirt, her hair beautifully brushed into a French twist.

"Don't be so surprised," she said, kissing me. "How could I let you graduate without being here. Part of me is graduating with you!"

I hugged my father who was already crying. Getting out from behind the steering wheel of the family Chevrolet, my mother seemed smaller than I remembered in her neat print dress, her graying hair in a bun. I invited everybody up to my room for a sip of Jack Daniels before my parents registered at the Stowe House, where they'd be staying. The Waddells, who had come upstairs to meet everyone, offered Leslie a bed down the hall from me.

"After all, it's graduation," Professor Waddell said, rubbing his bald head. "We've enjoyed having you for two years."

That night Murray and Aune joined us for dinner at the Stowe House, jammed with graduating seniors and their families. My father and Murray hit it off immediately, once Murray said a few words in Greek to him that he'd picked up in Chicago. Later, Dad confided that when I got to be Murray's age I could have my "whiskers."

Aune was radiant in a white Mexican dress embroidered with turquoise. For a graduation gift she had created an enormous monotype of a phoenix, rising in red, black and gold splendor from a bed of ashes. Under it she'd lettered Lawrence's words: "I rise in flames cried the phoenix!"

"This is your real diploma," she said.

Leslie handed me the Grove Press edition of Henry James's *Italian Hours*.

"You've had your Lawrence period," she said. "Now you'd better confront James."

"*Touché!*" Murray shouted, as we raised our wine glasses.

"Maybe we'll do it together," I said. "Murray just got his advance. Let's drink to it!"

"There's still some work to do here on the farm," he said. "By next spring we should be ready for a little trip to Italy."

After dinner Leslie and I walked back to 83 Federal Street across the rickety wooden railroad bridge we'd often stood on, looking at the tracks as they disappeared into the distance.

"I'm still speechless," I said, feeling awkward now that we were alone.

"Jason, I just wanted to be with you. I know how important this graduation is. Besides, I couldn't miss your address."

"I'm not too happy with it," I said.

"O bosh! I bet it's just splendid."

We kissed at the door of Leslie's room and I trudged back to my own, wishing desperately we could spend the night together. As I lay naked in my own bed for the last time, I thought I heard some noise in the corridor. I pictured Leslie coming to my door in the yellow nightgown I knew so well. But it was only the wind or someone stirring downstairs in the Waddell's part of the house.

How strange to have Leslie so close to me yet so distant. I thought of getting up, of going to her room. Maybe she was waiting there for me in her warm bed, in the dark. But no, Leslie had made it clear how things stood between us, not so much with words as with the gentleness of a kiss. It was a kiss between friends and that is how I had to accept it.

Still, I couldn't sleep. I kept turning my commencement address over in my mind. I felt that there was something unsaid in it, something I needed to add. I got up, my eyes smarting from the strong light of the old gooseneck. My books were all packed, the typewriter safe in its case beside the bare desk. But I grabbed the oak tag folder that held my speech and I began to read it.

I recalled some remarks from Carter's Baccalaureate address the week before, something that had disturbed me.

"If this country is to be changed, if our public life is to be renewed," he had asserted, seeming to look directly down at me from the pulpit of the First Parish Church, "it will not be through the agency of bearded bohemianism."

I wanted to respond to that. I needed to reply, even though I didn't think Carter meant to attack me and my friends directly. I began to write by hand on a sheet of legal foolscap.

"The writers and artists of the Beat Generation have not given us a vision for a new society, but they have shown the way to one. They have opened the doors and windows of our lives of musty conformity, letting fresh air blow through the national edifice, a structure many of us have thought was always built of cards..."

I wrote and I revised, the stillness of night around me like a blanket. Then I got out the typewriter and recopied what I had written to add to my address. When I looked out the window, the first light was just beginning to show between the trees along Federal Street. I went to the bathroom and, as I turned from the toilet, I saw my face in the mirror, the whites of my eyes bloodshot from exhaustion. I let the sink fill up with hot water. Then I took the shaving brush I hadn't used for almost a year out of the medicine cabinet and began to lather my face with a dried up soap stick.

It was hard work scraping away at my beard. I stood in front of the mirror as the morning light came into the bathroom. Changing blades in my safety razor, I went over my face once again, starting down at my throat. After I'd finished, I found some Bay Rum and splashed it all over my face and neck. It stung like crazy. While I was inspecting my handiwork, wondering if I hadn't been foolish to shave off the best beard I'd ever grown, Leslie came into the bathroom in her nightgown.

"Oh, Jason, I'm sorry," she said. And then she looked at me again.

"I did it," I said. "I don't really know why. Maybe just because this part of my life is over."

"You look so different, so handsome."

"My face seems fat," I said. "I guess I'm not used to it."

Leslie hugged me.

"Hurry," she said. "Everyone will be here for breakfast."

✠ As I sat in cap and gown with my class, high up above the audience at the First Parish Church, I could see Leslie near the front row next to my parents. Murray and Aune were seated farther down toward the rear. We had marched in and been seated. We'd heard the prayer by the pastor of the church. And now the Bowdoin choir was singing Croce's *Cantate Domino*. As Quoins rose to give his address, I felt the palms of my hands begin to perspire. The oak tag folder that held my talk was damp at the edges.

Quoins' address was the story of a young man, Tim, facing the trials of growing up. It was in the form of an interior monologue and Quoins delivered it in a flat, emotionless tone that was quite effective. I found myself listening carefully to the words rather than attempting, as I often did with his work, to criticize it as he read it, cancelling out its meaning in the process.

It was the unknown we faced upon leaving college, Quoins seemed to be saying, even though we thought we knew what kind of world we were entering and what kinds of places we expected to find for ourselves in it. To deny the importance of the unknown in our lives, he said, was to deny the beautiful and terrifying quality of life itself.

Finishing, Quoins received a warm ovation. After the choir sang Byrd's *Sacerdotes Domini,* Roy Lusignuol, one of our many classmates who were heading to medical school, spoke about the role of science in our lives. What the talk lacked in imagination it made up for in the sensibleness of its conclusion. In order not to be feared, Roy asserted, science must be understood but not revered. Everyone clapped.

Then it was my turn. Trembling, I left my seat and walked to the podium. We were allowed to have the manuscript of our address in front of us, but Professor Chasson had insisted it be memorized. Once I began to speak, my mind went blank, so I tried both to read my address and to deliver it as though it were memorized. I spoke slowly, as I'd been coached to do, looking down at my listeners.

"Ours is not the best of all possible worlds," I began. "This is not even the best of all possible countries—if ever one existed; this land of rolling wheat fields and chrome-plated egg cartons, propelled by viciously powerful engines, sweeping down highways of concrete and steel: indestructible, ingenious, boring…"

I got a few laughs at my crack about big American cars before launching into the main part of my address.

I spoke of the paradox of a society in which radical gains in science and technology coexisted with a stultifying political conservatism and social conformity. I said that it was the responsibility of the artist, indeed, his very duty, "to look critically at his age. And with the insight and the technique, which take half a lifetime to acquire, the artist must reshape the world in his own vision."

"We need the artist," I continued, "to help us define and redefine ourselves and our values—to show us exactly where he thinks we are going wrong."

"But the artist, whether visual or literary, must be more than a social critic," I added. "Art which is basically social criticism, while it may have an exciting immediacy, often lacks the depth and the timeless quality inherent in a good work of art."

"The artist must be a thinker," I said. "His work must have the validity of a philosophical basis. Our age is sadly deficient in this art, especially in America."

I went on to read the short section I had inserted about the Beats.

"Don't think for a minute that the Beats have not had something important to say," I noted. "Just as Dada and Surrealism were necessary in clearing the cobwebs out of the dusty museums and galleries of Europe, out of the muddled heads of Academy poets and painters, so the Beats in America and the Angry Young Men in England have become the vanguard of a new way of looking at the world. They have fired the first salvos of a long-needed social criticism. We may laugh at Time magazine's satirical reports of Beat readings where Allen Ginsburg disrobes and Gregory Corso shouts 'Fried shoes!' at the audience. But Time, in its infinite rectitude, also knows that something heretical is happening in our social and aesthetic life, something that threatens the Luce Corporation's hegemony over national consciousness and values. The Beats are merely the harbingers of this change. It is they who have opened the doors and windows of our society. What will enter these newly aired rooms is up to us who stand before you.

"Most important of all," I went on, "the artist can compel us to look into ourselves, to understand ourselves. For if we cannot understand our own motives, we cannot minister to the minds and hearts of others; indeed, we have no business attempting to do so.

"When all is said and done," I concluded, "the unexamined life is not worth living."

As I looked down into the audience that was applauding vigorously, I saw Murray with a big smile on his face. My hands were dripping wet and I felt perspiration all over my body as I took my seat.

"Jonathan Edwards, even without your beard!" I heard St. Pierre whisper from a couple of rows above me. But I was still so caught up in the tensions of having delivered the address that I heard nothing else for the remainder of the ceremony until my name was called for me to receive my degree.

At the commencement luncheon they announced that I had been awarded both first and second prizes in the Brown Extemporaneous Essay competition. Quoins received the prize for the best commencement address. Having broken the rules and read mine, after adding to it, I knew I wouldn't get the prize and I really didn't care. Nevertheless, Carter congratulated me. Crossing the room quickly after the luncheon, the President told my parents they should feel proud of their son. Then Schrebner approached me in a crimson gown, beaming his approval.

"Go to Europe. Yes, go to that benighted place if you must," he said, in his thick accent. "But remember, the hope is here. America is the regeneration of the world!"

"Content wise, yours was head and shoulders above the other addresses." Murray had his arm around me as we made our way outside in the crowd. "You're not an orator, you're a writer and that's what counts."

Outside the Arena where the luncheon had taken place, I stopped to shake St. Pierre's hand and to introduce his parents to mine.

"You see," I said, holding onto his hand, "they came after all. And we both graduated."

"I must have passed my orals!" he shouted.

Before I turned to greet St. Pierre and his parents, I'd caught sight of Mendel, who had graduated *summa cum laude*, standing stiffly near the gym with his mother and father. After saying goodbye to the St. Pierres, I ran over to greet him, but he had disappeared. It was odd, the way Mendel had looked, like a little boy again, standing politely but unhappily with parents who doted on him.

Back at my room, Murray and I carried the cartons containing my books and records down to the car. Together we loaded them into the trunk along with my record player and typewriter, placing my clothing on top. We hugged goodbye and Aune gave me a big kiss.

"See you in Europe!" they both shouted, waving us on our way.

During the drive to Gloucester Leslie held my hand.

"I'm proud of you, too," she said.

Sleepily I sat watching the familiar landmarks appear and disappear as we made our way slowly home.

14

*T*wo days after I got home I went to work at Gorton's. At first they put me on utility shift at $1.55 an hour. I had to get up at five to be at work in the pen rooms by six a.m., shoveling red fish on a conveyor belt through the processors that converted it into mink food. After mug-up at nine, we worked straight through to noon when we broke for lunch. By two-thirty, when the second shift came on, I was exhausted and I stunk to high heaven from the oily fish. Sometimes, instead of shoveling, I was sent with the younger permanent help to load the processed mink food in hundred pound bags onto freight cars at the railroad station. From there it was shipped to farms in Minnesota and Michigan where the mink were raised. On that job we took turns, some of us doing the heavy work while others had a cigarette break or ran across the street to the variety store for a cold drink. I liked working the freight cars, but shortly after I got started I was transferred to the Seafood Center on Rogers Street, just up from the Inner Harbor.

I would remain there for the duration of the summer at $2.00 an hour. Initially my job was to pack corrugated cartons with boxes of deep-fried fish sticks and to glue the flaps down on the cartons once they were full. I stacked the filled cartons on a wooden pallet, each row separated by a pine rack. When I had achieved a dozen rows of twelve cartons each, someone came by with a fork lift and loaded the pallet into the freezer where the day's work was flash frozen and stored for distribution. The first thing I learned was that the cod sticks we used didn't come from Gloucester, or even from America. They were shipped in on immense cargo vessels from Iceland and Norway.

Next I was sent downstairs. My job there was opening the cardboard covered slabs of frozen cod so that they could be sawed into manageable pieces. A crew of men fed them through a gang-saw that cut them into the actual fish sticks. Since I was new I wasn't allowed to operate the machines. From the bottom floor the sticks were sent on a belt to the floor above. In that department they were battered and fried by women, who packed them individually in the boxes that had been my responsibility to place in cartons for freezing.

I was on the second shift. We started at two-thirty, finishing at 11 p.m. with a half hour for lunch and two fifteen minute mug-ups. Like everyone else, I had to wear khaki pants and a matching tan workshirt. The women all wore hair nets, while the men were issued paper caps with the company's Man-at-the-Wheel logo on them to keep our hair from getting into the products. By the time I got home my entire body smelled of fried fish. The odor seemed to remain in the pores of my skin even after I took a shower.

I worked through most of July, moving between the air-conditioned levels of the Seafood Center and the heat of the old flake wharves directly on the waterfront. The help took their breaks where the company had once laid out salted cod fillets to cure in the sun. I ate my dinner outside, either on the flake wharves with the women or with the men on a loading platform in front of the center. It was usually a sandwich, which my mother prepared for me. At first I sat alone. But when Sooky Simmons, a kid I'd known in elementary school, was transferred to the Center from the canning factory, where they made chowder and cod fish cakes, I started eating with him. Sooky wore his hair in the same crew cut he had in fifth grade. He hadn't changed much from the pudgy, good-natured kid I'd walked to school with each day. Once I was known to be a friend of Sooky's, the other men began talking to me. Some even offered me cigarettes from their own packs.

There was Brownie, a man who'd worked at Gorton's ever since his discharge from the infantry. Brownie talked a lot, mostly about the daily numbers game everyone played and the extra-marital sex he appeared to relish. Gus, who'd been on the wharf since the 1930s and had a bald head and no teeth, was quiet. I liked him better. Brownie reminded me of the bullies I'd known at the Hovey School. Mostly I stayed clear of him. He called me "college" when it got out that I'd just graduated from Bowdoin. At first I didn't tell anyone that I was bound for Italy in the fall. I let them think I was regular help. Actually, I was; for I'd been required to join Local 15 of the Amalgamated Meat Cutters and Packers Union, AFL-CIO. Working on the waterfront in previous summers, I'd gotten a student waiver; but it made me feel proud to be a dues-paying member of the seafood workers' union.

After I started eating with the men, they invited me out with them on payday nights to have supper at Patrican's restaurant, down the street from the Seafood Center. On those Thursdays they usually stopped for a drink at the Paramount Café, returning after work to drink there until closing time. Then they'd weave their way home on foot or fall into their cars, peeling out of the adjacent parking lots like teenagers. Usually I had an excuse not to join the men after work if my mother, who needed the car during the day, came to pick me up.

Sometimes, though, Sooky would offer to drive me home. He had a girlfriend named Tina, who worked for the telephone company. Each week Tina made him turn his paycheck over to her. Then she doled out some gas money to him for the maroon and gray Buick Sooky kept constantly polished, and for his lunch and smokes. The rest she put into a savings account for when they got married. They had been engaged since high school. Sooky said they were saving for a house, too. They only went out on weekends and Sooky was always complaining to me that Tina wouldn't have sex with him.

"Shit," he said, "I can't even get a good feel. She says we have to wait until we're married. What if it don't work out between us? What then?"

I didn't tell him I no longer went steady with Leslie. I would mention her name to let him and the others think I still had a girlfriend, but in reality I was lucky if we saw each other at a distance. Nevertheless, I still thought about Leslie. I thought about her when I was working over the cold fish slabs and when I was in the men's locker room smoking during mug-up. I thought about her after I'd come home from work and was trying to write, the Four Freshmen's "It's a Blue World without You" playing repeatedly on the hi-fi. It was then that I imagined Leslie with Karl in all the places she and I had shared.

I got up the courage to call Leslie a couple of times in July, on mornings when I was alone in the house and I knew she wasn't working. Our talks were perfunctory, as if she were in a hurry or didn't want to talk with me. And I hung up the phone feeling sadder and more rejected. Even so, I pictured her getting ready for work, walking around her house in the yellow cotton nightgown she'd worn the summer before when I visited her in the morning and we'd kiss with her sitting on my lap and I could almost smell her scented soap again, mingling with the smell of her sleep. I yearned to lift up her gown and kiss her breasts, as I had once been privileged to do.

Now Boulton must be doing that. I figured they had to be making love, while it had been my fault not to be more aggressive. I thought about these things when I was alone and I lay on my bed and masturbated. I got out photographs from the summer before of Leslie in her black bathing suit and I held them up, sweating in the July heat of the bedroom, worried that my mother would find out what I was doing upstairs by myself. I brooded constantly about Leslie and me and about what I'd done to alienate her. I was sick over it, sick from having lost her and sick that I'd decided to go to Italy.

That's when I thought about canceling my plans, even though I'd already applied for my passport and booked passage on the TSS Olympia out of Boston on September 20th. It was a ten-day sail to Naples. From there I planned to travel by train to Florence in time to start classes at the university in October. But I didn't care any more, even though I told my new friend Emiliano Sorrini that I couldn't wait. Emiliano was a graphic artist from Urbino, who was working in a studio on Rocky Neck. We spoke Italian together. He'd studied in Florence and he told me stories about student life in the clubs and *pensioni* of the city. He talked excitedly about the writer, Cesare Pavese, whose powerful novels of post-war disaffection he encouraged me to read.

"If you like Moravia," he said, "you will die for Pavese."

Our conversations on weekend nights when I wasn't working were the only company I had. My high school friends lived in other cities now or they'd gone into the service. There was only Leslie at home and she was with Karl. I knew that because I sometimes went looking for them in my mother's car. I would drive to Rockport to discover Boulton's Ford in front of the Peg Leg, as he waited to pick Leslie up after work at night. Those were late nights and my mother often wondered where I was. Usually I'd tell her that I'd gone to the movies or that Sookie and I had stopped for a beer after work.

It all nauseated me. I couldn't take a swim for fear of running into Leslie and Boulton at the beach. I couldn't go to the flicks for the same reason, nor to the art galleries I had once haunted. Consequently I became a hermit. I devoured Iris Origo's biography of Leopardi, identifying strongly with the reclusive poet of Recanati. Or I had fantasies. There was a dark-skinned woman on the packing line I used to think about a lot. Her name was Francine Lopes. She was Portuguese and she had an incredible body. The men joked about the leopard skin panties she wore under her white uniform. Francine came to work bare-legged, with her hair in a pony tail, and she wasn't afraid to banter with the men.

At first I just listened to the exchanges. But once in a while I'd catch her looking at me with a complicitous smile, as if she knew I saw through the stupidity of the others. I wanted to be friends with her. She was different from Leslie or Mary; older, more mature, tougher but not cheap, even though the men made cracks about her colored panties. Actually she'd only worn them once that I knew of.

I tried to figure out a way to get closer to Francine. Some nights I'd see her walking home up toward Portagee Hill. I imagined being able to talk with her about Leslie. I even had a sense that she wanted to speak with me but that the circumstances of the work situation made it difficult for both of us to communicate. So I just bided my time. At night I had fantasies of her beautiful brown body naked and close to mine, the two of us lying in her bed, smoking, maybe after making love. It helped me feel less desperate about having lost Leslie.

But then I ran into Leslie in my own territory. It was late on a Sunday night. I'd been taking one of my customary walks down to the marine railways on Rocky Neck before going to bed. On my way back I happened to pass the Studio restaurant. When I looked through the double screen doors of the cocktail lounge, Leslie and Boulton were sitting at a table near the door, their heads close together.

Without thinking I shoved the door open and sat down with them at a table shaped like an artist's palette. Boulton, who had never seen me, looked defensive. Leslie turned scarlet.

"What a surprise," she said, putting her hand out to touch mine. "Karl, this is Jason."

"Oh, yes," he said, reaching his hand across the table.

I didn't shake hands. I just sat there not knowing what to say. I felt foolish I'd barged in on them like that. Seeing Leslie in her Black Watch Bermudas, her hair all combed out as if she'd just dried it after a swim, made my heart beat wildly.

A waitress came over.

"Give me a bourbon and water," I said through my teeth. "Jack Daniels." Then I remembered I didn't have my wallet. I glared at Leslie. "Lend me two bucks."

"Of course," she answered. There was a sadness in her voice, a quality of distress. Boulton picked up on it, shifted in his chair.

"Jason," he said. "I've heard a lot about you."

"I'll bet," I said, looking right through him.

"Leslie says you're quite a writer."

"It's a matter of opinion."

"No, really," he said. "She tells me you've written some wonderful plays. I admire that. Plays are hard to write."

"Everything's hard to write," I said, "especially after you've been bird-dogged."

"Jason," Boulton said gently, his blond hair and eyebrows white in the bright overheard lights of the lounge. "I understand how you feel. I'm glad we saw you. I've wanted to get to know you. I've wanted to tell you that it isn't the way you might think it is. I mean, between Leslie and me. I love her deeply."

"So do I!" I shouted.

"Really, Jason. I want to marry Leslie."

I looked at Leslie, who sat silently as Boulton and I faced off. My drink came and she reached for her pocket book on the floor. It was the brown, tooled leather one I had bought her for Christmas in Harvard Square.

"Let *me*," Boulton offered. "I'd like to buy you a drink."

"I asked Leslie for the loan," I said, feeling my hands clench under the table. My voice was hoarse.

"Give me a cigarette," I demanded of Leslie.

She offered her Marlboros.

"I hate those."

"It's all I have," she said distraughtly. "Karl doesn't smoke." Leslie put the two dollars down on the table.

"I was saying," Boulton began again.

"*What?*"

"I was trying to explain."

I looked him in the face. I noticed how fat he was around the eyes.

"There's nothing to say," I said. "You steal someone's girl friend and then you try to make excuses for it."

"I don't quite see it that way," he answered.

"Well, I do," I said, pushing my chair back, the bourbon untouched.

"Jason," Leslie pleaded. She tried to cover my hand with hers.

"Let him go," Boulton said. "If he doesn't want to be civil, then let him walk out."

"You bet your sweet ass I'm going."

"Please stay, Jason," Leslie said.

I pushed my way through the doors, turning just as Leslie lowered her head. She was starting to cry. Boulton reached out to comfort her, but she was shaking her head in refusal. I could hear her sobs from the sidewalk. A couple of doors down the street, I found the unlighted Marlboro between my fingers and I flung it into the cove. Then I remembered it was Leslie's.

As soon as I got home I poured myself a bourbon from Dad's liquor cabinet and carried it upstairs to my desk. Switching on the gooseneck lamp in my otherwise dark and close bedroom, I pulled my typewriter over and began to write a long disjointed letter to Leslie. I asked her how she could possibly stand to be with someone as overweight and fatuous as Boulton, even though he claimed to be a writer and loved Dostoevsky. I repeated all the aggrieved things I'd begun writing her in the spring. I wrote until the first light, page after page: apologizing, pleading, demanding, until I was so tired I couldn't see the type any longer and I fell into bed, knowing that I'd sleep until noon, knowing, too, that it was hopeless, that instead of making things better between Leslie and me I'd only made them worse.

My grades followed me home from Bowdoin, along with a postcard from George, forwarded from 83 Federal Street. After fleeing Brunswick, he'd hitchhiked to Southern California. He was working at a bowling alley in Venice. "I've got my own pad, $20 a week," he wrote, "a chick who's ten years older than me, and plenty of tea." I received A's in everything except my major, in which I'd been given a B plus. But all that was behind me now.

My mother had taken my sheepskin to the frame shop. It hung now on the wall above my bed like any other picture in the house.

✠ August was just as bad as July, only hotter, more empty. I couldn't enjoy even the simplest summer pleasures because Leslie wasn't there to share them with me. I had sent her my letter, regretting that act the minute I'd dropped the thick, hand-addressed envelope into the mail box on the Causeway. Of course, she didn't answer it. And I didn't blame her. I took to drinking with the men at work, with Sooky and Brownie and Gus. The nights were cooling off now as I left the Paramount, sometimes walking the two miles home in the dark, walking off my inebriation or just relishing the time by myself to think, as I took the same streets I'd once so happily taken on the way back from Leslie's house.

One night toward the end of August the rain began beating down with the particular ferocity of a late summer storm. I was drinking again at the Paramount. As usual the talk was of "tail" and who got it from whom. The names of people I barely knew or remembered came and went in our conversation, as Dal Mitchell's baritone saxophone resonated in the background, my old piano teacher Don Oakes at the keyboard. It was like a scene from our high school dances frozen in time, the men sitting there in their khaki workclothes the way we all once appeared in our ROTC uniforms. At that point I was glad I'd soon be leaving for Italy. I only told a few of the women and Sooky, who took my arm tenderly as we were having mug-up one day.

"Lucky stiff," he said. "You deserve to go. I'm stuck here for life. All's I got to look forward to is the winter lay-off."

"You'll be getting married," I said.

"Big fucking deal!"

That night I had my mother's car. As I turned on impulse up Prospect Street, I noticed a woman in a red kerchief and white uniform walking toward Friend Street in the slanting rain. It was Francine and I stopped to offer her a ride. At first she hesitated, but when she recognized me, she smiled, getting into the car.

"Jason!" she said. "I feel like a drowned rat."

She explained that she'd been working overtime to help clean the fryers. We drove half way up Friend Street before she told me to stop in front of a triple-decker that was shingled in pink asbestos.

"My apartment's right here," she said. "Why don't you come up for coffee?"

I was so amazed I didn't answer.

"I won't bite," she laughed.

Francine's apartment was small and meticulously kept. There were two framed Impressionist prints on the wall and a beautiful old photograph of Gloucester harbor taken at the turn of the century. She had a small bookcase in the living room filled equally with paperbacks and hardbound novels. As I moved to examine the titles, Francine laughed again.

"Please don't embarrass me. I'm not a college graduate, but I love to read. I belong to the Book-of-the-Month Club. Here, come in the kitchen while I put on the water for the coffee. It's only instant."

With her kerchief off, her hair was damp but smooth around her face. Her dark brown eyes were sharp and alive. She seemed perfectly comfortable having me there.

"Sit, please sit," she said, pulling a kitchen chair out for me. We both plopped down in our work clothes. I could smell the fried seafood on her. I assumed I smelled just as fishy from the splinters of frozen cod that were thrown off by the saws around my work station.

Confronted with my fantasy made flesh, I didn't know what to say. But Francine offered me one of her cigarettes, an unfiltered Philip Morris. Kicking off her wet moccasins she smiled.

"This is fun," she said, putting her exquisite dark feet up on the chair next to mine. "I've been waiting to talk with you all summer. Is it true you're going to Europe?"

"I tried to keep it a secret."

"I won't tell anyone," she said. "I think it's great. I've always wanted to travel."

"Haven't you?"

"Oh, I went out to California once, when my husband was stationed there. I hated it."

"I didn't know you were married." I found myself looking at her fingers, now bare of any rings.

"Right after high school," she said. "Then Joe was drafted. They sent him to Korea."

Close up, the skin of her face had tiny pock marks in it. Her profile was everything I'd imagined it to be from a distance, her nose as amazing as the Florentine woman's in the Pollaiuolo portrait.

She reached around behind her to get the whistling kettle. Slowly she poured boiling water onto the crystals of coffee in our cups.

"What I like about you," she said, motioning me to help myself to the sugar and milk she'd placed on the table, "is that you never tease me the way the other men do. You're always a gentleman."

"I hate it when the men get that way," I said.

"I'm not a slut." Francine looked at me with a sudden sadness in her eyes. "Just because I'm divorced and live alone I don't have loose morals the way those jerks would like me to have."

I felt like touching her hands, but I didn't dare.

"Guys at the plant ask me out. But I know damn well if I accepted I'd get a reputation as a pushover."

"How long were you married?" I asked.

"Long enough to realize that I'd married the wrong person. We were just kids. There didn't seem to be anything else worth doing. I thought about going to college, I even took the college prep course. I bet we had the same English teachers, Miss Harris, Miss McGrew. But my parents didn't have any money. Besides, a Portuguese girl didn't go to college. She got married and raised a family."

Francine hesitated.

"I did one but not the other. Actually I had a miscarriage after Joe pushed me down a flight of stairs once when he came home drunk."

I found myself looking at her lips as she spoke, her voice gentler than it was on the floor of the plant, her beauty so much finer than when she wore a white paper floret pinned above her pony tail.

"I should hate men, I suppose." She went on as though she'd been waiting to say these things to someone for a long time. "I don't go out. There's no one to go out with. I come home and I read or I watch TV until I'm tired."

Her arms were quite shapely up close, as were her ears. Her voice was husky but soft as we spoke in the small kitchen, the sound of the rain still pelting against the window screens.

"I can't imagine you getting beaten up," I said. "I mean, you're so tough at work when the men insult you."

"I've learned how to defend myself since I left Joe."

"Where is he now?"

"I haven't got the faintest idea," she said with satisfaction. "And I could care less. When I left him my parents were furious. They wanted me to stay with him. They said he'd get over it. I grew up with a drunken father so I knew better. I knew it would only get worse. He'd apologize on the morning after a bender. That same night he'd smash me across the face if I so much as suggested he have one drink less. Once, when we were visiting some friends, he asked me to get him a beer out of their ice box. When I reached in, he leaned over and slammed the door shut on my arm. It hurt terribly and I begged him to stop. 'See this?' he said to me, looking at our friends, who were sitting there with their mouths hanging open, 'It's nothing compared to what will happen to you if I ever catch you stepping out on me.' I told him I'd never been unfaithful to him, I wasn't that kind of woman. But he kept the door shut tight on my arm until I nearly fainted and our friends finally made him stop. The next day I saw a lawyer. An hour later I had a restraining order. Joe never set foot in the house again."

"You must despise men," I said.

"I don't," Francine said. "I hate myself for letting that happen to me."

"We could be friends," I offered, wishing I could put my arm around her.

She smiled.

"I'm almost thirty. How old are you, twenty-one, twenty-two?"

"I'll be twenty-two in November."

"Wouldn't it be nice," she said, looking me full in the face. "I read about your play in the paper. You could talk to me about books and we could go to the movies. But you know what would happen? They'd kill us at work. They'd make us regret every minute we spent together. Those sons of bitches would grill you until they knew everything about our relationship. Then they'd parrot it all over the plant. Even if we never kissed, they'd have us fucking!"

She spoke bitterly.

"I don't mean to be cynical," she said, "but you know what I'm talking about."

I nodded in agreement, but, in reality, I could only imagine the denigration she was alluding to.

"Anyway," she said. "I'm not going to spend my life in that dump. I've applied to nursing school for next year. I've got most of the money saved up. My family thinks I'm crazy, but I've got to leave this town. It's now or never."

She kissed me softly on the lips as I left. I wanted to reach out and hug her in that white uniform, stained and wrinkled from a day's work. I wanted to return her kiss. I thought she might respond if I only had the courage. I yearned for her dark hands to caress me, imagining how we might undress each other slowly and make love. I felt there was something between us, some intensity I'd never felt with Leslie, something both sweet and reckless. I pictured myself with Francine in the pink covered bed I'd glimpsed though her open bedroom door, expending myself, forgetting myself, transcending my loss and my craziness in the midst of our shared cries. But as I went quietly down her stairs and unlocked the car, driving home now in the clear night, windows open to the moist air, I knew I wasn't ready for whatever that might be, even though it beckoned to me in my ignorance.

✝ A cold front came in after the rain storm and the next day felt like September. I was called off the floor by the foreman. In the lobby by the punch-out clock stood St. Pierre. For a minute I didn't recognize him with several day's growth of beard and his black leather jacket.

"You old Greek bastard!" he said, coming to shake my hand.

"I'm on my way to the Apple. I stopped by your house to say goodbye. Your mother told me where to find you."

"Here I am," I said, feeling awkward in my fish-stained khakis.

"I've got a job waiting on table at Minetta's in the Village." His eyes danced with delight. "Classes at the Actor's Studio start in October. When do you leave?"

"In a couple weeks."

"Listen, I've got an amazing story for you."

I motioned St. Pierre out onto the loading platform where we both sat on a pile of crates.

"You won't believe this," he said, offering me a Lucky. We lit up, the afternoon light slanting more obliquely across the parking lot in the waning summer. "Mendel showed up a couple of days ago. He was riding a huge Harley, loaded down with leather bags. Annegret sat right behind him. She was dressed in leather, too, and she had a crash helmet on. It turns out Mendel never started that job at the Pentagon. He never even showed his face in Washington. He sold everything he owned in New York—his hi-fi, all his books and records. He bought this big bike and he's been traveling around all summer long. Annegret told her parents she wasn't going to college. Then she ran away from home. She and Mendel were on their way to Canada when they stopped in Waterville. Beyond that they had no plans. 'We're drifting,' Mendel said. 'We might end up out west.'"

After Henri had left, I made my way back to the floor. Stopping at the men's locker room, I sat for a minute at the lunch table. Strewn all around me were ashtrays with butts spilling over onto the table top. Seeing St. Pierre seemed somehow out of context now that neither of us was in college. It was as if I didn't know him anymore and, like strangers, or friends who had taken different paths, we were awkward around each other, tongue-tied. I'd watched him drive away in the '49 Ford we did so many crazy things together in, only I was no longer in the car with him. I was the one left behind.

✛ Labor Day came and went. I had two weeks before I left for Italy, but I continued working to keep my mind busy. One chilly night I was awakened from a claustrophobic sleep by the sound

262

of fire engines and police sirens. My mother came running up the stairs to my bedroom.

"There's a fire somewhere on Eastern Point Road. My God, the whole sky is red!" She stood there in her nightgown. Suddenly she appeared old to me, even though she was barely fifty.

I pulled on a pair of shorts and a sweatshirt and I rushed out the front door to Wonson Street, my sneakers still unlaced. I ran up the Causeway toward the smoke and the color of the flames. When I reached Eastern Point Road, I found groups of excited people. Sleep still showing in their faces, they struggled up the hill and around the corner toward the Hawthorne Inn, just above Niles Beach. The entire hotel property was on fire. The delicatessen and casino directly on the road, and the stately, old, white clapboarded inn down by the water were all ablaze. The flames were so hot they appeared to singe our faces; sulphurous smoke filled the air. The police were trying to keep everyone away from the fire, but the spectators drew closer in their curiosity.

I stood across the street in front of a gray stucco apartment building where the help was housed in the summertime. People around me were remarking on how lucky it was that the hotel had been closed since Labor Day, literally boarded up, so that there would be no loss of life. I looked back in the direction from which I'd come to see the police diverting cars down Grapevine Road, a block away. With the flames leaping out to the street and the fire engines pumping away, no car could possibly have continued on to Niles Beach or to Eastern Point beyond it. As I peered through the smoke, I caught sight of Leslie getting out of a Ford coup like St. Pierre's. She began walking toward me, still dressed in her waitress uniform. I ran toward her.

"Leslie," I shouted, "it's me! Stay where you are!"

The driver of the Ford backed up as if to protect her. I saw that it was Boulton.

"I've been thinking about you," I said, rushing over to her. "I need to talk to you."

When I reached Leslie, who seemed surprised to see me, Boulton had his car stalled in the middle of the road. People were squeezing around it to get to the fire. He rolled his window down and looked angrily at me.

"Please talk to me," I said. "I've missed you so much."

Leslie stared at me and then back at Boulton.

"Leave her alone," he shouted from the car. Someone was blowing a horn for him to get moving.

"Shut up, you asshole!" I screamed. "I've known Leslie a thousand times longer than you have. I won't let you talk to me like that!"

I ran over to the car and rammed my fist in the open window. The blow glanced off Boulton's cheek. Looking enraged, he started to get out of the car when a cop came over and told him to move it immediately. Furiously he drove off down Grapevine Road. Leslie disappeared after him. At first I followed the white of her waitress uniform. All around us people were staring at me.

"Come back, Les. Please come back!" I shouted.

Then I stopped. I knew she wouldn't speak to me after what I'd done. So I turned around and walked back quickly through the crowd, away from the fire, away from Leslie and Boulton. At home I tossed in my bed until dawn, the smell of smoke and the sound of fire engines, the rumble of their pumps, reaching me from across the cove.

When I came down from bed at eleven the next morning, I told my mother what happened. I explained everything about Leslie and me to her. She encouraged me to call Boulton as we sat over coffee in the breakfast nook, leaving me alone as I dialed his number in Rockport. Karl came on sleepily, surprised to hear from me. I apologized for having struck him, for having acted so rudely at the Studio when he tried to be friendly.

"I'll admit I woke up thinking I'd file a complaint against you," he said. "But I understand why you did it. I probably would have done the same thing myself."

We talked for a while. His voice was strong but gentle. He told me he knew Leslie and I had been together for a long time and that her decision to break it off had been a blow to me.

"You'll have to understand that I wasn't in the picture, Jason. Leslie and I didn't start seeing each other until after she'd made her decision. It was painful to her. She talked about it constantly. I took your side, if you'll believe it."

I felt better after I'd gotten off the phone. My mother came in and gave me a hug.

"It was very big of you," she said. "Why don't you get ready and I'll drive you to work."

That night after work I walked down to Niles Beach past the ruins of the Hawthorne Inn, the smell of fresh smoke and charred timbers everywhere. It was a cool, clear night. The stars were massed in the sky the way they are in September. There was a hint of fall in the air. And the ocean, washing among the boulders below me on the beach, was like the sound of distant drums.

I sat on the old stone wall, my legs dangling above the sand. I sat reflecting on everything that had happened. Words, images, faces passed in review like a movie whose frames I could freeze at will. I thought about St. Pierre living in the Village now, of crazy Mendel tearing around Canada with Annegret on his motorcycle—Mendel the quietest and smartest of us all. I wondered if Mary had been able to leave home for the University of Maine and if she'd stay once she got there. I no longer felt angry at her for being in the car with Hosmer that night. In fact, I felt grateful for what we'd shared. Sex with Mary, even if it wasn't the way I first imagined it, was a liberation.

I thought of Roonie and Mueller in North Beach under a sun far warmer than mine. I pictured them taking coffee in the sidewalk cafes of San Francisco or browsing among the latest books of poetry at City Lights. I could almost hear the jazz coming out of the jukeboxes of nearby bars. I recalled our time together in New York, the otherworldly sound of Sonny Stitt's tenor and the mad party the night before we'd left the city. And through it all I imagined Dell searching for his elusive love under the neon lights of Times Square.

I thought of Murray and Aune who'd be joining me in Florence in less than a year, of how much they'd given me by just being themselves. I thought of Bowdoin, of those years gone by so quickly as if they'd never happened. And I thought again of everyone I'd been close to in college, especially of Frank, now lying in the alien soil of a Cuban jungle; old Frank, who had taught me that we are condemned to be free if only we can accept the responsibility it entails. Yes, Frank, now gone forever, along with his mildewed books and his endless games of bridge; his squeaky voice stilled. Who would remember all that?

And then there was Leslie and me. I felt her close by as I looked out across the water I'd soon be sailing away on.

Sitting above the beach, I said my quiet goodbyes. I said goodbye to Gloucester, where so much of my past twenty-one years had been lived, and to my parents, who had somehow understood this tormented child of theirs, this son who was going away from them just as he'd achieved their dream of graduating from college. Perhaps, like Lawrence, I was now condemned to be a wanderer, and my voyage to the Mediterranean was merely the first stage of an endless journey. I pictured myself on the high seas for the first time in my life. I imagined myself docking in Naples, from where I would take a train to Rome for a few days' sightseeing before arriving, finally, in Florence. Then I walked back in the cold dark to my lonely bed.

✢ I was awakened by the telephone the next morning. Jeff Cotton was on the line from Brunswick. Schrebner had killed himself.

"Anton slashed his wrists the day classes were to begin," Jeff said hopelessly.

When I didn't answer right away, Jeff apologized for calling me out of the blue. According to Jewish custom, Schrebner had been buried immediately. But there was going to be a memorial service at Harvard that Saturday at noon.

"I know you cared about Anton," he said. "He asked for news of you the last time I saw him. Ilsa and Michael would appreciate it if you came."

On Saturday I put on a suit and drove my parents' car to Cambridge. Parking off Mt. Auburn Street, I walked nervously up Plympton and crossed Massachusetts Avenue to the Yard.

When I entered Appleton Chapel, I saw a large number of Bowdoin faculty, but I only recognized a few students, mostly graduates. Ilsa and the Schrebners' fourteen-year-old son Michael were sitting in the front row with Carter and his wife and the Dean. Jeff motioned me over next to him and his wife Jeanne.

After some opening words from the Harvard chaplain, Carter spoke briefly about the loss to the College of a dedicated teacher. The two main speakers were friends of the Schrebner's and former colleagues of his at Harvard, where he had once taught German before coming to Bowdoin to teach philosophy. The first spoke of Anton as a philosopher, recalling his brilliant paper on Cassirer and Galileo, which many had hoped would become a book. The second, who introduced himself as Frederick Hazen, chairman of the German Department, noted how Anton hated having to teach German, even though it had been his own language.

"Everything Teutonic was abhorrent to him," Professor Hazen said, "after the ordeal of losing his parents. He couldn't believe that people who spoke the language of Goethe could also have created the Final Solution."

He went on to relate how Schrebner had been prevented from taking his doctorate at Hamburg because of the proscription against Jews. Having lost his fellowship, he had attempted, with Cassirer's help, to emigrate to England where a research position awaited him at the Warburg Institute in London. Once there, he hoped to bring his parents to England along with his sister, who was a medical student. But family friends, who managed to escape to Portugal, wrote him that his parents had been arrested and deported. It was only after the fall of Germany that he learned of their deaths at Auschwitz. His sister died at Ravensbruck, where the Nazi doctors Clauberg and Schumann conducted experiments in sterilization on women and children. Schrebner and Ilsa, also a refugee, had met in London.

"It was Ilsa who gave him life again," Hazen said, "at least for as long as she could."

"Like his mentor Cassirer," he concluded, "Anton became an itinerant scholar. He left no letter or note, but on his desk at Adams Hall colleagues found a single slip of paper on which he had copied out these words of Cassirer's:

"'In our life, in the life of a modern Jew, there is no room left for any joy or complacency. All this has gone forever. No Jew whatsoever can and will overcome the terrible ordeal of these last years.'"

After the brief service I went up to pay my respects to Ilsa and Michael, stopping for a quiet handshake with Carter and the Dean, both of whose hands I had not expected to shake for some time. On the way out, Jeff told me that Schrebner had suffered from depression for many years and that the condition seemed to be worsening. He had apparently never been able to forgive himself for having, in his mind, abandoned his family in Europe. His doctor wanted him to enter McLean hospital, but Anton, who lived for his teaching, wouldn't countenance the advice.

"And yet he knew he couldn't give to his students the way he was feeling," Jeff said. "That morning he took his usual bath. When he didn't come down for breakfast, Ilsa rushed upstairs and found him in the tub of bloody water. By the time the ambulance came he was dead."

Driving back to Gloucester, all I could think of was that there would no longer be a light burning in the window of Adams Hall far into the night.

✠ On the Wednesday before I was set to leave, Leslie called asking me to meet her in Boston for what she called a *bon-vivant voyage* drink. I took the Thursday afternoon train to North Station and we sat at a quiet table in the deserted bar of the Hotel Manger. Leslie wore a tightly fitting pearl gray skirt, her hair still looking wonderful in the French twist. She carried her books, having just come from the first classes of the semester. We talked about the courses she'd be taking and she asked me about what I expected to study in Florence.

"You won't believe this," Leslie said excitedly, "but I actually managed to get into Albert J. Guerard's course on the forms of the modern novel!"

It was just like old times, although there was a heaviness about it all, a sense of our meeting for the last time. Over one bourbon after another, I apologized to Leslie about the incident with Boulton the night of the fire. I also told her I was sorry about my behavior at the Studio. She said she understood.

"I still love you, Jason," she said. And as she said it my heart sank.

"You have to go away," Leslie said. "I went to Europe. You need to go, too. I'm sorry I didn't realize that earlier. Don't think about Karl. Don't worry about us. Don't think about anything but yourself."

"I'll try," I said, as we kissed after she walked me to my train. All the way back to Gloucester I heard Chet Baker's voice in my head singing *"Just friends, lovers no more"* and I felt a million miles away from everything, even Leslie.

On Saturday I got a letter from her.

"Dear Jason," it began. "I couldn't say these things to you today so I have to write them. I might not have acted as though I did, but I love you deeply. I love you, but I have to let you go. I *had* to let you go. You are wonderful in many ways, but you are still so young and nothing I can do would make you change or grow. I knew I had to abandon you to time, to Italy, to whatever happened to you there without the merest hope of ever getting you back.

"So please go knowing how I feel. Don't write me now, don't write me for a long time. I can't tell you to forget me because I won't forget you. If you still think I left you for Karl, please don't. Karl is very nice to me and he cares about me, but I'm not going to marry him and I don't even know how long we will be together. Karl is not the force that came between us; our own natures and needs did that and I had to face up to it. I'm sorry I hurt you in trying to do that.

"But you will have your Europe and I will have my life here. You also have your writing. I still don't know what I have or what I will do. There is much more that I could tell you, but you would have to be here for me to do that in the old way we talked and were together. So I will only promise to tell you those things years from now when your sons are asleep and we are in our big warm bed, having just made marvelous love. Then I will turn to you and open my heart, only then; and we will have no secrets from each other and no one will love like we will love."

✢ The morning I was scheduled to leave, I got up as usual to help my father assemble the Sunday newspapers. It was a job we'd shared in the store every Sunday morning since I was a teenager. Whether or not I arrived home late the night before, I was always up at seven to help Dad get the papers ready for his eight o'clock customers. Dad began collating the various sections of the *Boston Herald* and the *Globe* that got delivered throughout the week. I concentrated on the *New York Times* and the *Herald Tribune*. As we worked together, Dad recalled how he'd come to America alone at the age of nine to join his father, who had left his family in Sparta to find work in the cotton mills of Lowell.

Dad had to lie about his age in order to enter the country. He arrived at Ellis Island wearing his mother's shoes, since he had no shoes of his own and they wouldn't let him on the boat in Greece without them. He described that anxious moment when he was about to be turned back at Piraeus. Suddenly his mother, a simple peasant woman, reached down, removed her own shoes, and handed them to her son.

When Dad got to Lowell, he discovered that his father had died from consumption, his lungs packed with textile fibers. Dad, who spoke no English, worked for a year at the Massachusetts Cotton Mill. It had been his job to clean out the spittoons into which the workers constantly spat their snuff and chewing tobacco. One day, when he saw a boy his own age hawking newspapers on the street, Dad left the boarding house where he was staying. With his possessions wrapped in a brown paper parcel, he took the train to Boston and presented himself at the office of the *Boston Evening Transcript*. That day he began selling newspapers. When he'd earned enough money for his own kit, he started shining shoes at the corner of State and Court streets. Relying on newspapers and a big *Webster's International Dictionary*, which he later gave to me, Dad taught himself English. From that time on, he vowed never to work for another man.

As he told me the story I'd heard many times before, the early morning light glinted off my father's rimless bifocals. Working side by side, we stacked the assembled newspapers on a rack near the entrance to the store. Then we went into the house for breakfast. That afternoon my parents drove me to Boston. When at dusk I finally sailed for Naples on the TSS Olympia, it felt to me like the end of something. Little did I know that it was only the beginning.

ABOUT THE AUTHOR

*P*eter Anastas was born in Gloucester, Massachusetts in 1937 and attended local schools. He holds degrees in English from Bowdoin College and Tufts University. His previous publications include *Glooskap's Children: Encounters with the Penobscot Indians of Maine* (Beacon Press), *Landscape with Boy*, a novella in the Boston University Fiction Series, *At the Cut,* a memoir of growing up in Gloucester in the 1940s (Dogtown Books), and *Broken Trip*, a novel (Glad Day Books), along with fiction and non-fiction in *Niobe, The Falmouth Review, Stations, America One, The Larcom Review, Polis, Split Shift, Café Review,* and *Sulfur.*